# SOMEWHERE TO CALL HOME

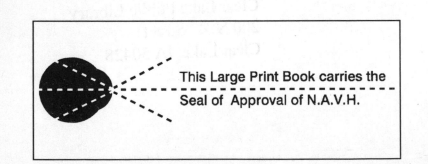

This Large Print Book carries the
Seal of Approval of N.A.V.H.

# SOMEWHERE TO CALL HOME

## JANET LEE BARTON

**THORNDIKE PRESS**
*A part of Gale, Cengage Learning*

GALE
CENGAGE Learning®

Detroit • New York • San Francisco • New Haven, Conn • Waterville, Maine • London

**GALE**
CENGAGE Learning·

Thorndike Press® Large Print Gentle Romance.
The text of this Large Print edition is unabridged.
Other aspects of the book may vary from the original edition.
Set in 16 pt. Plantin.

LIBRARY OF CONGRESS CATALOGING-IN-PUBLICATION DATA

Barton, Janet Lee.
    Somewhere to call home / by Janet Lee Barton.
        pages ; cm. — (Thorndike Press large print gentle romance)
    ISBN 978-1-4104-5789-9 (hardcover) — ISBN 1-4104-5789-3 (hardcover) 1.
Large type books. I. Title.
PS3602.A84228S67 2013
813'.6—dc23                                    2013004109

Published in 2013 by arrangement with Harlequin Books S.A.

Printed in the United States of America
1 2 3 4 5 6 7 17 16 15 14 13

And the Lord, he it is that doth go before thee; he will be with thee, he will not fail thee, neither forsake thee: fear not, neither be dismayed.

— *Deuteronomy* 31:8

To Tamela Hancock Murray and Tina James for making a dream come true;

To all my LI and LIH author friends, who have encouraged me to keep trying;

To the Bards of Faith and the OCFW chapter for their encouragement and support;

To my husband Dan and my family for their unending love and support;

And, most of all, to my Lord and Savior for showing me the way.

# PROLOGUE

*Ashland, Virginia*
*May 1895*

Violet Burton sighed with disappointment as she left the mercantile. How could things have changed so much in such a short time? Only moments ago, on her way to the post office, there'd been a help-wanted sign in the store's window and another one in the milliner's shop. Evidently, she wasn't the only one seeking employment in her small hometown, for both positions were filled by the time she got through picking up her mail.

She walked along the main street, her gaze searching the windows of the businesses on each side of the street. When she spotted a sign in the café across the way, a flicker of hope nudged her to gather up her skirts to clear them from the dirt road and hurry across. However, just before she reached the door, the sign was yanked right out of the window. Violet's hope sank once more, but she entered the establishment anyway.

She walked over to the proprietor, who was putting the sign under her cash box. "Good morning, Mrs. Wheeler. Has the position been filled already?"

The woman looked down at the floor and back up at Violet, her face a bright pink. "I'm sorry, dear. But I've decided I can't afford to take anyone on today."

It seemed an odd way to word the answer to her question, but Violet didn't feel she should press. Since her widowed mother's illness and death a few weeks earlier, she knew firsthand what it was not to be able to afford things. And if she didn't find employment soon, she'd be able to afford even less. Worst of all, she could lose her family home if she couldn't come up with the money to pay the mortgage her mother had taken out on the house as her illness progressed.

Violet nodded and sighed. "I understand. But if you should find that you do need someone after all, please keep me in mind."

The woman opened her mouth as if to say something, but seemed to change her mind, closed her mouth and only nodded instead.

Disheartened, Violet turned to leave, but just as she reached the door a thought came to her. She turned back and walked over to the woman she'd known all her life. Violet didn't want to put her on the spot, but she had to know. She kept her voice low and asked, "Mrs. Wheeler, by any chance, did Mr. Black tell you not to hire me?"

The older woman looked around to make sure none of her customers were within hearing distance before giving a curt nod. She motioned Violet closer and whispered, "He holds my mortgage, Violet. I can't afford to make him mad."

"I see." *All too well.*

"I'm sorry."

There were tears in Mrs. Wheeler's eyes, and Violet knew she was sincere. She reached out and patted her on the shoulder. "It's all right, Mrs. Wheeler. I don't blame you. Thank you for being honest with me."

Still, Violet felt the flush of anger flood her cheeks when she turned to leave, her stride strong and purposeful as she went outside and crossed the street to the bank. With each step she took, her outrage grew. If Harlan Black thought this was the way to win her heart, well, he had better think again!

"Miss Burton, how nice to see you," the receptionist said as she entered the building. "What can I do for you?"

"I'd like to speak with Mr. Black as soon

as possible, Miss Bancroft." Violet tried to keep the irritation out of her voice, but she had a feeling she failed as the woman took one look at her and stood.

"I'll tell him you are here."

"Yes, please do that."

The receptionist hurried back to the banker's private office while Violet tapped her foot as she waited.

In a matter of seconds Miss Bancroft was back. "He'll see you now, Miss Burton."

"Thank you." Violet held her head high and marched back to the office.

Harlan Black stood at the door, a smug smile on his face. Violet supposed many women would find him handsome with his thick blond hair and gray eyes. He was always impeccably dressed and one could not fault his manners, but there was something about his sinister smoothness that made her skin crawl.

He bowed slightly. "My dear Violet. How nice to see you today —"

"You might not think it is so nice once I tell you what I have to say. And, I am *not* your 'dear.' " Violet swept past him and stood in the middle of the room, smoothing her skirts as she waited for him to join her. Then she pinned her gaze on the man.

"Please, take a seat, Violet, and tell me

what has you so distressed." He motioned for her to take the chair across from his desk.

Violet chose to keep standing. "You and your deceitful ways of keeping me from finding employment so that I can pay off the mortgage on my home are what have me so upset. How dare you?"

Harlan's eyes narrowed, and the smile left his face. "Violet, dear, there is absolutely no reason for you to seek employment. I've told you I will forgive the mortgage, if only —"

"I will *not* marry you, Harlan Black. If my mind were not made up before, it certainly is now — after finding out that you've told the townspeople not to hire me." The very thought of marrying the man nauseated Violet. "I will pay off the mortgage to my home, even if I have to leave here to do it!"

Harlan raised an eyebrow and chuckled. "And go where? Think about it, Violet. I offer you freedom from debt and a life of comfort. No woman in her right mind would turn that down."

"Then I must have lost my mind, for I have no intention of marrying you. Not now, not ever!" Violet turned to leave, but Harlan beat her to the door.

He grabbed hold of her arm and pulled her near. His breath was hot on her face, and his nearness sent a cold shiver down her spine. "Don't be too hasty, my dear. I can make you happy. You know I can. You have two weeks until the next payment is due. I'll need your final word by then."

Bile rose in Violet's throat at his words and she willed herself not to heave as she jerked her arm away and yanked the door open. Never would she marry this contemptuous man. She'd lose the home she loved first — but not without a fight to keep it.

# CHAPTER ONE

*New York City*
*May 24, 1895*

As the train came to a grinding stop in Grand Central Depot, Violet Burton's heart beat in excitement at the same time her stomach fluttered with apprehension. She stood, shaking out the skirts of her brown-and-beige traveling outfit before joining the other passengers in the aisle and following them out of the train. Pausing on the top step of the car, she fought the urge to turn around and seek refuge back inside. Perhaps she could ask the porter to buy her a ticket right back home. And then what?

Go back and marry Harlan Black? Violet shuddered. No. Never. Instead, she should be thankful her mother's old friend had come up with a solution to her problem. Violet took a deep calming breath and let it out. Once . . . twice . . . and again.

"Hurry it up, miss," a man behind her

said. "Are you getting off or what?"

A woman beside him reached out and pushed Violet's shoulder. "Yeah, missy. You're holding up the line and we don't have all day."

Heat stole up Violet's face and her heart hammered in her ears as she gave her hand to the waiting porter and hurried down the steps and out of the way. She didn't know in which direction to look for Mrs. Heaton. There were more people here than she'd ever seen in one place, yet she'd never felt so totally alone in her life.

Mrs. Heaton had told her each railroad line had its own waiting room, baggage facilities and ticketing operation in the building, so Violet assumed it wouldn't be hard to spot her. But she'd been mistaken. She didn't know how she'd ever see her mother's friend among all the people coming and going from every direction.

"Your trunk and bags will be over at the New York Central baggage claim area, miss." The porter pointed across the way. "Over there, where all those people are gathered."

"Thank you."

He tipped his hat. "There's a waiting room there, too. I'm sure someone will be here to meet you soon, miss."

"Yes. I hope so." He'd been very helpful on the trip and she hated to see him turn away.

Violet tried not to panic. What was it Mrs. Heaton had said in her letter? She'd be there to meet her. But where was she? And what would she do if Mrs. Heaton didn't show up? Violet began to think she might have made the biggest mistake in her life by coming here. Her mother had always warned her about big cities, and Violet knew she would not be happy she'd come to New York City. Yet, she was certain Mama would not have wanted her to marry Harlan Black under any circumstances. Besides, she really had no choice.

She took another deep breath and looked around. The only way Violet could see how the name *Grand* could apply to this depot was its size. It certainly couldn't be considered a grand place to be — not with all the steam, smoke and ashes spewing from the locomotives, hovering overhead and condensing with the odors of people from so many walks of life. From the sweet scent of toilet water to the strongest perfumes, they all intermingled with the smell of unwashed bodies and sweat, pervading the huge room, making Violet more nauseated by the minute.

17

Grand Central Depot wasn't only the largest building she'd ever been in — it was also the busiest. No sooner had the train she'd just arrived on chugged away than another one arrived in its place. Passengers poured out of it, heading off in every direction. Some of the travelers looked as lost as she felt.

She glanced around again but there seemed to be more people than ever, many speaking languages she couldn't understand. There was all manner of dress, from elegant to almost threadbare. Men pulled out their watches to see if the time matched the huge clock in the depot while mothers tried to keep their children close to their sides. The noise level seemed to rise with each passing minute as Violet made her way across the room.

A man spit near one of the spittoons positioned all over the depot, but he didn't seem to have good aim as his spittle ran down the outside of the cuspidor and ended up on the floor beside the vessel. The sight, mixed with the smells, made Violet's stomach roll, and she picked up her pace.

Trying to tamp down her anxiety, Violet pulled a picture of Mrs. Heaton out of her reticule and looked at it once more, although she was certain she would recognize her old neighbor. Surely she couldn't have changed much in three years. She turned in a small circle, looking closely at each woman she saw. Finally, when she'd about given up hope, she saw a woman she thought was Martha Heaton hurrying across the building. The older woman waved, and Violet breathed a sigh of relief as her mother's good friend reached her.

"Violet? It is you, isn't it?"

Her eyes held such warmth Violet couldn't help but smile. "Yes, ma'am, it is."

Mrs. Heaton grasped Violet's hands in hers. "How lovely you are, all grown up. You look just like your mother when she was your age. You have her dark hair and blue eyes and even her coloring." Mrs. Heaton pulled her into a quick hug. "Oh, you bring back so many memories of my younger days."

The older woman's blue eyes sparkled, and her fading auburn hair was done up under a large hat that matched her afternoon dress of blue-and-green stripes.

"Thank you, Mrs. Heaton. It is good to see you again." An understatement to be sure. It warmed her heart to see the older woman's familiar face.

"I am sorry I'm a bit late." Mrs. Heaton shook her head and the green feathers on top of her blue hat bobbled to and fro. "Traffic is just awful today, and I'm so glad Michael came with me. Hopefully, it won't be so bad on the way home."

At the mention of her son, Violet looked over Mrs. Heaton's shoulder to see a man that looked very familiar, but so much . . . more, striding toward them. Dressed in a navy blue suit, a wing-collar white shirt and a blue silk cravat, his dark brown hair covered with a gray bowler, the young man she'd known back home seemed to have become a mature businessman. His warm brown eyes had an expression in them that made her wonder if he were as surprised at the changes in her as she was at his.

"Violet, how good it is to see you," Michael said, taking her gloved hand in his. "If Mother hadn't been talking to you, I'm not sure I would have recognized you. You've grown up since I last saw you."

If anything, Michael Heaton was even more handsome than Violet remembered. "I could say the same for you, Michael. It's so good to see you both."

"Mother has been looking forward to your arrival very much. She's been fussing over your room for days."

She slipped her hand from his and turned toward his mother. "Oh, you shouldn't have gone to any trouble, Mrs. Heaton."

"I've enjoyed every minute, Violet. I hope you'll like it and feel right at home."

Michael quickly took charge, and before Violet knew what had happened, he'd procured a man to fetch her bags and help carry them through the huge building. She barely registered walking across the marble floor and outside, as she dodged first one and then another person hurrying to or from the trains.

Michael helped them get seated in the hack waiting right outside for them, and once they were settled and he took his seat, Violet said, "Thank you for meeting me at the station. I'm not sure I would have known what to do otherwise." She shook her head and chuckled. "I've never seen so many people in one place. Or such hustle and bustle."

"The city can be intimidating at first. And for a woman alone, I'm sure it's quite frightening," Michael said.

As the driver flipped the reins and steered his hack out onto the street and into the traffic, Violet could well believe the city would overwhelm her for years to come.

Once they were on their way, Mrs. Heaton turned to her. "I am so very sorry about your loss, my dear. Your mother was like a sister to me, and while I know your loss is greater than mine, I will miss her tremendously." The older woman patted her hand as tears gathered in her eyes.

Violet's heart warmed at her sincerity. "Thank you. She missed you sorely after you left. She looked forward to each of your letters, and I read them over and over to her when she couldn't read them herself anymore."

Mrs. Heaton dabbed at her eyes with the delicate handkerchief she pulled from her sleeve. "I'm so glad your mother and I stayed close through our correspondence. I know these last few months must have been grueling for you, dear, but I want you to know you have a place with me for as long as you need it."

Violet swallowed around the sudden lump in her throat. The very day she'd walked out of Harlan Black's office, she'd written a letter accepting Mrs. Heaton's offer to help in any way she could and telling her why. In the two weeks since, she'd been so consumed with getting ready for the move and getting out of town without letting Harlan suspect what she was doing, she hadn't had time to even grieve. The woman's kind words were like balm to her battered heart. "Thank you. I can't tell you how much your kindness means to me."

Mrs. Heaton gave a brisk nod, as if to dismiss the sad thoughts. "I'm just glad to have you here with us."

Violet began to relax. She was here among friends — even though she barely recognized Michael. Just seeing him stride across the depot toward her had taken her breath away. Sitting across from him now, she tried to keep from stealing glances at him as he and his mother pointed out different sights to her.

She wasn't even sure she saw half of all the sights since she closed her eyes each time another horse-drawn vehicle seemed bent on running them down, just before it stopped or turned on another street. She'd never seen so many different modes of travel in her life. Mrs. Heaton pointed out omnibuses, landaus and the trolley.

"Traveling in the city is a bit harrowing the first few times," Michael said. "But you'll get used to it."

"Thankfully, Grand Central isn't far from Gramercy Park, where our home is located. We'll have plenty of time to show you the sights and teach you the best way to get around, once you're settled," Mrs. Heaton said.

Violet wasn't sure she'd ever learn how to

get around and was more than a little relieved when the hack pulled up outside a nice four-story brownstone on the corner of a quiet residential street. A small sign outside read Heaton House.

"We're home, dear," Mrs. Heaton said, patting her hand. "This is my boarding-house."

Michael and the driver took Violet's baggage to the door, which was quickly opened wide by a young woman near her own age. She was slightly plump and wearing an apron and cap, her blond hair curling out from under it.

"I was getting worried, ma'am," she said as Michael and the driver brought Violet's trunk and bags into the foyer.

The foyer was wide and long, the floors polished until they gleamed. A long table with a vase of fresh flowers in the center of it and a holder for calling cards stood against one wall. There were several hat racks and coatracks on the opposite wall, and Violet assumed they got a lot of use when all the boarders were there.

"The traffic was quite heavy today, Gretchen." Mrs. Heaton took off her hat and put it on the rack. "This is Violet Burton, a dear friend from home and our new boarder. Violet, this is Gretchen Finster. She and her sister, Maida, help me out in the house and the kitchen Monday through Friday, and then on Saturdays and Sundays one goes home and the other stays to help with meals and the boarders' laundry. I don't know what I'd do without the two of them."

"How do you do, Miss Burton?" Gretchen's smile was welcoming.

"I'm fine, thank you." Now that they were out of the traffic and congestion, she felt much better. "It's nice to meet you, Gretchen."

"Come, let me give you a quick tour of downstairs while Michael and Gretchen take your bags to your room," Mrs. Heaton said.

"I'll see you later at dinner, Violet. I must get back to work for a while," Michael said.

"I'm sorry I interrupted your day, I —"

"I was glad to take some time to come greet you, and we're glad to have you here." He kissed his mother on the cheek and smiled at Violet before heading up the stairs with Gretchen following.

"See you later, dear."

"I'll try to get home early," Michael said just as he disappeared on the landing.

Violet forced her thoughts off Michael and back to Mrs. Heaton as the woman turned and pointed to the right of the foyer. "This is the front parlor, Violet. Some, if not all, of the boarders gather here most evenings before and after dinner."

The room was quite lovely and large, with a piano in one corner and at least two very comfortable-looking parlor suites covered in a plush burgundy color, along with several rocking chairs upholstered in a gold-and-burgundy stripe, stationed around the room. The draperies were of the same material as the rocking chairs. She would have liked to look closer at the paintings and portraits on the wall, the framed pictures on the tables, but there wasn't time before Mrs. Heaton led her across the hall to the dining room.

This room was attractively furnished, as well. There were the same drapes on these windows and a beautifully carved sideboard along the opposite wall. The lace-covered table was huge — it must seat at least twelve people, and Violet wondered if there were that many boarders. Next came the kitchen, and her stomach rumbled at the wonderful aroma coming from the large range. The room was large and sunny with plenty of cupboards and a large worktable in the center.

"We're having roast chicken this evening."

Mrs. Heaton took up a pot holder and checked the contents of a large pan in the middle of the oven. There appeared to be at least two big hens in the pan. Mrs. Heaton seemed to determine all was well as she closed the oven door and motioned to Violet to follow her.

Across the hall from the kitchen was the back parlor. A bit smaller than the front parlor, it seemed cozy and inviting. It was decorated in greens and blues and was quite restful. "This parlor is more for reading or quiet conversation. Several of our boarders bring their callers here to visit with them. Gretchen or Maida are always glad to bring tea or coffee for our guests."

The next room, between both parlors, was Mrs. Heaton's private study. It was paneled with shelves reaching from floor to ceiling, packed full of books. "You're welcome to come see me here anytime, Violet. And the books are available for all the boarders."

Although she'd only gotten a glimpse of each room, the homey feel of the house comforted Violet. "It is quite lovely, Mrs. Heaton."

"Thank you, dear. I'll show you to your room now, as I'm sure you're longing for a rest after your trip." She led the way down the hall and it was then Violet noticed a telephone on a table in the curve of the staircase. Mrs. Heaton motioned to it as they passed by. "The telephone is for us all to use. Many times an employer will ring up to ask someone to come in early or change their schedule. And sometimes their families or friends need to contact them."

They continued up the staircase to the second floor. "All my lady boarders reside on the top floors. Michael and the gentlemen have rooms on the bottom floor. They may use the outside entry or come up through the kitchen stairs, but they are not allowed past the main floor. Most boardinghouses cater to gentlemen, but there is a great need for rooms to let for women and I wanted to help fill it."

She passed several rooms before stopping and opening a door. "I've given you a nice bright corner room. I hope you like it."

Violet smiled as she entered the room. Mrs. Heaton was right. Sunrays glinted through the windows, splashing the lavender-and-yellow wallpaper and the striped bedcoverings of the same colors. It reminded her of her own room at home, only it was larger.

This room easily held a nice bedstead and armoire to match, an upholstered chair with matching footstool in one corner, a round table and lamp beside it. A writing table stood in front of one of the windows, and a small sofa set was grouped in front of the fireplace. It seemed to be a combination sitting room and bedroom, and Violet had no doubt she would be quite comfortable in it.

"Oh, this is a wonderful room, Mrs. Heaton. I'm certain I'm going to feel right at home here."

"I hope so, my dear."

"How nice of you to remember my favorite colors."

"It wasn't hard. I remembered how pretty your room was in Ashland. The bathroom is just next door, and you'll be sharing it with another young woman. I'll introduce you to her at dinner. Gretchen may finish helping you unpack, if you like. Then we'll leave you to rest awhile. Dinner is at seven but, of course, you may come downstairs anytime before."

Violet looked around and found Gretchen was hanging up her nicer gowns. "Thank you for what you've already done, Gretchen. I think I'll wait to unpack the rest. I must admit I am a bit tired."

Mrs. Heaton motioned to Gretchen, who immediately left the room. "I understand, dear. You try to rest. We only dress up for meals on the weekends — Saturday evenings, Sundays and holidays. All of the boarders work, and they are much too tired at the end of the day to follow society's rules for dress during the week. A nice skirt and shirtwaist will suffice. If you aren't down by dinnertime, I'll send Gretchen up to fetch you."

"Thank you."

"You are quite welcome, Violet." Mrs. Heaton moved out into the hall and quietly shut the door behind her.

After all the noise and confusion, the sights, sounds and smells of the depot and then the ride to Mrs. Heaton's, Violet felt she needed some quiet time to take everything in. And she was more than a little nervous about meeting the other boarders. It certainly wouldn't hurt to get her bearings first.

For now, she was glad just to be at Mrs. Heaton's. She sank onto the bed and looked around the room once more. It did remind her of home. But would she ever have her family home free and clear from Harlan Black?

She'd paid this month's payment the day she walked out of his office. And she'd given her best friend the money to pay the next month's payment right before she left. Violet had barely had enough money left to get to

New York City and live on for a few months. She must find work as soon as possible.

Once more she wondered if she'd done the right thing by leaving — but she'd worry about that later.

Michael found his mother in her private study, sitting in her favorite chair with her Bible in her lap and with her eyes closed as if she were praying. He had turned to leave when she called his name.

"Michael, come in, dear. I'm not asleep."

He took a seat in the chair opposite his mother's and put his feet up. "I didn't want to disturb you."

She closed her Bible and laid it on the table between them. "I'm through with my conversation with the Lord, at least for now. I was just taking a few minutes to talk to Him about our new boarder and asking Him to make Violet's transition to our home an easy one."

"I'm sure it's been difficult for her since losing her mother just a month ago, especially after finding her home was mortgaged and not being able to find work. Having to leave her home couldn't have been easy, and New York is very different from Ashland."

His mother nodded. "I'm so glad she came here. But I think she was a bit overwhelmed today. My being late to meet her train didn't help, but she was very gracious about it."

"We'll do what we can to make things easy for her, Mother."

"I know. We can begin tonight. I'm sure she's a little apprehensive about meeting everyone. She's grown into quite a lovely young woman since the last time you saw her, hasn't she?"

"Yes, she has." Michael hadn't been able to quit thinking of Violet all afternoon. He couldn't remember when thoughts of a woman had interfered with his work so much, and he didn't know quite what to make of it.

The sound of doors opening and closing signaled that many of their boarders were home from work, and his mother got up from her chair. "I'd better go see to the finishing touches for dinner."

Michael stood, as well. "Good. My mouth has been watering ever since I walked in the door."

"I figured as much. You might want to go to the front parlor and greet Violet when she comes down. And make sure our gentlemen boarders behave themselves."

"That I will do." Michael bent and kissed his mother's cheek. "She reminds you of

Rebecca, doesn't she?"

His mother sighed and gave a quick nod. "She's the same age that Becca was when —"

He knew she couldn't bring herself to say the words. His sister had been missing for over three years now, and still they didn't know what had happened to her. "Is this going to be too hard for you . . . having Violet here, Mother?"

"Oh, no, dear. She does bring back memories of being in Ashland before Becca left to come here . . . but those memories are good ones and I welcome them."

Michael gave his mother a quick hug. "I'll be grateful that she's here then and do all I can to make the transition to the city easier for her."

"Thank you, son."

Michael watched his mother leave the room, hoping that she was right and that it would be good for her to have Violet here. She could use some joy.

Becca's sudden disappearance after she'd moved to New York City three years earlier had changed their lives forever. It'd been the catalyst for selling their home in Ashland, moving here and starting the boardinghouse. Thankfully, his father had provided for his mother well so that they could fulfill her wishes. She wanted to give safe haven to the people who lived under her roof, especially the young women. She wanted them to have a place they felt was home even while missing their own. And she wanted to make sure that their families would never have to hear that their loved one was missing, never to be heard from again.

Michael had been trained as a private investigator by the best. He'd worked for Pinkerton before opening his own detective agency, and now he made it his life's work to try to help his clients who had heard those same words — or others similar to them — and to follow each and every lead that might turn up about his sister.

That Violet was the daughter of his mother's best friend and their next-door neighbor was enough to make him want to watch her as closely as he would Becca, if she were here. Becca was several years older than Violet and while one wouldn't have called them best friends, he'd always considered them friends and had teased Violet as much as he had his own sister. He knew that if anything happened to Violet, his mother would blame herself, and Michael couldn't let that happen.

He stood and rubbed the back of his neck

before heading down the hall to the front parlor. Their boarders were a good group for the most part, but after what his mother had told him about Violet, he wanted to be there to try to put her at ease among strangers.

"Why, Michael, how nice of you to join us early tonight!" Lila Miller, a young woman who'd been with them for nearly a year, left the side of Luke Patterson and headed in his direction as soon as he entered the parlor.

"Good evening, Miss Miller, everyone," he said, trying to make eye contact with each person in the room.

"To what do we owe this honor, Michael?" Lila asked. "You've barely been on time for meals the last few weeks."

He'd like to tell her that it was her company he'd been trying to avoid lately, but that was out of the question, of course. Michael didn't want to offend her. He just didn't like the way she fawned over him.

"I thought I'd greet our new boarder when she comes down."

"Oh?" Lila raised a narrow brown eyebrow. "She's here then?"

"She arrived this afternoon."

"And she's here now." Elizabeth Anderson, one of his mother's favorite boarders, entered the room just ahead of Violet. "Everyone, meet Violet Burton. I met her at the landing. She seemed a bit hesitant to come down, but I promised her that we'd all be on our best behavior. At least until we get to know her better."

The young woman who'd followed Elizabeth into the room smiled at everyone and said, "I took her at her word."

That brought chuckles from the boarders gathering around her, and Michael quickly crossed the room to her side. "Violet, I hope you've been able to get some rest?"

His mother was right. This was not the Violet he remembered. That one had been a young girl and, while pretty and sweet, this Violet was a fully grown woman and a lovely one at that. Her black hair was swept up on top of her head, and when her gaze settled on him, he was struck by how brilliantly blue her eyes were.

"I did, thank you, Mr. Heaton."

She hadn't called him Mr. Heaton back home. It'd only been Michael . . . and that in an exasperated tone when he'd been teasing her and Becca. He chuckled at the memory. Perhaps she was only doing it now because of the boarders, but he didn't like it. "Oh, come now, Violet. Surely as long as we've known each other, we can dispense

36

with the formalities, can't we?"

She looked up at him and her smiled deepened. "I suppose we can . . . Michael."

But her smile didn't quite reach her eyes and the wary expression in them reminded him of all she'd been through so recently. Suddenly his protective instincts rose up full force, shocking him with their intensity. In that moment, Michael knew he'd do all he could to keep Violet Burton safe and to help her adjust to her new surroundings.

# CHAPTER TWO

"Dinner is served," Mrs. Heaton announced from the dining room. "Come along, everyone, we'll make the remaining introductions while we dine."

Michael held out his arm and Violet hesitated for a moment before taking it. This was Michael Heaton, after all, not a complete stranger. He'd been her neighbor for years and he was only escorting her across the hall to the dining room. Although he was several years older than Violet, she'd known him all of her life. And his teasing manner was just the same as it had been when she was growing up.

But Violet hadn't been prepared for the effect of his smile on her. The sheer force of it, with those twin dimples that hadn't been in evidence earlier that day, left her a little stunned and bewildered that she felt so drawn to him. She told herself it was because it was so good to see another familiar face in this strange city so far away from home, but she wasn't sure she was telling herself the truth. Her heartbeat hadn't slowed down since her gaze met his.

He led her across the foyer and into the dining room. Pulling out a chair, he seated Violet while another of the boarders seated his mother at the opposite end of the table. Then Michael took his own place at the head of the table; his chair was adjacent to the one Violet was sitting in.

The brown-haired, brown-eyed woman who'd been standing with her hand on Michael's forearm when Violet came into the parlor had slipped into the chair opposite Violet, but her attention was solely on Michael.

Others who were in the parlor took their seats at the table, and Violet was relieved to see that, just as Mrs. Heaton had said, most of the ladies were dressed in skirts and nice shirtwaists. Mrs. Heaton had changed into a dark brown skirt and beige shirtwaist as well, and Violet felt as if she fit in with the navy skirt and crisp white shirt she'd chosen. It had a lace insert at the top of the bodice and she'd worn her mother's cameo, which made her feel a little dressed up, but not so much that she felt out of place. She let out a small sigh of relief.

Once everyone was settled, they all looked to Mrs. Heaton for direction.

"Michael, will you please say grace?"

"Certainly."

Violet bowed her head while he said a simple prayer of thanksgiving. She was touched that he thanked the Lord for her safe travel as well as for the food. Once he'd finished the prayer, he began passing dishes family-style with some help from Gretchen and Maida. The other boarders began to talk amongst themselves as the dishes were passed around, and Violet felt herself begin to relax.

Michael held the tray while she selected a piece of chicken, and then he handed it off to the man beside her while Gretchen and Maida helped keep the rest of the dishes moving around the table. The side dishes were creamed potatoes, peas, carrots and baby onions. The rolls were crisp and hot, and Violet was glad there were so many small conversations going on that hopefully no one could hear her stomach growl.

When all the dishes had made the round of the table, and Gretchen and her sister had slipped into their chairs, Mrs. Heaton introduced Violet to the other boarders.

"This is Violet Burton, our new boarder. She's a dear friend of the family and we're very happy that she's come to live here." She then motioned to the young woman on her right. "Violet, this is Julia Olsen, who works at Ellis Island. It's a busy job she has."

The auburn-haired girl smiled down the table at Violet. Her green eyes sparkled. "It's certainly an interesting one, too. I've many stories to tell."

"I look forward to hearing them." Violet took some potatoes and passed them down.

"The gentleman next to her is Benjamin Roth, who is a teacher," Mrs. Heaton continued with the introductions. "And across from you is Lila Miller, who works at Butterick."

Benjamin had blond hair and blue eyes. "Good to have you with us, Miss Burton."

"Thank you, Mr. Roth." Violet then smiled at Lila. "Butterick! Oh, wonderful! Their patterns certainly have made it easier for the home seamstress to make garments that fit," Violet said.

Lila gave a half smile and slight nod while Mrs. Heaton continued, "On your right is Luke Patterson. Luke writes dime novels."

"Dime novels?" Violet asked. She'd never met a real writer before. "How interesting."

Luke's blue eyes seemed to twinkle as he brushed his brown hair off his brow and smiled. "I think so."

Mrs. Heaton continued, "And next to him is Elizabeth Anderson, who works for *The Delineator*. She's also the young woman you'll be sharing a bathroom with."

"We met at the landing, Mrs. Heaton," Elizabeth said with a smile. She had blond hair and hazel eyes.

"And Elizabeth was kind enough to accompany me down to the parlor," Violet added. "I love *The Delineator*. Mother subscribed to it and we pored over it, looking at all the newest styles." She looked from Elizabeth to Lila and back again. "Isn't *The Delineator* owned by Butterick? Do you two work together?"

Lila gave a brief shake of her head, but Elizabeth explained. "Butterick does own the magazine. And we joke about being coworkers, but *The Delineator* has its own offices at Butterick Publishing Company on Thirteenth Street."

"I see." Violet liked Elizabeth. She was quite friendly and helpful. She wished she could say the same about Lila, who only seemed to smile for Michael's benefit.

Mrs. Heaton continued with her introductions. "Of course you've met Gretchen and Maida. We have another boarder, but he's out for the evening. You'll meet him tomorrow."

"It's probably better this way. The whole bunch of us at one time might intimidate Miss Burton," Luke Patterson said.

"I'm sure she can handle being around us all, Luke." Julia took a roll from the basket Mrs. Heaton passed her and handed it to Benjamin. "She's got to be a brave woman to move to New York City on her own."

Violet almost laughed out loud. If Julia could have seen her at the train station today, she might not think she was so brave.

"Violet will be able to handle this household with ease. I'm certain of it." Mrs. Heaton smiled at Violet and then looked around the table. "What we need to do for her now, though, is try to come up with places that she can apply for employment. Do any of you know of any openings?"

"What is it you are trained to do, Miss Burton?" Julia asked from down the table.

"Well, I can't say I'm trained to do anything. I can cook and clean. And I can sew, but I'm not sure I could call myself a seamstress. I've only sewn for my mother or myself." Suddenly, Violet realized she wasn't really trained for any kind of employment. She'd been groomed to be a wife, but that wasn't anything she wanted any part of at the moment — if ever. "I really don't know what kind of work I'd be best suited for. . . ."

"Don't worry," Elizabeth said with a chuckle. "I most certainly wasn't trained to work for a magazine. Most of us have positions where we've been trained to do the job. I don't think *The Delineator* has any openings at present, but I'll check. I'm sure you'll find something, though."

"Lila, didn't you say recently that Butterick was needing help?" Michael asked.

Lila glanced over at Violet and chewed her bottom lip for a moment before looking back at Michael. Her smile brightened as she fluttered her eyelashes at him. "I believe they were needing help with folding and packaging the patterns or possibly with cutting them out. I know they hired one girl, but I can ask tomorrow if they still need help."

"Oh, would you, dear?" Mrs. Heaton asked. "I would think of it as a personal favor to me, if you would."

"As would I," Michael added.

"Then I will certainly ask." Lila batted her eyelashes once more.

"Thank you, Lila," Violet said. "That is very kind of you."

The other girl's smile dimmed somewhat as she glanced at Violet. "I'll let you know what I find out."

"Anyone else know of anything?" Michael asked.

"I have a friend who works at Tiffany Glass. They might not be hiring right now, but she says someone is always getting married and there are bound to be openings before too long," Elizabeth said.

"We can look at the classifieds in the morning paper, too," Michael suggested.

Several other ideas were mentioned as they ate their meal and Violet felt her hopes for employment grow. Surely in a city this large, she could find something before long. At least Harlan Black didn't have an influence here. He couldn't stop people from hiring her.

Coconut cake was served with coffee, and Violet enjoyed it while she listened to the others talk about their day. So far everyone seemed nice, but Violet couldn't help but notice that most all the women at the table seemed to hang on to every word that came out of Michael's mouth. And if Lila Miller batted her eyelashes at him each time he looked her way, she wasn't the only one doing so. Even with two other men at the table, Michael seemed to be the one who had the attention of every woman, and — much to Violet's dismay — that included her. She couldn't really blame them. Those dimples were hard not to watch for.

During the meal, Michael watched the interaction between the boarders and Violet. She listened more than she talked, and she seemed to be totally unaware that Luke and Benjamin were both taking in everything she did say. On the other hand, he hadn't missed the way the two men watched her every move.

A new woman in their midst was always of interest to the male boarders. Just as he supposed a new man would be to the females sitting at the table. But Luke and Benjamin appeared to be totally captivated by Violet. While he couldn't blame them — she was lovely and quite unpretentious — Michael felt a little out of sorts about the attention they were giving her.

He watched as Violet asked Luke about his writing and wondered, what would she think if she knew Luke sometimes did investigative work for Michael's detective agency? It was something few people knew about, which worked to Michael's benefit. No one would suspect one of his agents was the dime-novel writer living in his mother's boardinghouse. Violet seemed interested in Luke's writing — was she interested in him?

It shouldn't matter. Michael had made up

his mind never to become interested in any of the women living in his mother's boardinghouse — an easy thing to do since he'd been burned once and was determined never to let it happen again. But Violet wasn't just a boarder. They'd lived next door to each other, and their mothers had been best friends. He couldn't ignore that connection. Nor did he want to.

He glanced her way as she spoke to Elizabeth, and realized how much she'd changed since he last saw her. She seemed to have lost the smattering of freckles that once graced her nose, and her skin was smooth and flawless now, but he found he missed those freckles.

It took some effort to pull his thoughts back to the present and he was glad to see that most everyone seemed genuinely interested in helping Violet find employment, with the exception of Lila. She didn't seem enthused about assisting in the search — at least not where she worked. He was certain she'd mentioned that Butterick was expanding and needed more help just a week or so ago, and he'd almost laughed at the look on Lila's face when he'd backed her into a corner so she had no choice but to say she would check on it. However, he wasn't totally confident that she would keep her word.

He'd had no reason to check the classifieds, so he didn't know if Butterick might have placed an ad. Hopefully they'd find something in the paper tomorrow, whether it be Butterick or some other place. It would make things easier if Violet found a position where one of the other girls worked. She'd be able to learn her way around a little faster if she had someone to go to work and come home with. But this was New York City, after all. Violet would find something. He was sure of it.

When everyone adjourned to the parlor, Violet excused herself saying she had unpacking still to do. That was the truth, but the real reason she felt the need to escape to her room was that she was quite overwhelmed by her whole day. It had been a very long one and she hadn't had time to let it soak in that she really was going to make her home in New York City, in this house, with these people.

Mrs. Heaton followed her upstairs. "Are you all right, dear?"

"I'm fine. I'm just —"

"Not used to all that conversation and everyone talking at the same time, are you?"

"No, ma'am." She smiled. The older woman seemed to have a knack for knowing what she was thinking. "But I did enjoy it. I think I'm just very tired tonight."

"I'm sure you are. I wanted to show you where the towels are kept and make certain you weren't feeling poorly." She pointed out the linen closet in the hall and got out a fresh towel and washcloth for Violet. "My room is just across the hall from yours, should you need me. Please remember, Violet, that you are like family to me and —"

"I thank you so much for that. Your hospitality is more of a comfort than I can tell you. But that being said, I need to pay you my first month's rent. It's fifty dollars, isn't it?"

"That's the fee, but I want you to wait until the first of July to pay me."

"Oh, no." Violet shook her head. "I can't let you do that, Mrs. Heaton."

"You have no choice, dear. I don't want you worrying about money until you have a paying position, which I'm certain you will have by then. You have enough stress trying to find employment and getting used to everything. Think of yourself as my guest at least until July. Then you'll be a boarder."

"But —"

Mrs. Heaton held up her hand and smiled. "Not another word about it, dear. It's final."

"Thank you. I am so blessed that you wrote me offering your help. I had no intention of ever leaving Ashland, but with Harlan Black making it impossible for me to find work, your letter seemed an answer to my prayers. I can't thank you enough."

"Your being here is enough thanks. You bring back happy memories to me of times past and I cherish them. As for Harlan Black . . . I do remember him as well, and I am glad you got away from that horrid man!"

"Oh, so am I." The very thought of Harlan sickened her.

"Do you think he'll come after you?"

Violet's heart plummeted to her stomach at Mrs. Heaton's question. Thus far, she'd not let herself think along those lines, but now she realized that same question had been lying at the back of her mind just waiting to torment her. "I don't know. I certainly hope not."

Mrs. Heaton placed a hand on her ample chest. "I am so sorry, Violet. I didn't mean to bring up unpleasant thoughts for you."

"It's all right, Mrs. Heaton. I'm just glad to be out of Ashland and away from him." She shivered again thinking of the last time she'd seen him.

"Well, never you worry, dear. He won't bother you here." Mrs. Heaton waved her hand as if to dispel the thought of Harlan. "Enough of this depressing talk. I'll let you have some time to yourself. Breakfast is from six to nine. It's set out on the sideboard in the dining room. We'll take a look at the classifieds and see if we can find some positions for you to apply for tomorrow. Good night, dear."

"Good night."

Violet heard the sound of the piano being played and voices singing "The Sidewalks of New York" as Mrs. Heaton went back downstairs. For a moment she wished she'd stayed with everyone. Then she reminded herself that there would be other nights and much more time to get to know the others. For now, she needed some quiet time.

Violet finished her unpacking and then took a long soak in the big tub in the bathroom. Once she was back in her room, she settled herself into the chair by the window and listened to the singing from downstairs. She loved to sing and would be happy to join them around the piano one day.

The music faded and she heard footsteps on the stairs, doors opening and closing down the hall and the sound of water running in the bathroom she shared with Elizabeth. She found she liked the sounds of life around her and knowing she wasn't alone.

As the house quieted, Violet opened her Bible and read several of her favorite Psalms. Then she said her prayers before turning in, thanking the Lord for giving her safe travel and for Mrs. Heaton and her offer. Exhausted as she was, Violet felt certain she would drift right off to sleep.

Instead, she remembered the conversation with Mrs. Heaton earlier and before long, her thoughts were in such turmoil wondering what Harlan would do when he found she'd left town that she couldn't sleep. She tossed and turned for what seemed like hours before flinging back the covers. Violet got out of bed and paced around her bed and back again.

Harlan was not going to be happy, that was for sure. But would he try to find her? She prayed not. Still, afraid that he might look for her, she'd bought a ticket as far as Baltimore, then bought another one from there to New York City. She hoped it would be impossible for him to locate her, should he decide he must.

Violet stopped and pulled the curtain away from the window. Lights were still shining in some of the homes nearby and she could even see a light or two in the next street over. Somehow the light in the darkness comforted her, knowing others were up at this hour. Back home there wouldn't be a light shining anywhere this time of night, except for the taverns and the small police station. But this city was so large — surely Harlan would never find her here if he did decide to look for her.

She dropped the curtain and went back to bed. It wasn't going to do any good to worry about him. He'd either track her down or not. But he couldn't make her marry him. Worrying about him would serve no purpose; she'd just turn it over to the Lord and leave it in His hands.

The next morning Violet awakened to the sounds of doors opening and closing once more. She looked at the small clock on her bedside table. Six-thirty. She was used to sleeping a bit later than that on a Saturday, but she was eager to start the day.

Throwing back the covers, she hopped out of bed and hurried to the windows. The sun was up and it looked as if it were going to be a beautiful spring day.

Violet started to walk to the bathroom, but she heard water running. Elizabeth would be getting ready for work. She'd said she worked a half day today, and Violet was glad she hadn't hurried to the bathroom right away. It seemed everyone had a job or somewhere to go except her, and she certainly didn't want to hold Elizabeth up.

The water stopped running, but Violet waited until she heard the bathroom door shut from the other side, signaling that Elizabeth had finished washing up. Even then she knocked just to make sure the bathroom was empty before entering.

Once she'd finished freshening up, she went back to her room to dress in a burgundy skirt and ivory shirtwaist. She put her hair up, twisting it up into a knot on top of her head in one of the current styles, and made her bed before leaving the room. By the time she arrived downstairs, some of the boarders she'd met the evening before were heading out the door and they wished her well in her search for employment.

"Thank you," she called as she waved goodbye and entered the empty dining room. She took a plate and began to fill it from the sideboard, choosing a couple of slices of bacon, some scrambled eggs and a biscuit. Just as Violet took a seat at the table, Maida, or maybe it was Gretchen, came in the room. On closer inspection, Violet decided it was Maida. She was a little taller and her hair was a darker shade of blond.

"Good morning, Miss Burton."

"Good morning, Maida." Violet knew she got it right when she was rewarded with a smile.

"Did you sleep well last night?" the maid asked.

"I did."

"Would you like tea or coffee this morning?"

"Tea, please."

Maida poured her a steaming cup from the silver pot on the sideboard. "Mrs. Heaton asked me to let her know when you came down. She'll be joining you soon."

"Wonderful. Maida, do you know where the morning paper might be? I'd like to look over the classifieds."

Mrs. Heaton walked into the room just then, the newspaper in her hand. "It's right here, dear. I've been looking over them for you."

Maida poured Mrs. Heaton a cup of tea and set it at her place at the table. "Would you like me to prepare you anything, ma'am?"

Mrs. Heaton glanced at the offerings on the sideboard. "No, thank you, Maida. There is still plenty here to choose from."

After Maida replaced the pot on the sideboard and left the room, Mrs. Heaton handed Violet the paper. "There are several positions you might be interested in, dear. If you see anything you want to apply for, I'll be glad to accompany you on Monday to put in applications. However, I hope you will let yourself rest this weekend. Besides, some of the other boarders might come back with news about openings in their companies this evening."

"That would be wonderful." Violet took the folded *New York Tribune* Mrs. Heaton handed her. "I'm sure I will take you up on the offer to go with me on Monday. I wouldn't have the faintest idea on where anything is located."

"I thought you might enjoy a ride around town today so that I can show you several of the places you might want to apply at on Monday — if you see anything that appeals to you."

Remembering the terrible traffic of the day before, Violet didn't exactly look forward to getting out in it again, but she did want to see the city. While Mrs. Heaton filled her plate, Violet looked at some of the circled entries. There were several requests for shopkeeper positions, a straw-hat presser — whatever that was — and an opening for a correspondent. Those were the only ones Mrs. Heaton had circled, but Violet's gaze skimmed the rest. A lady wanted a person to do writing for her at home; another wanted a companion, but that meant living at the residence, and Violet knew she wouldn't want to do that.

She liked being right here. When she'd awakened this morning, it'd been quite comforting to know that she was in the home of someone she was acquainted with, someone she could call a friend.

"What do you think? Do any of those positions sound good to you?" Mrs. Heaton took her seat at the table.

"I'm not sure appealing to me is the important thing," Violet said. "I need work, so most likely I'll accept any decent position I'm offered."

"Don't feel you must rush into employment, Violet. I'd prefer you take your time and find something you believe you'll be happy at. One good thing about the Butterick position is that you'd know someone who works there, and you'd have company for the trips to and from work."

"But we don't know if that is still open, do we?"

"You didn't see it?" Mrs. Heaton jumped up and came over to her. "Oh, dear, it's on the top of the next page."

She took the paper from Violet and turned the page. There, at the top, was circled: "Pattern cutter/Pattern folder wanted. No experience necessary. Will train. Apply at 555 Broadway Monday through Friday, 8:00 a.m. to 4:00 p.m."

Violet looked up at Mrs. Heaton. "Oh, yes, I would like to apply there. They're willing to train me and that is exactly what I need."

"And once you are established here and meet more people, if this position isn't one you like, it will be easier to find another one. You'll know your way around the city and you'll have a résumé."

Violet couldn't help but chuckle. "You speak as if I already have this position. It may be filled by Monday."

"I don't think so. But we won't know until then. In the meantime, I'll show you around so that you can see where some of these places are. We'll be on our way as soon as we finish breakfast."

"Where is it you are off to so early in the day, Mother?"

Violet's breath caught in her throat at the sight of Michael striding into the room.

Even Mrs. Heaton seemed surprised to see her son. "Michael, I thought you left for work over an hour ago. What are you doing back home?"

"Good morning, Mother." Michael gave his mother a kiss on the cheek and grinned at Violet. "Good morning to you, too, Violet. I hope you slept well."

"I did, thank you."

"Michael, you haven't answered my question."

"I'm sorry, Mother. I did go to the office and I telephoned Butterick from there and found that they are indeed hiring, but they only take applications Monday through —"

"Friday." His mother laughed. "Well, I could have told you that!"

"How could you have known?"

"I read the paper this morning," she answered, waving it at him.

"So that is where it was!" He laughed. "I looked all over for it."

His mother grinned. "It was in my study. I'm sorry. It appears we're both anxious to find something for Violet."

Michael poured himself a cup of coffee from the pot Maida had left on the sideboard. He took his seat at the table and smiled at Violet. "Now that Mother has you here, she wants to make sure you stay."

"I have no plans to go anywhere other

than out to find work," Violet said. "And I am very grateful to your mother for coming up with a solution for me."

"I thought we could take a ride around the city this morning so that Violet could get a look at some of the places she might want to apply at on Monday," his mother said.

"If you don't mind the company, I'll escort the two of you."

"I hate to take you away from your work —"

"We'd love to have your company," his mother interrupted. "I'll feel better if you are the one explaining the El and the trolley to Violet."

"Good. And there is no need to worry about taking me away from my work, Violet. I am fortunate in that I get to set my own work schedule."

"Then I thank you both. I'll just go freshen up and be ready when you are," Violet said.

Michael pulled out her chair for her. Although she'd given in gracefully, he couldn't really tell if she was pleased or not that he'd be going with them.

"And I will talk to Maida about our dinner tonight," his mother said.

He pulled out her chair, as well. "All right.

But there is no need to rush, ladies. I'll sit here and have another one of Maida's biscuits while I wait for you."

Although Michael could set his own hours, it wasn't often he took a day off from work, and he was going to enjoy it. He buttered a biscuit, plopped a spoonful of apple jelly in the middle and took a bite. Delicious.

He wasn't sure exactly why he'd decided to come back home this early. He'd telephoned Butterick when he got to his office because, for some reason, he didn't quite trust that Lila would ask about openings at the company. Still, he could have waited until this evening to tell Violet about it; she couldn't apply there until Monday, anyway.

However, knowing his mother as he did, he was sure that she and Violet would be out and about today. He really was a little concerned about Violet learning her way around the city — after all, it was his mother's suggestion that brought her here and there was no denying that made him feel personally responsible for her safety. He couldn't let anything happen to her.

"I'm ready, dear, and I'm sure Violet will be coming down the stairs any moment now. I do appreciate you checking into the

Butterick position for her. I'm praying she gets it."

"So am I." For his mother's sake, if not for Violet's. "You like having her here, don't you?"

"I do," his mother answered. "Don't you?"

Michael hadn't expected that question, and he wasn't really sure he could answer it right now. After all, Violet had only been here one night and her presence meant more responsibility for him. But his mother looked so happy this morning, he wasn't about to tell her any of that. So he chose to be as truthful as he could at the moment. "I want you to be happy, Mother."

"Thank you, dear. I want the same for you, don't you know?"

"I —" Footsteps could be heard crossing the foyer and Michael was glad. He took one last sip of coffee and stood just as Violet entered the room.

"I hope I didn't keep you waiting long," Violet said, pulling her gloves on and smiling at them.

She did have a beautiful smile. Michael couldn't help but smile back. "Not at all. Are you ready to see the city?"

"I am."

"Then, I'm at your service, ladies."

# CHAPTER THREE

Violet thought it was a beautiful day as they sauntered down the street to Third Avenue, where she assumed they'd find a hack to take them around the city. She couldn't help but be pleased that Michael had come home to tell her about the Butterick opening and wanted to accompany them today. But she didn't want to be a burden to either of the Heatons. She hoped she got the job at Butterick. At least that way, she'd have Lila to help her learn her way to work and back, and Michael and his mother wouldn't be worrying about her.

"Is it a long walk to the Butterick Company from here?" she asked.

"It could be done in around a half hour. But it would be much quicker to take the El or another mode of transportation," Mrs. Heaton said.

"We'll be traveling by the El today." Michael smiled down at her. "I want you to get familiar with the stops and comfortable with getting on and off at the right places."

While the sound of the traffic she'd witnessed the day before couldn't be heard from Mrs. Heaton's boardinghouse, as they got closer to the avenue, the sounds of horses' hooves and drivers yelling became more and more noticeable. When they reached the corner, Violet pulled up short and inhaled sharply. Somehow the traffic seemed even worse when one was on foot.

"What is it? Is something wrong?" Michael asked, his hand at her back.

Violet put her hand to her throat and expelled a deep breath. She shook her head, but there were no words for what she was seeing or feeling as she watched people from all walks of life hurrying along the busy thoroughfare, some even crossing the street, dodging the horse-drawn vehicles as best they could. And that had to be taking their lives in their own hands, because there seemed to be every kind of vehicle imaginable, and some Violet had never seen before, racing up and down the street. Then she heard a train and had to look up to see it. There, high above the traffic down below, was the El. Mrs. Heaton had pointed it out to her the day before. She didn't know whether to laugh or exclaim.

"It's the traffic, Michael," Mrs. Heaton said, grasping her hand.

"Of course it is. I'm sorry, Violet. I didn't realize — it is quite a change from Ashland, isn't it? But don't worry. One day you'll know your way around and the traffic will just seem normal to you."

Violet hoped so, as she tried to get her breathing back to normal. But she had to admit that as much as it all frightened her, there was something about all the hustle and bustle of this place that exhilarated her and had her heart pounding to keep pace with all the sounds around them.

Michael led her and his mother up to what she supposed was an entry to get on the train, which had stopped only a block away. He handed the man a coin for a ticket, then gave a coin to her and his mother and they did the same. Then they were allowed to go through a turnstile into an area where they waited in front of doors with glass windows until they were allowed to enter the train on the other side.

"Take a window seat, Violet. You'll see more that way," Mrs. Heaton said.

Violet sat down and Mrs. Heaton took the seat across from her. Michael sat down beside Violet. A conductor collected their tickets and, as the train took off, Violet couldn't keep an excited giggle from escaping as she looked down on the street below.

"It is quite something, isn't it?" Michael asked. "Seeing your reaction reminds us of our own just a few years ago. Mother and I were just as amazed as you are."

His words made Violet feel better, but she didn't have time to say so, as he leaned across her and pointed. "Look, there's City Hall on your left."

The train stopped just then for some of the passengers to get out and others to get on, and Violet got a good look at where the city government was conducted. Then the train was on its way again. They made a sudden turn and Violet slid closer to Michael. His nearness and the scent of his cologne were hard to ignore as she tried to right herself. Trying to compose herself, she pointed to the tallest building she'd ever seen. "What is that?"

"That is the Tower Building over on Broadway. It's thirteen stories high and is one of the tallest buildings in the city at present."

Violet was certain she wouldn't want to be on the top floor looking down. She shuddered at the mere thought of it.

"We're on Sixth Avenue now and we'll get off at the next stop," Michael explained.

"Butterick isn't far from here."

"If we have time, I'd love for Violet to at least get a glimpse of the Ladies' Mile," his mother suggested.

"The Ladies' Mile? What is that?" Violet asked as the train came to a stop once more and Michael and his mother both stood. Violet scooted out of her seat, shook her skirts and stood beside Mrs. Heaton in the aisle.

"Oh, my dear, the Ladies' Mile is blocks and blocks of the most wonderful shops and department stores. Some weekends the girls and I come down just to window-shop. Even if one doesn't buy anything, it's the place to go to know what is in style. Besides, several of the shops that need help are there, so it will be helpful if you know where they're located," Mrs. Heaton said.

Violet followed them out of the train and down to ground level again. Michael hired a hack and off they went once more.

"Aren't we going to show her Central Park, Michael? We've come this far."

"Perhaps we can go there tomorrow after Sunday dinner?"

"That is a wonderful idea. She can't see New York City all in a day, that is for certain."

As the Heatons talked over her, Violet

began to believe she could live here the rest of her life and never see it all. Back on street level, in the traffic of a Saturday morning, Violet once again found herself closing her eyes from time to time as one or another vehicle seemed bound to run into them.

Michael was right. It wasn't far to Butterick on Broadway. Violet looked up at the building with the signs that said E. Butterick and Company. Ornate molding framed the windows and doors. The building was very nice, and Violet didn't think she would mind working there, but in her present circumstance she'd be glad to find any respectable position.

Michael pointed out all the El stops, but Violet had a feeling it would take a while before she knew exactly which one to take. He promised to draw her a map to keep with her, to make it easier for her to remember.

Mrs. Heaton pointed out Brooks Brothers, Tiffany's Jewelry and Lord & Taylor along with other stores on Broadway. Michael had the driver turn up and down several different blocks and, new as she was to the city, even Violet could tell when they got close to the Ladies' Mile.

Traffic slowed and became more congested. Carriages of all kinds, landaus, rockaways and phaetons moved slowly, giving them a glimpse of the ladies inside. That these women belonged to society was evident by the gowns they wore and the fact that many had liveried men driving them.

But there were others — everyday women dressed much like Violet and Mrs. Heaton — who were there, too. They were lined up, looking in the shop windows of Macy's, Le Boutellier Brothers, Hearns Department Store and Orbach's on Fourteenth Street. Violet remembered that Macy's and Hearns both had ads in the classifieds. She'd apply at them on Monday as well as Butterick.

Part of Violet wanted to be looking in the windows along with all of those other women, and the other part of her could not have been more relieved when Michael told the driver to take them back to the boardinghouse.

If anything, traffic was even more frenzied than earlier in the day, and Violet closed her eyes at more than one intersection. When Michael chuckled, she opened them to find him looking at her with a smile on his face.

"I'm sorry, Violet, it is just so entertaining to watch you try *not* to watch the traffic."

"I can't seem to help it. I fear a calamity is bound to happen at any moment, and I don't want to see it or be part of it."

"Oh, accidents do happen, and frequently. But most times they aren't all that serious." He grinned at her. "However, it might be best if you try *not* to shut your eyes, or pray that our driver doesn't shut his, as well."

Violet laughed with him. "Yes, I can see how that might help. I'll try, but I can't promise."

Just then, an omnibus careened around a corner and seemed to be heading straight for them. Violet scrunched her eyes shut tight and screamed.

After a much-needed nap, Violet woke refreshed and looking forward to dinner, in spite of feeling horrible about screaming in Mrs. Heaton's ear. When that omnibus had come straight toward their hack, she'd been certain it was going to topple them over. Thankfully, the Lord had been with them and, just in the nick of time, their driver had avoided the calamity.

The Heatons had assured her, over and over again, that they understood, and told her that if not for her scream, their driver might not have acted so quickly. Still, she felt a bit silly and embarrassed about it all. Hopefully, it wouldn't be a topic of conversation at dinner.

She chose a gown of purple moiré that

was several years old, but still in style. At least it had been back home. She only hoped it wasn't terribly outdated here in New York City.

After dressing her hair into a psyche knot, Violet turned this way and that in front of the standing mirror in the corner. The dress had an ivory lace inset in the bodice and a high collar and waistband of a darker shade of purple. It showed little wear, and, well, it would have to do. Even if she chose another gown, it would not be new.

After Mama had her stroke there'd been no money for new clothes, not even home-made ones, and Violet had no interest in them anyway. All she'd wanted was for her mother to get well. But that wasn't to be and, oh, how she missed her. Grief, sudden and sharp, threatened to engulf Violet, until she remembered the promise she'd made to her mother just before she had passed away.

Mama had been so alert for just those few moments as she'd grasped her hand and said, "Violet, now don't you give yourself over to grief once I'm gone. You've been a blessing to me and I don't know what I would have done without you. I want you to get on with your life. The Lord has great plans for you. I know you'll miss me, but I pray your days will be full of life and joy and living according to the Lord's will. When you start to give in to the grief, think of me in Heaven. Promise me, Violet, for I'm ready to go."

"I promise, Mama," Violet had said. Her mother had squeezed her hand, closed her eyes and slipped away. Remembering how peaceful her mother had looked, Violet let one last sob escape before she wiped at her tears. They wouldn't bring her mother back, and Violet wouldn't have wanted her to suffer just to stay here for her sake.

She let out a huge sigh and nodded to herself. Enough of this — it wasn't what Mama would want. She would honor her mother's wishes and her promise to her. But, oh, how she wished she'd been with her today to see all the sights and hubbub of this city. It comforted her to think that maybe she saw it all from Heaven.

Hearing the sounds of the other boarders begin to make their way downstairs, Violet hurried into the bathroom to splash water on her face, trying to get rid of the telltale tears. She pinched her cheeks to give them color and took a deep breath before stepping out into the hall.

Violet hoped she wasn't overdressed, or underdressed, as she headed down to the parlor to join everyone. She was relieved to see that Elizabeth was dressed much as she was in a pale blue gown, and she put her worries about how she looked away.

"Violet, did you have a good day?" Elizabeth asked as she led the way downstairs. "I asked my friend about openings at Tiffany Glass, and as I suspected, there aren't any at present. Still, she said she'd let me know when one comes up. Evidently it's fairly often."

"Thank you for asking about it, Elizabeth. I did have a good day. I rode on the El for the first time and I know where several companies are that I'll apply at on Monday, including Butterick."

Elizabeth chuckled. "Riding on the El for the first time is an experience, but you get used to it very quickly. I'm so glad there is an opening at Butterick. I'll be praying you get that position and then we can be co-workers, too."

They were both laughing when they joined the others in the parlor just as Mrs. Heaton called them to the dining room. Again, Violet found herself sitting adjacent to Michael and across from Lila.

After Michael said the blessing and began carving the large ham Gretchen had set before him, Mrs. Heaton introduced a new man at the table as John Talbot, a reporter for the *New York Tribune.* He'd been covering a charity ball the night before.

"Pleased to meet you, Miss Burton," he said. He was about her age and clean-shaven, with rust-colored hair and greenish-blue eyes. He didn't have the rough demeanor she'd thought a seasoned reporter might possess; instead, he looked like someone she could have gone to school with.

"Thank you, Mr. Talbot. I'm pleased to meet you, as well."

"How are you enjoying our city?"

"With her eyes closed." Michael chuckled and winked at Violet as he handed her a plate with a slice of ham.

His wink sent her heart into a little dive and dip and she felt color flood her cheeks, but she couldn't help but join in his laughter as she passed the plate down. "I'm not sure I'll ever get used to the traffic."

That brought laughter from all at the table and several nods of agreement.

"Oh . . . yes, well, that can take some getting used to. But it is easier with your eyes open," John said. "Did you apply for any positions today?"

"Not today, but I found several I'll apply for come Monday."

"Oh!" Lila put a hand over her mouth,

then removed it to say, "I am so sorry. I forgot to ask if there are any open positions at Butterick today. We were very busy and it totally slipped my mind. But, I'll be sure to ask on Monday." She ladled a spoonful of scalloped potatoes onto her plate.

"No need to worry, Lila. There was an ad in the classifieds today," Mrs. Heaton said. "Violet is going to apply there first thing."

"Oh . . ." Lila nearly dropped the casserole dish she was passing down the table. "That's good. Maybe we'll be coworkers after all."

Violet didn't know if she meant it or not, but Lila did smile across the table at her. For some reason she didn't think Lila liked her very much. Then she told herself that she had no way of knowing that. Still, it didn't dispel the feeling she had that Lila wished she hadn't come to live at the Heatons' boardinghouse. Violet thought it might have something to do with Michael. Lila tried to catch his attention at every opportunity, and it was obvious that she was very interested in him, but so far he didn't seem to be giving her any more attention than he gave the other women. Violet hoped to become friends with all the boarders, but she wasn't sure it was going to happen with Lila. Only time would tell.

She was relieved when the conversation turned from her to the other boarders. She liked hearing about their days and the rest of the meal was quite enjoyable for Violet. Mr. Talbot entertained them with stories from the ball he'd covered the night before.

Up until now the names he mentioned were those that Violet had occasionally seen in the newspaper, but none of their activities mattered much to her. However, they seemed to mean a lot to those around the dinner table. He was plied with questions about what the ladies wore, what was served and whom they talked to.

The conversation took them through a dessert of cherry pie à la mode and into the parlor afterward. This time Violet stayed for a while and, although she didn't join in on the conversations, she enjoyed listening and learning more about this city she would be calling home.

When everyone began heading to their rooms, Violet found herself going up the stairs with Elizabeth, Julia and Lila.

"What are you going to do tomorrow, Violet?" Julia asked. "If you don't have any plans, you are welcome to come home with me and have Sunday dinner with my family. Lila and Elizabeth are coming, and my mother always has plenty."

"Oh, thank you so much, Julia. But Michael and his mother mentioned something about showing me Central Park after church and Sunday dinner."

"Oh?" Lila arched an eyebrow and seemed to be waiting for an answer of some kind.

Violet didn't know what to say except, "I believe so."

"Oh, you'll love that, won't she, Lila?" Julia turned to the other girl. "We often go there as a group."

"I'd love to go with you all sometime." Violet was a little disappointed at having to miss the opportunity to get to know the girls better.

"Oh, there will be other times — don't you worry. We go on outings together quite frequently, don't we, Lila?" Elizabeth nudged the girl.

Lila gave a very brief smile. It was so quick, Violet was certain that had she blinked, she might have missed it.

On the other hand, maybe it was better that she couldn't spend the day with them. Besides, she'd had such a good time with Michael and his mother that she was really looking forward to the next day. "I'm sorry I can't go with you to meet your family tomorrow, but thank you for the invitation."

"You're welcome. There'll be another

time," Julia said.

They'd reached the top of the stairs when Lila said, "Elizabeth, could you come to my room, please? I want you to help me pick out what to wear tomorrow."

"Of course," Elizabeth said before turning to Violet and Julia. "Good night, Violet. We'll see you tomorrow evening. I hope you have a wonderful time. Night, Julia."

"Good night, all," Julia said from her doorway.

"I hope you all have a wonderful time, too," Violet said. "Good night, Julia, Elizabeth and Li—"

"Come on, Elizabeth," Lila said, pulling the young woman into her room and shutting the door.

Julia smiled at Violet and shrugged. "Obviously, Lila is in a tizzy about something. Don't let her bother you. She's just like that."

"No. I won't. Good night."

"Good night." Julia yawned and shut her door.

Violet opened the door to her room more certain than ever that Lila did not like her. And she had a feeling she was the cause of whatever kind of tizzy Lila was in.

Violet joined the Heatons for church the

next morning, and they introduced her to some of their friends and neighbors. She felt welcomed and it was good to be with friends on this Lord's day.

Since her mother's death, Violet had questioned the Lord as to why He'd taken her away, and then when she'd found out that Harlan Black held the mortgage to their home, she had even more questions on why the Lord would let that happen, causing her to leave the home she'd been raised in and her lifelong friends.

If the Lord had answered, she hadn't heard it yet. And deep down, much as she hated to admit it, she was afraid. Afraid that Harlan would come after her, afraid of this city that was so huge, afraid of being alone — afraid of so many things for the first time in her life.

She was truly thankful that she had Mrs. Heaton and Michael to turn to, that she had a place to stay. She was hopeful that she would find work in the coming week and would soon find the city not so strange and that she would begin to have the same confidence she'd felt in her hometown. She wasn't used to feeling vulnerable, and she didn't like it one bit.

A peace she hadn't felt in a long time settled over her as she sat between Michael and his mother, and the minister began his sermon. Taken from Isaiah, it comforted her for it said not to fear, not to be dismayed, that the Lord was her God and that He would strengthen and help her. That He would uphold her with His righteous hand. Violet wanted to believe it, but it'd been so hard in the past few months. Still, she would try to hang on to her faith, shaky as it seemed lately. She desperately needed to believe that the Lord was with her now.

# CHAPTER FOUR

After a wonderful Sunday lunch shared by some, but not all, of the boarders — Julia, Lila and Elizabeth were gone of course — Violet was quite pleased that Michael followed through with his mother's suggestion to show her Central Park. He'd made arrangements to hire a surrey so that he could drive, and Mrs. Heaton had him help her into the backseat, insisting that Violet ride up front beside him so that she could see better.

Michael helped her into the buggy and then went around and hopped in beside her. Violet wasn't sure why she felt safer with him handling the reins instead of a paid driver, but she did.

They headed down the street to Fifth Avenue, and although there was traffic, Violet was pleased that it didn't seem quite as hectic as the day before. There were many people out and about, but the pace of the traffic was slower as they turned onto the avenue and headed north past Madison Square Park and the Fifth Avenue Hotel.

"Look, Violet."

Violet looked back to see that Mrs. Heaton was pointing to the left.

"There is Delmonico's. It is supposed to be one of the best restaurants in the city and, from what I hear, it is quite the place to see and be seen."

"Perhaps we'll stop there for dinner on the way home and see whom we can see and be seen by." Michael laughed and winked at Violet, who couldn't contain her chuckle — or the flush of heat that crept up her cheeks.

"Perhaps we should," Mrs. Heaton said somberly. But then she joined in the laughter.

They passed several large churches, including the Marble Collegiate Church and the Brick Presbyterian.

Michael pointed out the Waldorf Hotel, explaining that rumor had it that it had resulted from a family feud between William Waldorf Astor and his aunt, Caroline Astor. "William, the nephew, had always resented that even though he had more money than his aunt did, she held the social leadership of the family. So to spite her, he had his own house razed and the hotel built. It opened in '93. It must have provoked his aunt, because just last year she had a home built on down the avenue next to Central Park."

Mrs. Heaton took up the story from there, pointing to construction going on next to the hotel. "Now her son, John Jacob Astor IV, has had her old mansion next to the Waldorf torn down and is building a hotel of his own." She shook her head. "There is no telling how it will all end up."

"Probably not," Violet agreed although she knew absolutely no more than she'd been told about the families. Nonetheless, it was all very entertaining.

There were many carriages out and about on the avenue, and it was quite obvious when they passed those of great wealth. Their vehicles were larger and grander, for one thing. And many of them were open so that one could see from the way the occupants were dressed that they were of the upper echelon of society.

However, there were many others who appeared to be dressed as she and Mrs. Heaton were — still in their Sunday best, but far less elegant than the rich. Violet felt quite comfortable traveling in the company she was with.

They passed several more mansions and churches before Michael said, "This is known as Vanderbilt Row."

The mansions occupied a whole block, and Violet was so impressed at the size and the design of the elegant buildings, she had to remind herself to close her gaping mouth. There were balconied windows with intricately carved trims around the windows and between each floor, and moldings everywhere.

Michael leaned a little closer to Violet. "A far cry from what we're used to, isn't it?"

"Oh, yes." Violet shook her head. "I can't imagine living in anything that size or that grand. Why, one could get lost."

"I'm sure I would." Michael chuckled.

"Well, I think I much prefer my small family home in Ashland or your mother's boardinghouse to such opulence."

"Why, thank you, Violet," Michael's mother said from the backseat.

Soon they arrived at Central Park and Michael drove the surrey into it. They passed from the city into a tree-lined road that ran through the park until the scene before them opened up to a huge space, beautiful and unspoiled.

"It looks untouched, as if it's been here from the first," Violet said.

Michael shook his head. "Every bit of the park has been landscaped. None of it is like it was to begin with and, from what I've heard, that's a good thing."

As they kept riding, Violet was taken aback by the sheer size of it. "I had no idea it was this large or this beautiful."

They passed waterways and ponds, and at the north end there was a huge lake where she could see couples boating. There were trails leading off in all kinds of directions, and people walking, riding or sitting on park benches. The perfume of blooming flowers of all kinds permeated the air around them, and Violet sighed at the beauty of it all. She couldn't wait to spend a whole day here.

"There are outdoor music concerts this time of year, and, oh, the ice-skating in the winter is wonderful," Mrs. Heaton said.

"Ice-skating?"

"Yes," Michael said. "We'll have to go, if you're still here by then."

Violet wasn't sure what to say. She'd love to go ice-skating here, but her goal was to stay only long enough to pay off the mortgage on her home. She couldn't imagine living here for any longer.

"New Yorkers of every nationality and status love this park," his mother said, saving Violet from having to say anything.

"I can well see why," Violet agreed. "It is simply amazing right here in the middle of the city."

"It didn't start that way," Michael said. "At first, the wealthy were the ones who mostly took advantage of it and there was a lot of discussion on just whose park it was. But with the El and all manner of other transportation, it's easier for all New Yorkers to enjoy fresh air and sunshine these days, and now the park is enjoyed by anyone who can get to it."

"I'm glad," Violet said. It didn't seem right that only the wealthy should enjoy something so beautiful.

As they left the park and started back down Fifth Avenue, Michael said, "It's about dinnertime. How does Delmonico's sound? Should we see and be seen?"

"Oh, Michael, I was just teasing about that," Mrs. Heaton said. "Besides, I should get back and see about the boarders' meal."

"Mother, you know the boarders realize that our Sunday night suppers are whatever you, Gretchen or Maida decide to put out for them. Maida will take care of it and they will be fine."

"But it's expensive, Michael —"

"No buts. I may not be able to afford a mansion on Fifth Avenue, but I think I can

86

manage to take us to Delmonico's. We're going."

Violet wasn't quite sure how she felt about it, but Mrs. Heaton seemed quite pleased, and she didn't have the heart to object and take the smile from her face.

Once at the elegant restaurant, they were shown to a table and given menus. Thankfully, the interior was dimly lit, because while a few other female diners were dressed in the manner that she and Mrs. Heaton were, most were dressed in gowns the likes of which Violet had never even dreamed of owning.

She felt a bit out of place, but if Mrs. Heaton did, it never showed, and Violet tried to relax and enjoy herself. There were so many offerings on the menu, both in English and French, Violet wasn't sure what to order and asked Michael to choose. He chose lobster bisque to begin the meal of the Delmonico steak with asparagus and creamed potatoes.

Violet had never seen the evidence of so much wealth in her life from both the sights she'd seen on Fifth Avenue to the clientele of Delmonico's. Once the waiter left them alone, she said so.

"There is a lot of wealth in New York City, to be sure. But there is also great poverty.

You just can't see it from here," Michael said. "You will, though. You can't live in the city for long and not become aware of it."

"That's true," Mrs. Heaton agreed. "It is a shame, but a fact that cannot be disputed."

"I think I'm glad I belong to neither group . . . although if I don't find work soon, I could certainly become one of the impoverished," Violet said.

"That isn't going to happen, dear. Neither Michael nor I would see you turned out on the streets."

"Oh, I didn't mean . . . I know I have a place to stay and I'll find work. What I meant was that I'm a lot closer to being poor than I am to being rich, and I don't think I'd like to be either."

Michael said, "I understand, and I must admit it is a great comfort to know that I have enough to enjoy my life, but not so much that someone would want to take it from me — or so little I'd want to take it from someone else."

"Michael! You'd never do that."

"I would not, Mother. But in this city, many do just that. I own a detective agency, Violet, and I've seen it all. Many who are poor will do most anything to survive, and some of the rich will do most anything to keep what they have."

■ ■ ■ ■

On the ride home Violet couldn't remember ever having enjoyed a day more. The meal had been excellent, although she didn't want to even think of how much it must have cost Michael to indulge in that way.

"Thank you for such a wonderful day. I only wish my mother could have been here to take it all in."

"Oh, so do I, my dear," Mrs. Heaton said. "She would have loved being here with us all."

"Yes, she would have."

Violet's mother had told her that Mr. Heaton had left his wife and son fairly well off when he passed away. They weren't wealthy like the Astors and the Vanderbilts she was learning so much about, but she had a feeling they could have been living in a style above that of running a boarding-house. Mrs. Heaton still didn't know what had happened to her daughter or even if she was still alive. And yet, she'd chosen to come to this city and reach out to others. That Mrs. Heaton chose to do that, to be there for young women who needed a place to feel safe, and that her son chose to support her in that endeavor, was proof enough for Violet that her sweet landlady sought to do the Lord's will in her life. And Michael seemed to do the same.

All she knew about Rebecca's disappearance was what her mother had told her. According to her, Rebecca had been talking about going to New York City for months before she actually did. Mrs. Heaton hadn't been happy about it, but Becca was determined and of age and there wasn't anything she could really do stop her from going. She'd evidently written to tell her mother that she was settled in a boardinghouse and would keep in touch. But that was the last they had heard from her. Finally after a couple of months with no answers from Rebecca, Mrs. Heaton received a packet with all her letters returned to her unopened with a note from the landlady saying that Rebecca hadn't lived there in over a month. Violet couldn't even imagine coming to this city without knowing anyone as Rebecca Heaton had done, and she was very thankful that the Heatons were here for her now.

Michael took his mother and Violet back to the boardinghouse before taking the surrey back to the livery and then walking back home. He helped his mother out first and then gave a hand to Violet to help her.

"I hope you enjoyed your day, Violet."

"Oh, I enjoyed every minute. Thank you for dinner, Michael. It was wonderful."

"I enjoyed it, too." He stood there looking down at her for a moment before clearing his throat and taking a step back. "I'll be back home soon."

But he watched her and his mother get to the front door before taking up the reins and heading out.

When she and Mrs. Heaton entered the house, Violet realized that if it didn't feel like home yet, it was beginning to feel very close to it. And once she thought about being alone back in Ashland, it felt even better to be here.

Several of the boarders were in the front parlor, including Lila. She didn't look the least bit happy, and Violet wondered if it was only her Lila wasn't happy to see.

"We were getting a bit worried about the three of you, Mrs. Heaton," Lila said. "It isn't like you to miss Sunday night supper."

"I know, Lila. I'm sorry to have caused you concern, but Michael convinced me that Maida was perfectly capable of taking care of you all."

"Oh? And where is Michael?"

"He's gone back to the livery. He'll be along shortly," Mrs. Heaton answered. "We had a treat this evening. Michael took us to

Delmonico's for dinner."

"Oh, my, Delmonico's?" Julia said. "What's it like? Who all did you see there?"

Violet found an empty chair and let Mrs. Heaton describe their outing. "Well, it is very dim in there so I can't be sure, but I think I saw Mr. and Mrs. William Waldorf Astor along with the Carnegies." She named several other people that Violet had never heard of, but the others in the room seemed to know exactly whom she was talking about.

More and more questions were asked, and Mrs. Heaton glowed recounting the people she thought she'd seen and the meals they'd ordered. Michael slipped into the room and listened to his mother's account of dining and grinned. Catching Violet's eye, he gave her smile. It was obvious that he was pleased his mother enjoyed herself so much. He was a good son.

Mrs. Heaton held everyone's attention from the beginning to the end of her report. "I hope you all get a chance to go there at least once. The interior was so elegant, and the food was truly delicious. I'm sure I'll not forget this day anytime soon."

"From your wonderful description, Mrs. Heaton, I feel I've just been there. I'm so glad you enjoyed yourself," Elizabeth said.

"Thank you, dear. I wish you all could have been there. It certainly wasn't something we planned."

"No, it was not," Michael said. "But if I'd known you would like it this much, I'd have taken you long before now."

"I'm glad you enjoyed it, Mrs. Heaton," Lila said. But the look she shot Violet seemed to say that she wasn't happy that Violet had been there with her.

Julia came to sit beside Violet. "I'm so glad you had a great day. How did you like Central Park?"

"It was wonderful. It's so beautiful and peaceful. I look forward to spending more time there soon. I hope you had a good time with your family."

"Oh, I did, thank you. I told Mama about you and she said you must come with me next time." She glanced over at Lila, who had made her way over to Michael and was talking to him. "I think Lila would rather have been with the Heatons and had you go with me."

Violet looked at the couple. Lila was leaning toward Michael and talking to him in earnest. Maybe there was more between them than she'd first thought. "Oh? Are they courting? I mean —"

"Not that I know of." Julia chuckled. "Lila

might wish for that, but as far as I know Michael has never given her any reason to think that he might want to court her. He is very conscious of the fact that his mother runs this boardinghouse, and he behaves with the utmost propriety toward all of us."

Violet felt a relief she didn't quite understand. She had no claim on Michael Heaton. And she was determined not to let herself care about any man. Although Michael didn't know it, she'd had a childhood crush on him and he *had* broken her young heart when he got engaged to Amanda Cabot before his sister disappeared. Then there was Nick — she'd really thought he might become a beau, but when her mother had her stroke, he took off in a hurry, leaving her alone when she needed someone to turn to the most. Then there was Harlan, who tried to blackmail her into marriage. She saw no reason to trust any man with her heart.

Still, she was glad Michael wasn't considered taken by anyone. Especially Lila. But as she watched Lila bat those eyelashes at him from across the room, she knew the girl was trying as hard as she could to change that status.

"I just wondered."

Julia laughed. "It's quite understandable.

We've all wondered the same thing."

"It is none of my business, really." And she wasn't sure why it seemed to matter so much, but it did.

Julia shrugged. "One can't help but wonder these things. Michael would be quite a catch. I don't think many women would turn his attentions aside."

"No. I don't think they would. He's very nice."

"Has he always been that way?"

Violet thought back to before he and his mother had left Ashland. Because Michael was older than her, they hadn't traveled in the same circles, but she had seen him and talked to him on many occasions. Although she'd been infatuated with him, he'd always been kind in a big-brotherly, teasing way, and if she were totally honest she'd missed running into him after he'd moved away. "Yes, I believe he always has."

"Somehow that doesn't surprise me. I think I'll call it a night. I hope you find a position you'll love tomorrow. And I'll say a prayer that you do."

"Thank you, Julia. I hope to have good news tomorrow evening."

"I look forward to hearing it." Julia stood and left the room after saying good-night to everyone.

Violet decided it was time to turn in, too. She wanted to be fresh for her interviews the next morning. She thought to slip out of the room unnoticed, but Michael called to her just as she got to the foyer.

She turned to him. "Yes?"

He quickly joined her in the foyer. "I hope you have a better feel for the city after yesterday and today."

"Oh, I do. And I thank you again for taking the time to show me around and the delicious dinner."

"It was my pleasure. I'll have a hack here to take you and Mother around to Butterick and the other places you'd like to apply at in the morning. What time do you wish to leave here?"

"Butterick's advertisement said to apply from eight to four. I'd like to be there by around nine anyway, if it isn't too much trouble and if the time is all right with your mother."

"If what is all right with me?" Mrs. Heaton joined them at the bottom of the stairs.

"To leave here about eight-thirty so that Violet can apply at Butterick first thing."

"Of course. I'll be ready."

"I'm sure that if I can hire a driver, I'll be fine. You don't have to go with me, Mrs. —"

"Oh, I want to. If we have time, maybe we can stop at a shop or two along Ladies' Mile after you make your applications. Besides, I want to celebrate with you when you get a position."

"I'd be glad to have someone to celebrate with, Mrs. Heaton, and I hope we'll be able to. I can't thank you and Michael enough for all the help you're giving me."

"Oh, my dear, seeing this city through your eyes is enough, thank you. It's like seeing it again for the first time. I can't remember when I've had a better time than I've had today. It has been a very long time."

Violet's heart swelled with gratitude that this woman had invited her to New York City and that she and her son had been so kind and willing to help her. Much as she missed her mother and her home, she felt blessed to have friends like these.

"I —"

"Violet, wait." Lila caught her attention as she sashayed across the foyer and joined her and the Heatons. "I just wanted to wish you well tomorrow. You'll probably be meeting with Mr. Pollard or Mr. Wilder. They are both very nice men and I'm sure either of them will give your application good consideration. You can give me as a reference if you like."

Violet wondered if she looked as surprised as she felt at Lila's sudden change in attitude. "Why, thank you, Lila. That is very nice of you."

"Yes, well, I hope you come home with good news tomorrow."

"Thank you. So do I."

"I think I'll turn in now," Lila said with a big smile. "Good night."

"Good night." Violet watched Lila head up the stairs. She couldn't help but wonder if Lila was putting on an act for Michael and his mother. Then she felt guilty for thinking such a thought. She shouldn't be so judgmental.

"Well, I — that Lila never fails to surprise me," Mrs. Heaton said as Lila disappeared at the landing.

Violet felt a little better that Mrs. Heaton seemed as surprised as she was at Lila's change in attitude. But Michael's expression was unreadable, and it was hard to tell what he was thinking about the other woman.

# CHAPTER FIVE

The next morning, Violet dressed to apply for work in a blue serge skirt and white shirtwaist. She thought back over the evening before as she twisted her hair up into a knot and pinned it at the back of her head. She was still a little stunned at Lila's offer to help her get a position. The young woman's whole attitude toward her seemed to have changed so suddenly. One moment Violet thought Lila was glaring at her, and the next she was wishing Violet well and acting as if she would be pleased if they were coworkers. Acting. That's what it all seemed like. For, deep down, Violet still felt that the other woman didn't like her at all.

She pinned her mother's cameo to her shirtwaist. But what if she was wrong? Perhaps she had misjudged Lila. If so, she needed to pray about it and ask the Lord's forgiveness. It would be nice if she and Lila could become friends, perhaps not best friends, but good enough that Violet could think the other girl didn't dislike her as she'd been doing the past few days.

She took one last look in the mirror and said a silent prayer that she'd get a position today — and asking for forgiveness if she'd been wrong about Lila. Leaving it in the Lord's hands, she left her room and hurried downstairs. Most of the boarders had left for work, and Mr. Talbot was just getting up from his place at the table when Violet entered the dining room.

"Good morning, Miss Burton. I hope you have good results from your job hunt this morning."

"Thank you, Mr. Talbot. I hope so, too." Violet smiled at the man. "I hope you have a good day."

"Thank you." He slid his chair back under the table and left the room.

Violet fixed herself a plate of strawberries and pancakes, with a small slice of ham on the side. Just as she set her plate on the table, Gretchen came in the room.

"Good morning, Miss Burton. Did you have a good weekend?"

"I did, Gretchen. I hope you did, also."

"May I get you some juice or tea or coffee?"

"Tea, please."

"Mrs. Heaton said she'd be taking you around to put in applications today and that you'll be eating lunch out. I wish you well with your interviews." Gretchen poured her tea and brought it to her.

"Thank you. I am hopeful that I'll have good news to share this evening."

Gretchen bobbed her head up and down, her curls bouncing out from under her cap. "I'll pray that you do."

"I appreciate your prayers on my behalf. I know that is the best help I can have."

Just as Gretchen left the room, Mrs. Heaton entered from the foyer. "Violet, dear, I trust you slept well."

"I did, thank you. I didn't think I would, thinking about today. But the Lord saw to it that I slept like a baby and I didn't lie awake worrying about what today would bring."

"I'm hopeful it's going to bring you a job." Mrs. Heaton laid the folded paper down beside Violet's plate. "The Butterick position is still open, and there are a few more I've circled that might be of interest to you."

Violet skimmed the classifieds while Mrs. Heaton filled her plate and brought it to the table. Along with the Butterick opening, there was also a new opening for a typist that Mrs. Heaton had circled and one for a receptionist at a bank.

The older woman poured her tea and brought the pot to the table, warming up Violet's cup. "What do you think?"

"Well, I don't know how to type —"

"Oh, that might make a difference. But should you wish to learn, typing, along with other clerical skills, is offered at the YWCA and several business schools in the area."

"Really? That's very good to know."

"Yes. There are so many positions opening up in that field of work that the YWCA felt it was a need they could fill."

"Should I not be able to find employment this week, that might be something I'll consider looking into."

"Hopefully you'll find something today. But if not, we can find out more about what the YWCA offers." Mrs. Heaton pulled an envelope out of her pocket and slid it to Violet. "This is a letter of recommendation, Violet. It may not be needed, but just in case."

"Thank you, Mrs. Heaton. I —"

Mrs. Heaton held up her hand in a manner that Violet had come to realize meant "say no more." "You're more than welcome, dear. I just want to help in any way I can. But we must hurry with our breakfast. The hack driver will be here soon."

Violet took Mrs. Heaton's suggestion and

they finished their breakfast in a companionable silence until Michael surprised her by entering the dinning room.

"Mother, I took a call for you. Mrs. Wentworth wanted to remind you of the meeting today."

Mrs. Heaton gasped. "Oh, dear, I forgot all about that meeting. And it is important I be there. Oh, Violet —"

"It's fine, Mrs. Heaton. I'm sure the hack driver will take me wherever I ask him to and back home. Please don't miss your meeting on my account."

"Oh, but I —"

"Mother, there is no need to miss your meeting. I'll be glad to accompany Violet on her job search."

"Michael, you gave up a day of work last week, I can't let you —"

"Violet, Mother will miss the meeting if you don't let me. Besides, I've been working much too hard lately and it will be good for me to take another day off."

Mrs. Heaton chuckled. "He's right on both accounts, Violet. So, what's it to be? Do I miss my meeting and deprive Michael of a much-needed day off?"

Violet shook her head at the two of them. "You two are a pair for sure. Thank you for the offer, Michael. I believe I'll take you up on it."

"Good. The hack should be here any minute now."

The hack he'd hired did show up right at eight-thirty, and Violet couldn't deny that she was a bit relieved not to have to find the places she'd be applying to alone. Nor could she deny that she was happy to have Michael's company once more.

He helped her into the hack and sat down beside her. "Where would you like me to tell the driver to go first?"

In spite of Lila's offer to help the night before, Violet still had a feeling that she did not want her working at the same company — no matter what she said around the Heatons. Because of that, she asked Michael to have the driver stop at the bank that'd advertised for a receptionist first.

"I thought you wanted to start with Butterick first."

"Well, I have no real experience, and surely being a receptionist won't take a lot of training. I believe I could handle greeting people without too much trouble."

"I'm sure you can do anything you set your mind to, Violet. If you want to start with the bank, that is what we will do." He gave instructions to the driver and it seemed no time before they pulled up in front of a very imposing building.

"Would you like me to accompany you?" Michael asked.

"I think I'll be fine, but thank you for the offer."

"I'll just wait here, then. Good luck, Violet."

"Thank you." Violet hurried inside, but her confidence quickly deflated once she found that they were only looking for someone with several years' experience.

"I'm sorry, Violet. Didn't they state that in the advertisement?" Michael asked when Violet returned and told him what happened.

"No. But I suppose I should have known."

"I don't know how you would have without them saying so."

"Thank you for being so kind, Michael."

The next stop along the way was at Hearns Department Store, where she was treated much more kindly and told that they would get back to her, as did Macy's when she put in her application there.

"I'm sure both places will be ringing you up on the telephone by the time we get back home, Violet," Michael said. "But why don't you try Butterick next?"

Violet agreed. She couldn't very well tell

him that Lila didn't seem too happy about them possibly working together . . . not after she'd acted as though she'd love it just the night before. Her hopes starting out this morning had been dashed, but she might as well get it over with. If her earlier interviews were any indication of how this one would go, Lila wouldn't have to worry about it.

By the time the hack arrived at Butterick and Company, Violet was so nervous she wished she hadn't eaten that morning. Her stomach felt as if a hundred butterflies had been taken captive and were all trying to escape at the same time.

"I'll wait here for you, Violet," Michael said. "You'll do fine, I'm sure."

"If this is like the others, you won't have to wait too long," Violet said as Michael helped her out of the hack.

"I'll say a prayer all goes well."

"Thank you, Michael," Violet said. "It helps to know that I have you and your mother praying for me. Gretchen said she would be praying, also."

The knowledge that she had people talking to the Lord on her behalf suddenly calmed the flutters in her stomach, and Violet felt at peace as she entered the building.

A young woman about Violet's age was

sitting at a desk and looked up as she entered. Violet assumed she was the receptionist and walked up to her.

The young woman smiled. "Good morning, miss. What may I help you with today?"

"I'd like to apply for the position advertised in the paper, please."

"Of course. Your name, please?" The young lady motioned to another young woman and had her come forward.

"Violet Burton."

"Miss Rogers, this is Miss Burton. She would like to apply for employment. Mr. Wilder is taking interviews today. Would you take her to his office, please?"

"Of course. Come this way, Miss Burton."

Miss Rogers led her up a staircase to the second floor. "Don't be too nervous, Miss Burton. Mr. Wilder is very nice and we do need help."

Her kind words helped keep Violet calm as she followed the woman down the wide hall. At the end of the hall, Miss Rogers knocked briskly on a door.

"Enter," a male voice said.

Miss Rogers opened the door and led Violet inside a room that was paneled in beautiful hardwood, with windows that looked out onto Broadway. There were two people there, a man and a woman. The man sat behind the desk and the woman in one of two chairs in front of the desk. "Mr. Wilder, Miss Carter, this is Miss Burton and she's come to apply for the cutting/folding position."

Mr. Wilder stood as Violet and Miss Rogers came farther into the room. "Pleased to meet you, Miss Burton. Take a seat and we'll talk."

Violet wasn't sure what she was expecting, but it wasn't a talk. Still, she took the seat Mr. Wilder motioned to, and was encouraged a little by the smile Miss Carter gave her as Violet took the chair beside her and Mr. Wilder sat back down.

"You may go, Miss Rogers. Miss Carter will show Miss Burton out when we are finished."

"Yes, sir." Miss Rogers smiled at Violet before taking her leave.

"Now, Miss Burton, what makes you want to work at Butterick?" Mr. Wilder asked.

What to tell him? How much should she tell him? Violet set up straighter in her chair and cleared her throat. "Well, sir, I'm new to the city and I need work."

"Where are you from, Miss Burton?" Miss Carter asked, her pencil poised above a stenographer's pad.

"I'm from Ashland, Virginia."

"And why did you decide to move here?" It was Mr. Wilder asking this time. Perhaps they were going to take turns.

"My mother passed away recently and, to be honest, I have family debts to pay and there was no work to be found in my small hometown." Violet grasped her shaking fingers together. Her nervousness was threatening to come back much quicker than it went away.

Miss Carter looked at her in a sympathetic manner. "And why did you decide that Butterick is a place you wanted to apply to?"

Violet laughed and she wondered if she sounded as anxious as she felt. "Butterick is a familiar name to me. I love the patterns and *The Delineator* magazine. My mother and I spent many an hour poring over the pages of it, looking at the patterns and —"

"You are a seamstress, Miss Burton?" Mr. Wilder asked.

"Not a professional one. Just a home seamstress who loves your patterns because they make it possible for the everyday woman to make clothing for her family that actually fits them well."

Mr. Wilder leaned back in his chair, placed his fingertips together over his chest and rocked back and forth. He had a huge smile on his face. "That is music to our ears, Miss

Burton."

"Indeed, it is," a voice from behind Violet said. She turned to find an older man sitting in a chair in one corner of the room. He was dressed in a black suit and sported a long white beard. He stood and walked toward them. "I'm Ebenezer Butterick, and I believe you've just found yourself a position at Butterick and Company, Miss Burton."

Violet looked from Mr. Butterick to Mr. Wilder and then to Miss Carter. All three were nodding and smiling. "But . . . but I don't know if I am qualified for the work and —"

"Most everything we do here can be learned, Miss Burton," Mr. Wilder said. "And I have a feeling you already know what you need to, to work here."

A wave of relief washed over her at his words.

"And we do like to help those who need work, and we love to hire those who understand what it is my wife and I started out to do when this company was formed in '68," Mr. Butterick said. "You are hired, Miss Burton. Miss Carter will help you fill out all the information we need from you and you can start tomorrow at eight o'clock sharp. You'll be shown how our operation

110

works and then we'll start you working."

"Oh, I —" She remembered the letter Mrs. Heaton had given her and pulled it out of her reticule. "I do have a letter of recommendation from my landlady. She used to be a neighbor of ours and —"

"The fact that you are willing to give us a letter of recommendation and are concerned that we might want one is enough, Miss Burton." Mr. Wilder waved away the letter. "You are hired."

"Oh . . . thank you so much!" Violet didn't know what else to say. She'd never thought to be hired so quickly — especially after her earlier interviews. She could only give credit to the prayers that Mrs. Heaton and Gretchen were saying on her behalf, for she knew she did nothing to get hired on her own. *Thank You, Lord, for answered prayers.*

"You are quite welcome, Miss Burton," Mr. Butterick said. "I've pretty much retired from the daily overseeing of things. But Mr. Wilder and Mr. Pollard are doing a fine job of taking care of the business. However, I'm glad I was here today, to be in on your interview."

"I'm glad as well, sir."

"Come this way, Miss Burton," Miss Carter said.

Violet stood and followed her. But just

111

before they left by a side door leading to another office, she turned back. "Thank you again!"

"You are quite welcome, young lady," Mr. Butterick said.

Violet fought the urge to run back into the room and hug the man. She couldn't believe it. She had a job at Butterick. She would be able to pay off the mortgage on her home. Violet couldn't wait to share the news with Michael.

# CHAPTER SIX

Michael jumped out of the hack as soon as Violet came out of Butterick. She didn't try to hide her smile and he grinned at her. "You got the job, didn't you?"

"They hired me. I start tomorrow, Michael." She placed a hand over her hammering heart.

"Oh, Violet, that's great news. I've been out here praying that you would be hired, but never did I dream that you would find out today, especially not after —" Michael stopped speaking and looked at Violet apologetically.

"My earlier interviews today." Violet smiled and said the words for him. "It's all right, Michael. I was thinking the very same thing. I'm finding it hard to take in, but it's true. I really have work. I still can't believe it! But they were so very nice, and Mr. Butterick himself told me I was hired!"

"From what Lila has told us, I thought he

was retired now."

"I think he is. But evidently he comes in from time to time to see how things are going and today was one of those days. I didn't even realize he was in the room until he spoke up from behind me."

Michael chuckled. "I'm sure that surprised you."

"Oh, it did!"

"You must have impressed him as one who will work hard and do your best for the company."

"I'm not sure about that. I think he might have had some sympathy for me with my mother's passing and all."

"Well, for whatever reason you were hired, I am sure they'll never regret it."

"I certainly hope not."

Michael helped her back into the hack and took his seat beside her. "You know, Mother probably isn't even home yet, and I'm taking at least half a day off. Why don't you let me take you to lunch to celebrate?"

Violet loved his suggestion, but she didn't want to impose on his time any more than she already had. "Oh, Michael, you don't have to do that."

"I know I don't, but I'd like to. Unless you don't want to —"

"Oh, I'd love to have lunch with you, Michael. And I must admit I'm in the mood to celebrate."

"Well, then. That's what we'll do. And you'll be doing a lot of it this week. Mother loves to have something to celebrate."

Michael leaned forward and said something to the driver, but Violet couldn't understand what he said. And it really didn't matter where they went, she was just glad to get to spend more time with him.

The hack moved out into traffic, and the route he took was one Violet hadn't seen before. Of course, as large as New York City was, she doubted that she'd ever see it all. Still, she loved looking at the buildings, seeing all the hustle and bustle on the streets.

Michael turned to her. "You know, Violet, now that you have a job, I must admit to not knowing a lot about why you came here to find employment instead of staying in Virginia — not that we're not glad you did, but —"

"Your mother didn't tell you?"

"Not really, only that you needed to come here and find work to pay off the mortgage on your family home because you couldn't find employment there. When I asked why, she said it was your story to tell. And if you'd rather not tell me, that's all right."

Violet shook her head. She was impressed

that Mrs. Heaton hadn't told even Michael all about Harlan. Since she was staying at his mother's and he'd been such a help to her, she felt she owed it to Michael to tell him what had happened.

"No, I don't mind. I just thought you knew. I couldn't find a position in Ashland because, well, the banker who holds the mortgage to my home made it impossible for me to find work."

"Why would he do that? Seems to me he'd be helping you and not trying to hinder you."

"One would think so. But he had other plans. He thought that if I couldn't find a position at home, I'd give in and marry him. Said he'd forgive the loan if I did."

"He tried to blackmail you into marrying him?"

"Why, yes, I suppose that is what he did. But I couldn't bear for him to . . ." Violet shuddered, remembering that last time she'd talked to him.

"Violet, he didn't try to — He didn't hurt you did he?"

"No. Other than grab my arm and try to convince me. But I must admit I wonder what might happen if he ever finds out where I am."

"He doesn't know?"

"Not that I know of. And I hope not. I went to some lengths to keep him from knowing."

"I see. And who is this banker? What's his name?"

"Harlan Black. Do you remember him?"

"I do. I'm glad you turned his offer down, Violet."

"Yes, so am I. Now I just want to get that mortgage paid off so that I can have my family home back free and clear."

Suddenly, a crash was heard up ahead, and their driver brought the hack to an abrupt stop, jostling her and throwing her against Michael.

"Are you all right?" Michael asked as he gently helped her sit back up.

Violet nodded and Michael turned to the driver. "What is it? What's happened?"

"I'm sorry, sir, but it seems there has been an accident up the street." He stood to get a better look before turning to Michael. "Could be a while. Looks like there's been a pileup of vehicles in the intersection."

"Oh, dear. Is anyone hurt?" Violet asked.

"Don't look like it, ma'am. But traffic is piled up ever which away. Don't you worry none. I'll get us around it all." He sat back down and quickly turned the horse to go back the way they'd come. Then he took a detour along one of the side streets, turning the hack this way and that into areas Violet knew she hadn't seen.

She noticed that the area seemed to be more residential than commercial, yet there were buildings, not homes, up and down the blocks. When their driver stopped at the next intersection she asked, "What are these buildings, Michael? It looks as if people live here."

"You're right. They do. These are apartment buildings and multiple-family residents. Some are two- and three-family dwellings along here and some much larger. On farther down there are what we refer to as the tenements, where many immigrant families live. There is much crowding together there and the living conditions for so many have been atrocious."

Violet craned her neck to look down the street as their driver took the hack into the intersection and turned once more. Soon they were in what must be the middle of what Michael had called the tenements. Violet could see all manner of trash piled up in front of many of the homes. And the smell was . . . Violet prayed she didn't gag before they got out of the area.

She saw young children playing in the streets, even in the trash, and some just standing on the street corner. Two little boys in particular caught her eye as they stood, holding hands and looking sadder than any children should.

"Oh, Michael, look at those two little boys."

"Stop, driver," Michael said. He motioned to the two little boys to come closer, and at first they started to move forward and then they stopped. Their eyes were big and blue and looked as if they'd been crying.

"They're afraid to come near," Violet said. She pulled some coins from her reticule and held them out so that the boys could see, but they shook their heads. Then she dropped them on the street and Michael told the driver to be on his way.

Violet turned in her seat to watch the two little boys as they hurried into the street and gathered the coins. She waved and, after a moment, they waved back with the most wistful expression she'd ever seen in their eyes. Surely there was more to do there. She watched until the driver turned down another street and she didn't think she'd ever forget the look in their eyes.

"Driver, get us out of here — now," Michael said when he turned down one more wrong street. "Surely you could have found another way to go!"

"Sorry, sir! I took a wrong turn up there for sure. We'll be out of here soon." The driver flicked the reins and the hack picked up speed as he did as told.

"I'm sorry, Violet. You need to know this way of life exists here, but I never wanted you to see it like this. I know it's nothing like you've seen back in Ashland." Michael sighed and shook his head. "Sadly, this is as much a part of the city as the mansions we passed the other day are."

Violet could see the sorrow in Michael's eyes as he went on, "It is absolutely horrible what some in this city endure. But with the publication of Jacob Riis's manuscript called *How the Other Half Lives,* many have been fighting to change things for the poor."

"I'm relieved to hear that. I can't imagine living in those conditions." She'd really had only a glimpse of it, but it'd been enough to throw her imagination into high gear and now she felt she must know more.

"The reality of it is heartbreaking. And sometimes, I wonder if Becca could have been caught up in . . . If she might be —" Michael broke off and shook his head.

"Michael? Surely you don't think Rebecca could be living in that kind of . . ." Violet didn't even know how to continue the thought. Didn't want to.

"I simply don't know, Violet."

His voice was hoarse and his eyes so sorrowful, Violet wished she'd kept her mouth shut. "I'm sorry, Michael."

As if it were too painful to talk about, he shook his head. He continued as if his sister hadn't been mentioned. "With the right people finally in office, things are changing, thank the Lord. Since Mayor Strong was voted into office last November, real effort is being put into cleaning up the streets and helping to make living conditions somewhat easier for those who must live in such crowded spaces. But living in the tenements is nothing like what you and I are used to, Violet. The streets have been much worse than you see now — filled with rubbish, trash . . . so much so that vehicles could barely get down them. It's a shame what the city allowed."

"It's that bad?" Violet asked. Her heart broke for those children and the people living in such dire conditions as Michael described. The overcrowding, the filth and disease they were forced to live with. What she'd seen was bad enough; she hated to think of it being worse.

"Yes. Of course, it is a big city and I suppose it is to be expected. And I'm hopeful that with Theodore Roosevelt, the new police commissioner in charge of fighting the crime in the city, the crime rate will come down. Much has been done since the elections, but more must be accomplished." Michael sighed. "So much more."

Hearing that things had been even worse than what she'd seen, Violet could only nod in agreement.

"Do you have that book you mentioned, Michael? May I borrow it?"

"I do. It's in Mother's study, and of course you may borrow it."

Curious as she was about the tenements and those that lived in them, Violet felt even more blessed that she had the Heatons to turn to in this city and she was eager to get out of this area of it.

As they made it back to Fifth Avenue, Violet breathed a deep sigh of relief. But the comparison between the tenements they'd passed through earlier and the wealth in this part of the city — not to mention the conversation about Rebecca — was almost more than she could take in. Violet tried to put the sights she'd seen in the tenements out of her mind and concentrate on celebrating her new job. Besides, she didn't want to spoil Michael's plans.

Michael took Violet to one of his favorite

restaurants not far from his office. It catered to both men and women, so he felt sure Violet would feel comfortable. He tried to keep the conversation on lighter things.

He owed it to her. He hadn't meant to put a damper on her day by bringing up the reason for her move to the city, but he had. He had managed to bring up hurtful memories for her — to think any man had treated her that way had him clenching his teeth.

And then — how they'd ended up in the part of town they had was beyond him — but it had only served to diminish her joy in finding a job even further . . . and brought up memories of the sister he couldn't find. He couldn't believe he'd opened up and confided his fears to Violet. He rarely talked about Rebecca to anyone anymore. Maybe it was because she'd been open with him — or maybe it was simply because she knew Rebecca and no one in this city did. But the fact remained that he'd managed to make her smile disappear and he wanted it back.

"Would you like to help me surprise Mother, Violet?"

"Surprise her?" Violet leaned her head to the side and smiled at him. "What do you have in mind?"

"Well, I feel sure she would have wanted to take you to the Ladies' Mile to celebrate your good news — did she mention it?"

"She might have. But it's all right, Michael. I'll get to go another day."

"Why don't you let me take you?"

"Oh, Michael, I've imposed enough on your time. I'd never ask you to take me to the Ladies' Mile." She giggled. "But thank you for the offer."

"You haven't imposed on me. I believe it was my suggestion to take you and Mother around the other day, and I know it was my suggestion to go with you today. And you're right to assume I might be a bit uncomfortable visiting most of the shops in the Ladies' Mile. But we could go to Macy's. It has most everything anyone — man, woman or child — might need or want. Would you like to go there?"

"Michael, really you don't have to —"

"Actually, I could use a new cravat, and you could help me choose one." He'd gotten her to smile again, but now, his goal seemed to be to get her to let him take her to Macy's. "Please."

Violet's laugh was light and melodious. "Well, if you put it that way, I'd be glad to go to Macy's with you, Michael."

"Let's go, then."

He pulled out her chair. As they headed out of the restaurant, he couldn't ignore the admiring glances Violet received from the men at other tables. But she seemed oblivious to them and he smiled. She truly was like a breath of fresh air in this city.

He hired a hack to take them to Macy's and once inside, watching Violet's expression as she saw all that was offered in the store, Michael couldn't remember when he'd enjoyed shopping so much.

And Violet did help him choose a new cravat — a red one no less. He wasn't sure where he'd wear it, but she seemed to like it. "It will look wonderful with the black suit you wore on Sunday or the gray one you have on now," she said.

He was flattered that she remembered what he wore and once he'd made his purchase, he turned to her. "Now, what would *you* like to look for?"

"Oh, I don't need anything right now, but I do like browsing. I've never seen so much merchandise in one place in my life."

He laughed. "No, it's not like anything back home, is it?"

"Do you miss Ashland, Michael?"

"Sometimes I miss the times I lived there. But nothing there is the same now and I've come to love living here in the city. It took a while, but now I feel this is home. What about you? Do you plan on going back to

Ashland or —"

"Oh, it's still home for me. And, of course, once I pay off the mortgage, I'll be returning."

Her words didn't really surprise him, though they did seem to put a pall on his mood. He knew the whole reason she was here was to earn enough money to get her home paid off. But he was going to have to warn his mother against becoming too attached to Violet so that she didn't take it too hard when she did leave. And he couldn't let himself enjoy her company too much for the very same reason.

"Well, you don't have Macy's back in Ashland, so you might as well see what it has to offer. We'll take a tour so that if something should catch your fancy, you'll know where to find it when you come back with Mother."

"All right. I'd like that."

They spent the better part of an hour going from one floor to another, browsing in the book department, the jewelry department and on to the fine-art and china department. Then Violet turned to him. "One truly could spend a whole day here and not see it all, I'm sure."

"Mother says the same thing, and I can tell you that you haven't seen anywhere near half of it yet."

"Well, I've taken up enough of your time for today, and I really need to make sure that my clothes are ready for work. I suppose we should be going."

Michael had a feeling Violet avoided browsing the women's department for fear of embarrassing him, and he had to admit he appreciated her thoughtfulness. Still, he almost hated to leave. It was the most time he'd ever spent with Violet alone and he'd thoroughly enjoyed getting to know her better.

By the time they returned to Heaton House, Violet's heart felt lighter than it had since she learned Harlan Black held the deed to her home. Now she had hope that she could pay off the debt against it. And even if she stayed here, she would have a home to keep in her family as part of a dowry if she should ever —

Violet caught her breath. Where in all the world did that thought come from? She had no need for a dowry, nor did she want to have need of one. She'd been disillusioned by Nick and then Harlan and wasn't sure she could trust any man. All she wanted now was to have her family home free and clear of the likes of Harlan. What she did with it could be decided when that was accomplished.

She'd had a wonderful time with Michael, seeing a side of him she'd never known. She'd enjoyed lunch and the shopping trip and she'd been surprised at how easy it was to open up to Michael about Harlan and her fears. Maybe it was because she had known him a long time and she trusted him and his mother. After all they'd done for her, how could she not?

Violet kept busy for the rest of the afternoon, and by the time she started downstairs that evening, she was confident she was ready to start work the next morning. She'd pressed and brushed her clothing, deciding exactly what she would wear each day. She was nervous, to be sure, but excited, too. She looked forward to beginning this new phase of her life more than she'd thought she might.

Michael asking her if she would be returning to Virginia had given her a lot to think about. She was a bit bothered that the thought of returning home didn't fill her with joy, but told herself that it was because she had no family living to return to. She did love her home and she wanted to keep it, but she wasn't quite so certain that she would be happy to leave here when the time came. Violet sighed. Now was not the time to be worrying about it all. She needed to be thankful that she had work and would be able to keep her home.

"Violet, wait!"

Violet stopped her descent and turned to see Elizabeth hurrying down the stairs.

"How did your interviews go today? I've been praying off and on all day."

"Thank you for asking and especially for praying for me, Elizabeth. The first one didn't go well at all. The next two said they'd be in touch with me."

Elizabeth sighed. "I'm so sorry. I thought for sure that you would have several and come home with a position."

"But I did come home with a position." Violet smiled at her new friend.

"You did? Oh, I am so happy. Where are you going to work?"

"The fourth interview was at Butterick. And I got the position. I'm still finding it hard to believe that I start tomorrow. It seems we'll be coworkers now . . . just like you and Lila."

They were both laughing when they stepped into the parlor.

"What is so funny?" Ben asked.

Violet was just about to announce her good news when Michael came into the room and announced, "Mother says dinner is ready, everyone."

There seemed to be a mass exit from the room, but Violet stayed put as Michael walked over to her. "Mother was quite pleased that I took you to lunch and shopping, Violet. Thank you for making me the son she can be proud of today."

Violet laughed. "She's proud of you every day, Michael."

"That may be, but she was quite pleased and surprised that I'd thought of it."

"So was I. It was very nice of you, and it made the day even more special for me." She took the arm he held out and let him lead her across the foyer and seat her at what had become her place at the table.

Ben seated Mrs. Heaton. When everyone else had taken their seats, she looked to her son. "Michael, will you say grace, please?"

Everyone bowed their heads as he thanked the Lord for the day and the food and for Violet's good news. He'd barely finished with an "Amen" before everyone started asking questions.

"What good news?" Lila asked from across the table. "You found a job?"

"Did you find a position?" Luke leaned forward from down the table.

"I did. I applied at Butterick this morning

and it looks like we'll be working together, Lila."

The other girl looked a little stunned, and Elizabeth rushed in to fill the silence. "It appears we have another 'coworker,' Lila. Or at least you really will." Her chuckle drew laughter at the running joke between the two women and even Lila managed a giggle — if it did seem a bit forced.

Everyone else congratulated her heartily as Michael began serving the main course and Gretchen began to pass the side dishes around.

"When do you start?" Lila asked as she took the bowl of creamed potatoes and served herself.

"First thing tomorrow morning."

Lila surprised Violet once more by saying, "I usually leave at seven-thirty. If you're ready by then we can go to work together."

Maybe there was hope for a friendship with Lila. Her change of heart from the evening before seemed genuine. "Thank you, Lila. I'll be ready."

"That's nice of you, Lila," Mrs. Heaton said from the other end of the table.

"Well, there's no sense in her going by herself when we can keep each other company on the way." Lila looked back to Violet. "Did you give me as a reference? If so, I wasn't asked about you."

"They didn't seem to need any references," Violet said. "They didn't even take the nice letter Mrs. Heaton gave me."

"Hmm, that's odd. Who did the interview?"

"Mr. Wilder and Miss Carter both interviewed me. But Mr. Butterick was there, too, and he seemed to have the final word."

"Oh!" Lila seemed a bit surprised as she continued. "Well, how nice. I —"

"I'm sure it's a relief to know that you have employment," Luke interrupted.

Violet was glad of the interruption. She wasn't sure she wanted to hear what Lila was going to say next. "Oh, yes. It is."

"We're all very happy for you, Violet," Elizabeth said.

"Thank you. I feel blessed to know I have everyone's good wishes and prayers." Looking around the table, Violet realized she was among friends, and she sent up a silent prayer, thanking the Lord above for Mrs. Heaton and her boarders.

# CHAPTER SEVEN

Michael watched as everyone congratulated Violet on finding work. He'd been pleasantly surprised by Lila's offer to accompany Violet to work, even though he'd been hoping she would. Had she not, he'd been prepared to suggest it.

What he hadn't been prepared for was the relief he felt that Violet had gotten the position, which meant that she would be staying with them. She'd never given any indication that she would go back home, but he'd wondered if she might if she didn't find something right away. Many who came to New York City did just that if they couldn't find employment quickly. He was glad Violet wouldn't be one of them, because his mother seemed to have perked up considerably since Violet's arrival and he wanted to make sure she stayed that way.

He had to admit he liked having Violet around, too. But he and his mother had to keep in mind that she would be leaving at some point. Her only reason for coming here in the first place was to find a job to be able to pay off her family home and go back to Virginia. And Michael had no intention of moving back to Ashland. His life was here in the city now. If his sister was still alive she was out there somewhere, and he'd never find her if he left. Besides, his mother's life was here, helping other young women. So he'd best keep reminding himself that Violet's stay here wouldn't be permanent. It wouldn't be wise to let himself become too attached to her.

"Did you go on other interviews, Violet?" Julia asked.

"Yes, I did. The first three came up empty, and I was sure Butterick wouldn't be any different. But I was hired before I left."

"Oh! I thought perhaps they'd telephoned you to let you know you had the position."

Violet looked lovely — her face was flushed with color and her eyes sparkled. She looked as relieved as Michael felt about her getting the position.

"Well, actually, you did receive a telephone call this afternoon. Gretchen remembered to tell me just before dinner," his mother said. "There seemed to be no hurry to let you know, with you getting the position at

Butterick. It was the personnel director at Macy's asking that you come in and have another interview tomorrow. Gretchen told her she'd give you the message."

"Thank you for letting me know, but you were right that there needn't be any hurry to tell me. I'm quite pleased that I was hired by Butterick."

"And I'm so glad you and Michael celebrated your good news by going to lunch and Macy's, since I didn't get to go with you," Mrs. Heaton said.

"Oh? Michael took you around?" Lila raised a thin eyebrow and looked at Violet. "That must have been a real treat."

Michael had a feeling Lila wasn't very happy about the time he and Violet had spent together. And in spite of the fact that she seemed to be trying to befriend Violet, he didn't feel any of it was genuine. But at least he wouldn't have to worry about Violet finding her way to work and home alone, and for that he was thankful.

"Oh, it was — at least after Violet had an unexpected tour of the tenements," Michael said.

"How did that come about?" his mother asked.

"There was an awful accident and our hack driver was trying to avoid the worst of the traffic, but I think he went entirely the wrong way about it. Needless to say, Violet saw that mansions and wealth are not all this city is made up of. It is something one needs to know. I just hadn't planned on her seeing it all up close yet."

"But after that we saw the other side of life," Violet said. "I couldn't believe the size of Macy's. I've never seen so much merchandise in one place. Do society women really need all of that finery?"

All the men at the table chuckled, including Michael.

"They seem to think they do," John Talbot said with a laugh.

"Well, you would know, covering all the society goings-on as you do," Elizabeth said, cocking her head to the side.

John only smiled at her. As always, there seemed to be an undercurrent between those two, and numerous times in the past few months Michael had caught them stealing glances at each other when they didn't think the other was looking. He couldn't help but wonder if Elizabeth was sweet on John or if it was the other way around, but they'd certainly make a nice-looking couple if they ever became one. At least John wasn't hanging on to every word that came out of Violet's mouth as Luke and Ben were.

Michael didn't like the attention the two men were giving Violet tonight any more than he had the first night she arrived. Not one bit. He told himself that it was because he felt responsible for her . . . as he always had his sister, Rebecca. But that didn't ring true either and, deep down, he knew it. There was something about Violet, something — thing —

"Michael, what are you so deep in thought about down there?" his mother asked.

"I'm sorry. I was just woolgathering, I suppose." He laughed and hoped he'd thrown his mother off track. She was very good at reading him, and he wasn't ready for a barrage of questions he didn't have the answers to.

Being on time the next morning was not a problem for Violet. She woke just after dawn and was in and out of the bathroom before she heard anyone else stirring. She took time dressing with care, at last feeling confident she was dressed in the same manner as the women she'd seen at Butterick the day before. She'd chosen a gray-and-black-striped skirt and a crisp white shirtwaist with a black ribbon trim. She tied her mother's cameo with a black ribbon and wore it around her neck.

Violet made her bed and took one last look at the room she'd come to feel was almost like home before hurrying downstairs to join the others for breakfast. She was pleased to find she'd made it down before Lila this morning in particular, and that Michael was still at the table when she entered the dining room.

"Good morning, everyone. Now I really feel as if I belong, seeing you all here this morning."

"Good morning, Violet," Michael said, adding his voice to the others around the table.

He smiled, flashing those dimples, and Violet tried to ignore the way her pulse raced as she hurried to the sideboard and began to fill her plate with bacon, scrambled eggs and a muffin.

Michael stood to pull out her chair and once he took his own, he slid a piece of paper to her. His fingers brushed hers as she took it, sending a spark of electricity straight up her arm to the vicinity of her heart, taking her breath away. She quickly looked at Michael and was relieved that he didn't seem to notice as he began to explain the map he'd drawn.

"This is the map I told you I would make for you. Just in case you and Lila should get separated at some point. This will show you where the El and trolley stops are." He pointed them out to her on the map while she tried to get her breathing back to normal. "None are far apart, and you should be able to get back home by yourself easily enough."

"Thank you, Michael." Violet sounded a little breathless to her own ears but he didn't seen to realize the effect his brief touch had on her, and for that she was extremely thankful. "I'll keep it with me until I know my way around by heart."

"If it isn't clear to you, let me know, and I'll do my best to make it easier for you to read."

"I'm sure it will be fine." She was touched that he'd remembered his promise to her. And she felt a little less nervous knowing she'd have the map with her at all times.

"Are you nervous this morning?" Michael asked.

She let out a shaky sigh. "I have to admit that I am."

"I'm sure it will all go well for you," he said.

"Having a case of nerves is normal for the first day," Elizabeth assured her. "You are already doing better than I did on my first day at *The Delineator.* I was afraid to eat anything, and by noon I was starving. But I'd forgotten to take my lunch with me! Thankfully one of my coworkers shared hers."

"Oh. I hadn't thought about what to do about lunch," Violet said.

"No need to worry, dear." Mrs. Heaton came in from the kitchen to hear her last words. "Gretchen packs a very nice lunch for all the boarders. She puts them on the table in the foyer. Just pick one up when you leave. I look forward to seeing how your first day goes this evening. I'm sure all will go well, but I think everyone is nervous that first day."

"Thank you all for your encouragement. I must admit that this is one *first* I'll be glad to have over with." Violet smiled around the table and her eyes came to rest on the woman she'd come to think of as family.

"Well, good morning, everyone!" Lila said as she entered the room.

Somehow Lila's greeting didn't seem to match the expression on her face. She looked a bit out of sorts as she went to the sideboard. Violet joined the others in greeting her. "Good morning, Lila."

"Are you ready for today? I warn you that it will be a busy one," Lila said as she took her seat across from Violet.

"Good. That means I'll get the first day over with quickly," Violet said, grinning at the other woman.

"Hmm. I suppose you are right," Lila answered. "Actually that's one thing I like about working there. Most days go by very fast."

Violet was glad to hear it. Not that she minded working. She was looking forward to making her way in this city. But she was beginning to enjoy the company of the other boarders more each day, and she looked forward to hearing about their days and getting to know them all better.

Michael slid his seat back and stood. "I suppose it is time to go. I hope you have a really great first day, Violet."

The smile he gave her made her heart beat faster and do a little flip that she tried to ignore, but those dimples were just too hard to avoid. "Thank you, Michael."

He was on his way out the door when he turned back. "And, Lila, thank you for seeing to it that Violet will know her way to and from work."

"Why, you're welcome, Michael. I'm glad to do it." For the first time that morning, Lila's smile seemed genuine as she batted her eyelashes at him.

Violet had no doubt that Lila was attracted to Michael, but did he feel that way about her? Suddenly she felt a little sick to her stomach. She quickly put it down to nerves about her first day of work and chided herself for wondering if there might be something going on between Lila and Michael. It wasn't any of her business anyway. But the thought didn't sit well with her. Not at all.

Violet was more than a little relieved when they arrived at Butterick and Company. Although Lila had smiled a time or two, she'd barely spoken to Violet once they left the boardinghouse, and Violet wondered if she would ever feel comfortable around the other young woman.

Lila had hurried her along, saying they must rush or they'd be late when they got to the trolley stop. But it turned out that they waited about five minutes before the trolley arrived and there were several others waiting with them.

Violet had expected to ride the El as she and Michael and Mrs. Heaton had, but she found the trolley ride quite interesting. At this time of the day, she was sure that most of the men and women were on their way to work just as she and Lila were. She enjoyed wondering what kind of jobs they held and if they'd all get off at the same stop. But each time they came to a standstill, one or two got off and several more hurried to get on.

Perhaps it was all the stopping and starting, but for some reason the traffic didn't bother Violet quite as much today. Maybe she would get used to it, after all.

When they arrived at Butterick, Miss Carter was at the base of the stairs. "Good morning, ladies. Traffic must not have been too bad this morning. You're right on time."

"Good morning, Miss Carter," Lila said before Violet had a chance to say anything. "Traffic wasn't nearly as awful as usual."

Her tone was much more exuberant than it had been that morning. Perhaps Lila was the kind of person who needed time to wake up and get her thoughts together in the morning. Violet didn't know her well enough to be sure.

"Violet and I live at the same boarding-house. I've taken her under my wing to show her how to get here and back home," Lila informed Miss Carter.

"That's good of you, Lila. It's always nice to have company on the way to work and home."

"I really appreciate it," Violet said. "Everything seems so different to me."

"I'm sure it does, just moving to the city and away from what is familiar." Miss Carter smiled at her. "Well, let's get started. I'll show you around and then assign your work duties and introduce you to your supervisor."

Lila was still standing listening to what Miss Carter had to say. The older woman turned to her. "Lila, dear, you may go on to work now."

"Yes, ma'am. I'll look for you when the lunch bell rings, Violet. Good luck!" With that she pivoted and headed in the other direction. Something about her demeanor made Violet wonder if Lila and Miss Carter didn't quite get along.

"Have you and Lila become good friends?" Miss Carter asked as they watched her walk away.

"I don't think you could call us that. At least not yet. But we do reside at the same boardinghouse. She was kind enough to tell me I could use her as a reference when I applied for the position, but I forgot to mention it yesterday."

"You made a fine impression on your own, Violet. I'm not sure a recommendation from Miss Miller would have done as much as just talking to you did." Miss Carter smiled and motioned for Violet to follow her up the same stairs she'd climbed the day before.

For the next half hour Miss Carter gave her a quick tour, showing her where the designers and pattern makers worked. They watched for a while before going out into the hall once more.

"The templates are then sent to the cutting room, where they're placed on a stack of tissue paper and cut out. The markings are then transferred to each piece by hand. The pieces are identified by letters marked on it with small holes. Once that is done, the pieces are sorted, folded together and labeled with an image of the garments and brief instructions."

"I never realized just how much work went into making the patterns I've come to count on," Violet said.

"It is a lot." Miss Carter chuckled. They went down another floor and entered a room where seamstresses were working on different outfits, and then they entered another room where artists were sketching the finished products that were placed on mannequins.

"This is where the drawings you see in *The Delineator* and other magazines come to life. After the sketches are finished, some are done in pen and ink and others are colored in for templates to make into prints that are then put into the magazine."

Miss Carter led Violet around the room so she could get a good look at what was being done. She'd never imagined how many steps it took to get a pattern made and to be able to show it in a way that made her and her mother think that an outfit would look good on them.

Everyone she met was very nice and Violet looked forward to getting to know them all better.

"Come along. We'll go to the cutting and folding room and get you started." Miss Carter led her to a huge workroom. "This is where the cutting and folding operations take place. As you can see, it takes a lot of people to keep up with it."

Violet looked at the floor below and saw both men and women at work. She saw that most of those doing the folding were young women of about her age, including Lila, who looked up and gave her a wave before whispering to the girl next to her.

Violet followed Miss Carter down the stairs and into the room where she introduced her to Mr. Hanson, the floor supervisor. "Mr. Hanson, this is our newest employee, Miss Violet Burton."

Mr. Hanson sported a dark brown beard

and mustache, and he had a nice smile. "Pleased to meet you, Miss Burton. How do you like what you've seen of our operation?"

"Oh, I am quite impressed. I never dreamed of how much work it took to make a pattern. I'm looking forward to working with everyone."

"Now, that is the kind of attitude we like around here. I'm sure you are going to fit right in, Miss Burton."

Violet was beginning to feel that she might.

# CHAPTER EIGHT

Michael had watched the clock all day, wondering how Violet's day was going. She'd seemed quite nervous this morning, and he'd prayed that she'd come to feel at ease in her new surroundings. It was well-known that Mr. Butterick was one of the kindest, more generous men in the city. He gave much to the poor, in particular to needy children, and his company had always had a reputation for treating its employees well.

He gazed out the window of his office and jangled the coins in his pocket as he watched the traffic on Third Avenue. He'd felt a restless energy all morning — one would think he was the one starting a new job today instead of Violet.

In spite of the fact that there were times when she looked very vulnerable and Michael had wanted to ease her fears about the city, the traffic and her decision to move here, Violet Burton was a strong woman. A weak woman would not have made the decision to leave all she knew and move to New York City to find a way to keep her family home instead of entering into a loveless marriage.

After Violet had told him about what Harlan Black had tried to do, he was certain she could take care of herself. After all, she'd decided to chance losing her inheritance rather than marrying the likes of Black. Still, it infuriated Michael that the man had tried to blackmail Violet into marrying him.

He clenched his fists, wishing he could get ahold of Black. Michael remembered Harlan and his reputation. There weren't many in Ashland who liked the banker. He misused his position in town to get what he wanted, and it didn't matter to him if others had to suffer. But he did have a reputation as a ladies' man. In fact, at one time Michael had feared Becca might be attracted to him, but that was before she'd left to come here. At least she hadn't come under his influence. And neither had Violet. He was thankful for that.

Still, Black held Violet's inheritance in his hand, and Michael didn't like that one bit. One of the things that bothered him was why Mrs. Burton had had any need to go to Black for money in the first place. His mother had said that she thought Mr. Burton had made provisions for his wife and daughter in his will. She'd been under the impression that while they might not have been well-off, they had enough money to provide for them in the manner they'd been accustomed to.

Evidently it had been much on his mother's mind, because just this morning, she'd mentioned that she wondered if Harlan Black had made Mrs. Burton believe something other than the truth about her money situation.

As always, when he heard something like that, Michael wanted to know more, get to the bottom of it. Maybe he should send one of his men to look into things in Ashland. Yes, it might be time to do just that. It was certainly something to think about.

That Violet had turned down Black's offer showed him that *weak* was not a term that applied to her. Even so, a strong woman could be naive in ways. This city was far different from their hometown. But after yesterday, she must realize there was a darker side that hid behind all the mansions, the businesses on the Ladies' Mile and the beauty of Central Park. The dangerous side that had swallowed up his sister. He couldn't let that happen to Violet. *Wouldn't* let it happen.

The noise of traffic seemed to intensify and Michael looked down to see that an omnibus had hit a street vendor's wagon. It didn't look as if anyone was seriously hurt from what he could tell three stories up, but he hoped traffic was better today and that no omnibuses came close to running into the streetcar Violet and Lila rode to work in.

Michael chuckled, remembering Violet's reaction to the near accident on Saturday. To give her credit, had it not been for her scream, they might well have been in a horrible accident. All in all, except for that near calamity, it had been the most enjoyable weekend he'd had in a very long time. And he'd enjoyed yesterday even more. He hoped Violet had enjoyed it as much as he had.

He decided to take off a little early so that he would be sure to be home when she and Lila returned. As soon as he let himself into the house, the aroma coming from the kitchen assured him that his mother planned a special dinner to celebrate Violet's first day of work.

That she was becoming attached to the

young woman was obvious. Violet was a link to their hometown, to the woman who'd been his mother's best friend and even to Rebecca, in his mother's mind. He couldn't blame her because he felt much the same way — only different — and definitely not brotherly.

Since the disappearance of his sister, Michael hadn't given much thought to his personal life. He'd been more concerned with helping his mother and trying to find his sister. And for propriety's sake, because of his mother's business, he'd made a conscious decision not to let himself become interested in any of the women boarding with her.

But Violet Burton could very well be the exception. If the amount of time he spent thinking about her was any indication, she already was. Since the moment he'd first seen Violet all grown up, there had been something about her that drew him to her. He wasn't comfortable with it, tried to ignore it — to no avail, but there it was. He enjoyed being around her. Already, he looked forward to seeing her each morning and evening.

And yet he had no intention of falling in love with her. Violet was going to return to Virginia when she got the mortgage paid off. She'd said as much. She had no intention of staying in New York City. And just as he wanted to warn his mother not to get too attached to her, he had to tell himself the same thing. Besides, after Amanda broke their engagement, refusing to postpone the wedding until he had a chance to look for his sister, he knew that not many women would accept his commitment to finding his sister or even helping his mother. There was no sense setting himself up for disappointment again.

Still, Violet was a family friend and he wanted to help her in any way he could. And he was curious to know how her day had gone.

Michael made his way down the hall, peeking into his mother's study only to find it empty. He headed to the kitchen. His mother was icing a three-layer coconut cake, and she looked up with a smile when he entered the room.

"Michael! You're home early today, son."

"I am." He joined her at the worktable and stuck a finger in the icing bowl before bringing it to his mouth. "Mmm. Love coconut cake."

His mother playfully slapped at his hand when he went for another dip in the icing. "You didn't know I was making this, so that isn't why you came home early."

"You're right. Actually, I wanted to see how Violet's first day went."

His mother chuckled. "I understand. I've been a bit nervous for her all day. I'm sure everything has gone well — still I'm anxious for her to get home to find out."

At the sound of the front door opening, Michael's heart seemed to do some kind of funny little jump and twist and he decided that *anxious* described how he felt perfectly. It was all he could do to let his mother hurry to the foyer before him.

"How did your first day go?" his mother asked as soon as she spotted Violet.

Michael didn't need to hear the answer. He could tell from the look on Violet's face. A deep sigh of relief left his lungs before she answered.

"It was wonderful. Everyone was so friendly and kind. I'm sure I'm going to like working there."

"Oh, yes," Lila said. "Violet is going to fit right in."

From the conflicting tone in Lila's voice and the almost smile on her face, Michael couldn't decide if she was being sarcastic or sincere.

"Lila was very kind to introduce me to everyone she could when we took lunch,"

Violet said, turning to smile at the other girl. "Just knowing someone there helped put me at ease."

Her words went a long way to convincing Michael that Lila was being genuine.

"I'm so glad everything went well," his mother said. "I was sure it would, but it's good to hear that I was right to plan a dinner to celebrate your first day. I remembered that coconut cake is one of your favorites and I'd best get back to icing it. You girls have plenty of time to freshen up."

"I believe I have the beginning of a migraine," Lila said abruptly. "If I'm not down for dinner, please don't be concerned. I think I might need to lie down and close my eyes for a bit."

"Oh, I'm sorry, Lila," Michael's mother said. "Would you like me to send you up some tea?"

"No, thank you." Lila turned to the stairs.

"I'll be sure to save a plate for you and a big slice of cake for later if you don't come down to dinner."

Lila said nothing as she began to climb the stairs.

"Is there anything I can get you?" Violet asked. "A cool cloth?"

"No. I just need some quiet and a dark room. I'll be fine." Her voice trailed off as she reached the landing.

"I hope she feels better soon. Does she have these headaches often?" Violet asked.

Mrs. Heaton shrugged. "Occasionally. But she usually recovers quickly."

"I'm sure she'll be fine," Michael said. Lila had looked more irritated than in pain, and he had a feeling that she didn't like all the attention Violet was getting. She'd acted much the same way when one of the other girls was getting more attention than she was.

"I hope so. Is there anything I can do to help in the kitchen, Mrs. Heaton?"

"No, dear. Dinner will be in about an hour and a half. You have time to relax and rest."

"Oh, I don't think I can rest. My mind is still in a whirl." Violet gave a light laugh. "There is so much going on at Butterick it's hard to take it all in. But I have much more appreciation to what goes into making the patterns to make it easier for the home sewer."

"Maybe you should go sit in the garden for a bit. It's very relaxing out there this time of day. I've got to go finish icing the cake." She started back to the kitchen and then turned back. "Michael, why don't you show Violet the garden? It's a nice place to relax."

Michael surprised himself by saying, "I'll be glad to, if you want to see it, Violet?"

"That would be nice," Violet said as Michael took her elbow and led her through the hall to the doors at the end.

"Mother's pride and joy is the garden. It is very small, but she's done a lot of work getting it just the way she likes it." He opened the door and let Violet go through first.

"Oh, it is beautiful." The air was sweet smelling from the roses and all the other flowers in bloom. It felt much cooler here than anywhere else she'd been that day.

Michael led her to a small bench and waited until she sat down before joining her. "I'm glad your first day went well."

"I am, too." Something about the way he was looking at her had her feeling warm and . . . fluttery. Michael was such a handsome man and very considerate of others. How could a woman's heart not beat a little faster when his attention was turned on her?

She told herself that he was just acting as any old friend would, being happy for her, as she continued, "I must admit I was very nervous. I hope I can live up to their expectations. I was so surprised when they offered me a position as a seamstress instead of the pattern folding."

Michael leaned a little closer and grinned down at her. "What? You're going to be a seamstress? You aren't going to be working alongside Lila in the pattern room?"

Violet tried not to think about how deep his dimples were up this close. She shook her head. "No. I don't think she's very happy about it, and I can understand how she might not be. I expected to be folding patterns right along with her, but after lunch I was summoned to the office and told that one of the seamstresses was leaving to get married. They asked if I would be interested in taking her place since I was familiar with sewing from their patterns."

"Violet, that is very good news for you. It pays better than the pattern folding, I'm sure."

She nodded. "It does, and I'm so glad. I think I'll be able to make an extra payment to the bank every other month or so. I just feel bad for Lila. And I'm a little apprehensive. I tried to tell them that I am not an excellent seamstress, but they said that since they target the home seamstress, that is exactly who should be making their sample wardrobes."

"Mother is going to be so excited for you. And so will the other boarders."

Violet sighed. "All except for Lila. I feel

so bad —"

"Don't worry about Lila. You didn't seek out the position and, besides, I'm pretty sure Lila doesn't know how to sew."

Violet jumped up from the bench as an idea came to her. "Maybe I could offer to teach her to sew, so that next time an opening comes up she could apply for it."

"That would be nice of you."

She let out a sigh and shook her head. "But I don't have my sewing machine with me."

"I'm sure Mother would loan you hers."

"Or maybe I could have Beth, my friend from home, send me mine."

"Either way would work. But don't be surprised if Lila doesn't take to your suggestion. She might not really want to learn. Or she might not want to —"

"Learn from me?" Violet finished for him.

Michael shrugged. "One can never tell how Lila is going to react to an idea. But it's very kind of you to want to make the offer."

"No, it's more selfish than anything. I'll feel better if I do. She was kind enough to introduce me to several coworkers today and, well, I might feel the same way if I'd been at the company first. In fact, I'm sure I would."

Violet saw no need to mention that Lila had barely spoken to her on the way home — or even on the way to work that morning. She might have known Michael and his mother longer than Lila had, but Lila had been living in their home longer than she. At this point Violet had no idea how close any of them were.

"That's understandable. Still, if she doesn't know how to sew, she wouldn't have gotten the position anyway. Try not to blame yourself for her attitude."

Violet had to ask, "How long has Lila lived here?"

"She's only been with us about eleven months."

"Oh. I thought she'd lived here much longer."

"No. Although sometimes it feels as if she has been here much longer."

Violet couldn't tell how he felt about Lila, and she told herself once more that it wasn't any of her business anyway. Still, she wished she knew. "I suppose I'd better go freshen up for dinner. Hopefully, Lila will feel better and come down."

"Mother will send something up if she doesn't. Don't worry about her. She'll be fine."

Violet was sure she would be, but today's

events weren't going to make it easier for them to become friends. And she might have to accept that they never would be. But it would make living in the same house much easier if they could get along.

They parted at the staircase. Violet had just reached the landing when Julia came out of Lila's room and hurried to give her a hug. "I heard about your wonderful news," she whispered. "I am so happy for you."

"Lila told you?"

Julia steered Violet down the hall away from Lila's room.

"How is her headache? I feel so bad —"

"Don't you feel that way for a minute. You thought you were being hired to be a pattern folder. You had no way of knowing they would be in need of a seamstress. But you can sew and Lila can't. For whatever reason you were asked to take the position, just rejoice and thank the good Lord for the blessing. That's what I'd do."

"Oh, thank you, Julia. I needed to hear those words. I do hate that Lila is upset, but I'm so very excited to begin my new position!"

"Good! You should be. Hopefully Lila will get a promotion one day soon. But don't blame yourself if she doesn't. Now, let's freshen up and get downstairs. I can't wait to see what Mrs. Heaton has prepared for your first-day-at-work celebration — it's bound to be delicious. She's so great to make all 'first days' special."

"She's a wonderful woman. I'm so thankful she suggested I come to New York when I couldn't find work at home."

"Well, I'm thankful she did, too. I'm glad you are here, Violet. So is everyone . . ." She grinned and shrugged. "Well, all except for one, maybe. It's impossible to please everyone, you know."

Julia was right. If Lila was determined to dislike her, there was nothing she could do to make her change her mind. Mrs. Heaton had put a lot of effort into this celebration dinner and Violet wasn't going to let Lila's attitude ruin it.

The table was set with the Sunday china, and as Michael pulled out her chair for her, Violet realized how much she was coming to look forward to dinnertime. She loved hearing him say the prayer before meals, and that he thanked the Lord for her quick promotion touched her heart.

As Michael began passing dishes around, there was a family feel to sharing meals with these people she was coming to know. Everyone seemed truly happy about the way her day had gone and wanted to know all about her new position.

"I would think that would be a more interesting position than the one you applied for," Elizabeth said. "How fortunate that you know how to sew."

"I am very thankful that I do. And the fact that I'd been using Butterick patterns to make mine and Mother's clothing the last few years seemed to help."

"I'm sure it did," John said. "Any company wants to have an employee who likes what they sell."

The dinner Mrs. Heaton served was one of Violet's very favorites and it made her feel even more at home than ever. Had her mother been alive, she would have prepared the exact same thing. Dinner was filet of beef with mushroom sauce, creamed potatoes and peas along with other side dishes. The dessert was a huge coconut layer cake.

"Thank you so much, Mrs. Heaton. Everything is delicious." Violet tried not to think of Lila missing out on it. Was she sulking? Violet sighed inwardly at her thoughts. There she went again — judging others. It was possible the other woman really did feel bad for reasons other than jealousy. She shouldn't be jumping to conclusions.

"I love it when someone has something to

celebrate on a weeknight," John Talbot said. "It feels like a holiday."

Elizabeth added, "We're blessed that Mrs. Heaton considers most pieces of good news a reason to celebrate."

"So, Violet, how did it come about that you've become a seamstress instead of a pattern cutter or folder?" Luke asked.

Violet explained about the young woman she'd be replacing getting married. "Evidently, from what I was told, openings come up quite often in all departments for that reason."

"They come up often in all businesses. I suppose there are some women who keep their positions once they are married, but I haven't known many," Julia said. "And, were I to get married, I don't think I'd want to work. Of course there are women who must take care of their families for various reasons and I would hope they would be able to find work, should they need it."

"Times are changing," Mrs. Heaton said. "There are many more opportunities for employment for women now that were not available when I was young. I was blessed in that I married for love, but I knew young women who weren't so fortunate. Their fathers arranged marriages for them or they felt forced to marry any available suitor. You have many more choices, particularly in this city. But you must always be aware of the dangers, too."

"Yes, we know. And we're all thankful to you, Mrs. Heaton. You've given us a safe haven and you watch over us so well," Elizabeth said.

"Even with my rules about not going out at night alone or without one of our male boarders accompanying you?"

"Even with those," Julia said. "I think that's part of why I feel so much at home here. I know you would give me the same advice my mother would. And I have no desire to go out by myself after dark."

"There's not one of us who objects to keeping you ladies company any evening." Luke grinned and winked at Violet.

"That is true," Michael said, capturing Violet's gaze. "Anytime."

The look in his eyes as his gaze met hers had a warm flush creeping up Violet's neck and cheeks.

"Why don't we all go to a concert at Carnegie Hall —" All conversation stopped as a loud series of knocks on the front door interrupted Michael.

Maida hurried to see who was interrupting their dinnertime. Then Michael and his mother were called to the door. The pocket doors were shut for but a few minutes and then Gretchen was summoned to the foyer. From the looks on the other boarders' faces, Violet was certain she wasn't the only one wondering what was going on.

# CHAPTER NINE

Everyone was waiting in silence when Michael opened the pocket doors once more. In fact, no one spoke until he and his mother had taken their seats.

"What is it, Michael? Has there been some kind of trouble?" John Talbot asked.

"No, at least not for any of us. Only for the young woman we're taking in for a while." Michael understood the intensity in John's voice. He wanted a big story to break. One that could get him out of covering those high-society festivities that he disliked so much. If he could break a big story, he could work for any newspaper in the country. But it had to be the right one, and John was always on the lookout. This wasn't it, unless one took a look at the bigger story — the overcrowding of the tenements, the corruption that couldn't be completely eradicated.

"I'm sorry about the interruption, everyone," Mrs. Heaton said. "I knew we were going to gain another temporary boarder, but I wasn't expecting her quite so soon."

"A temporary boarder?" Violet asked.

Michael could see the confusion in her eyes as his mother tried to explain.

"Yes. Sometimes we take in someone who needs a safe place to stay just for a while, until they can go back to the home they've left or move on to another more permanent place. I give them a room on the third floor. Anyway, Mrs. Clara Driscoll, who lives a few streets over and works for Tiffany Glass, asked her landlady, Mrs. Owens, to see if we could take in one of her girls for a short time, as there was no room at her boarding-house."

"And of course you said yes," Elizabeth said. "That's one of the things we all love about you, Mrs. Heaton. You are always willing to help out those less fortunate."

"Thank you, dear."

Michael's mother cleared her throat before going on and he knew Elizabeth's words had touched her deeply . . . along with the problems of the young woman they'd just taken in.

"You all know not to mention this to anyone, of course. This young lady has been treated very badly where she's been living."

She sighed and tears came to her eyes. "It seems her brother-in-law kicked her out of their tenement and she had no place to go. Clara says she's a hard worker and will help to find her a more permanent place. For now, though, she needs encouragement and the peace of knowing she's safe."

"How sad," Violet said.

"I'm sorry that I haven't gotten around to explaining all this to you, Violet."

"I'll explain to Violet later, Mother."

Mrs. Heaton took a deep breath. "Thank you, Michael. For now let's get on with our meal. I'll have something sent up to her after she's settled in her room."

"Oh, Mrs. Heaton, if you are needed upstairs, please don't give me another thought. We're nearly finished with our meal anyway. Thank you very much for making it so special."

"I'm not leaving until we have the cake. Michael, please bring it to me. And, Julia, would you be a dear and get the dessert plates, please?"

Michael and Julia hurried to do as requested. Once the cake was in front of her, his mother cut large slices and sent them around the table.

"Too bad Lila didn't feel like joining us," Elizabeth said. "Coconut cake is one of her favorites, too."

"She won't miss out," Michael said. "Mother will send a plate up to her."

"I already did — all except for the cake," Mrs. Heaton said. "But she sent it back down. I'll leave it in the kitchen in case she changes her mind, and I'll make sure there's a slice of cake for her."

"If she doesn't want it, I'll be glad to take her piece of cake so it doesn't go to waste," Benjamin said.

Everyone laughed at that. It'd been mentioned on more than one occasion that with men in the house, there wasn't much food that went to waste. From what his mother told him, Michael knew it was true. But she always took that into account and he was certain there would be plenty left for both Lila and the new boarder. And he was pretty sure Lila's appetite would be back before the evening was over — in fact she'd probably be starving by then. He had a feeling that migraine was only a ruse to keep from celebrating with Violet.

Violet joined the others in the front parlor after dinner, but her thoughts were on the young woman the Heatons had just taken in. What must it be like to be kicked out of your home . . . even if it was a tenement?

Thoughts of the area she and Michael had wound up in made her shudder. But still, it was home to many. It was all they had. And to be forced out . . . Where did one go from there?

It appeared they could possibly come here. Violet had known there were rooms on the third floor and that Gretchen and Maida stayed in two of them, but she really hadn't thought about the other empty rooms. Nor did she know how many there were. But she was pleased to know that the Heatons reached out to those in need. Much like they did her, only in a different way.

Mrs. Heaton went upstairs right after dessert to see about the young woman they'd taken in and Michael seemed to have disappeared. Violet wondered if it had anything to do with their new boarder. Everyone else was there, except for Lila, who still hadn't made an appearance.

Violet wondered if she should go check on her. She'd just decided to do that and had excused herself when Maida met her in the foyer.

"Miss Burton, Mr. Heaton would like to talk to you, if you have time for him. He is in Mrs. Heaton's study."

If she had time for him? Violet couldn't

imagine ever not having time for Michael Heaton. "Thank you, Maida." Violet headed down the hall to the study. She knocked lightly on the door frame and was pleased to be greeted with Michael's smile.

"Maida said you wanted to talk to me. If I've come at a bad time —"

"No, you haven't. Please, come in and take a seat, Violet. I didn't forget that I would try to explain about our temporary boarders to you. Would you like me to have Maida bring us some tea?"

"No, thank you. I'm still quite full from supper." She took a seat in one of the chairs by the fireplace. "And please don't feel you have to explain. It's really none of my business."

"Oh, but it is. You live here, and while most of our boarders know Mother takes people in from time to time, they don't know everything. But Mother and I want you to know what it is we do here besides take in boarders."

Michael took the seat on the other side of the fireplace. "It's been a busy evening. We were expecting this new boarder, but we didn't know exactly when she would arrive. There's been trouble in her family for a while now, but evidently things escalated last night and her brother-in-law insisted that she move out of the apartment she'd been sharing with her sister and him and their children."

"How sad." Violet's heart broke for the woman upstairs.

"It's a story we hear often. Families all crowded into a small apartment, with little income to provide for everyone." He shook his head and looked into the fire. "Tempers flare and relationships are sometimes damaged forever. This may be one of those cases."

"I hope not."

"So do I." Michael's gaze turned to her once more. "But to explain about how we came to take in temporary boarders —"

"Michael, you don't have to explain to me. This is your home. You have the right to do whatever you want with it. And I am the last person who would have a problem with you helping others less fortunate. Your mother came to *my* aid. It does not surprise me at all that she would do the same for others."

"It is a little different with you, Violet. You're a family friend and you've become very special to mother and . . ." Michael paused and chewed his bottom lip. He shook his head and continued, "I cannot thank you enough for moving here and becoming part of this household. Your presence has made my mother very happy. Since Becca's disappearance, she's poured herself into this house and helping others. But with each passing year, much of the hope of finding my sister has disappeared, and, well, you've brought joy back into my mother's life. I am so glad you are here."

"Why, thank you, Michael. But it's I who am blessed to be here."

Michael smiled and shook his head. "Shh. I'm trying to thank you for what your being here means to my mother. And I'm getting off track. I'm supposed to be telling you how this all came about."

"I just assumed it was because of Becca's disappearance that your mother decided to open the boardinghouse."

"And you'd be right in that assumption. From the first, Mother's goal has been to provide a place for young women to live where they could feel at home and safe." Michael got up and began to pace and Violet could tell it was hard for him to continue. She waited in silence, not knowing what to say.

Finally, he continued, "When it became obvious that Becca wasn't coming home, we came here and went to the boardinghouse where the last letter we'd received had come from. But it was only to find that she'd lived there just a week before disappearing. She'd never given them our address to contact us, if something happened, never even —" He shook his head and sighed.

Taking his seat once more, he looked at Violet. "It's been very hard on both Mother and me. Not to know where she is, for the few leads we had go nowhere. Still we look for her, but I'm not sure we'll ever get the answers to all the questions we have."

The sorrow in his voice had Violet blinking back tears as she reached out and touched his arm. "I'm so sorry, Michael."

"I pray you'll never have to know the feeling." His hand covered hers and he squeezed it before letting go. She quickly moved her hand back to her lap, her pulse racing up her arm and straight to her heart at his touch.

"So, Mother decided to move here and open a boardinghouse. I wasn't going to let her do it alone, so I came, too. She's comfortable with the number of boarders we have, but she's always wanted to have room for those in dire need, if only for a night, a week or a month or so. It took a year before she began to make the connections that let others of the same mind know she was willing to help in that way."

175

"How was she able to get the word out?"

"There are several boardinghouses in the area and many all over the city. She met the owners and let them know that she keeps some rooms available for such a need. In my work, I've come to know several policemen, firemen, others who came into contact with young women who needed help, and I let them know. After a few months, we began to get calls from boardinghouse owners who had no room and knew someone who needed a place for a night, then we'd have a knock on the door from a policeman or fireman who'd run across someone in real need for a temporary place to stay to get away from a situation . . . somewhere safe until they could decide what to do."

"What wonderful work you and your mother are doing, Michael. If there is any way I can help, please let me know." Violet paused. "After seeing only a small part of the other side of the city, I've not been able to get it or the little boys we saw out of my mind. I realize I've lived quite a sheltered life in Ashland."

"I understand. I realized the same thing. It is quite a shock at first — to know there is poverty at such high levels just blocks from here. Does it make you want to go back?"

"I don't like it. But no, it doesn't make me want to go back — at least not until I have the money to pay off the mortgage on my family's home. However, it does make me feel selfish for feeling sorry for myself. I never had to live in those kinds of conditions. Never had to worry about my next meal or having a roof over my head. Oh, I worry about not being able to keep my home . . . but if that happens, I'll be able to work and stay here. I worried about finding work, but I was blessed to find it so quickly. I've never had to live in squalor. I'd like to help in some way, if I can."

"You have the heart of my mother and the others who want to make a difference. And I'm sure you'll be able to. There are all kinds of opportunities and ways to help, Violet. We just wanted you to know how we came to the point that we take in more than just our regular boarders. You'll find there is a group of people working to help in many ways. We can't do it all, and there will always be more problems than we can solve, but we try to do our part, one person at a time."

Violet had never felt prouder to know this man than at that moment. "Thank you for explaining it all to me. I see now why this house feels like a home. It holds much love for those who come to it."

■ ■ ■ ■

Long after Violet went upstairs, Michael sat in his mother's study thinking about their conversation. Violet had a huge heart and he could tell she was sincere in wanting to help others. Well, she'd have plenty of opportunity in this house. And his mother would be thrilled to have her help.

Perhaps it was a good thing their hack driver had taken a wrong turn the other day. Although Violet just saw the tip of the iceberg, she at least knew for certain that New York wasn't all mansions and fancy shops. And she'd find out more the longer she lived here.

There were many who didn't want to see or even hear about those less fortunate. Sadly, a few of their boarders were like that. Lila came to mind. She was much too self-absorbed to care much about others.

Her actions this evening were a prime example. She might have had a headache, but he'd seen her act that way before and he was pretty sure that Lila was just plain jealous of Violet and didn't want to be part of her celebration tonight. If she had any idea how transparent she was, she'd see that her attitude was what actually made people less inclined to want to spend time with her. Lila wouldn't want to know about the temporary boarder. She would barely acknowledge her existence once she joined them downstairs.

She and Violet were total opposites, and it was no wonder that Violet was getting most of the attention Lila craved. Violet cared about the others in this house, how their day went, what was going on in their lives.

Michael had never felt about a woman quite the way he did about Violet. On one hand, it was as if he'd known her all his life, which he had. On the other, it was as if he was getting to know her for the very first time and he was aware of her presence in a way that made him feel more alive than ever. Not even his ex-fiancée, Amanda, had made him feel the way Violet did.

He wondered if he should have told her that he'd sent someone to Ashland to try to find out where her attorney had gone and to try to find out what Harlan Black was up to. He'd talked to his mother more about the Burtons' finances and she was quite sure there would have been no need to take out a loan. Not unless something had happened that her best friend hadn't told her.

It was enough to see what, if anything, could be found out. There would be time enough later to let Violet know if something turned up. Until then, he would just be glad that she was here and had a job and wouldn't be thinking about going back home.

The relief he felt when she'd said she didn't want to go back just yet had surprised him in its intensity. He didn't want Violet going back to Ashland. Certainly not until he knew what Black was up to. Truthfully, he didn't want her going back at all. He told himself it was for his mother's sake, but to be honest, he wanted her to stay right here where he could get to know her better. For him, it was a big admission to make. And he wasn't ready to make it to anyone but himself.

Violet half expected to meet the temporary boarder the next evening, but when they sat down to dinner Mrs. Heaton announced that she'd returned to her family. It saddened Violet to know the woman had gone back so soon. Would anything have changed by then? How would she be treated?

"I don't know why you bother yourself with these people, Mrs. Heaton." Lila shook her head. "All the trouble you go to for one night."

Violet opened her mouth to come to Mrs.

Heaton's defense, but the older woman quickly came to her own.

"Sometimes, in some instances, that is all that is needed to bring clearer thinking and for things to get better," Mrs. Heaton said. "And sometimes it is too soon. In this case, I feel it was. But all I can do is offer a safe place for however short or long a time is needed and pray it helps."

"Still —"

"We knew we wouldn't be able to help everyone who came here for a night or a week or longer when we began to open our home to those in need," Michael said. "But if we can help a few, then we've done what we set out to do and what we feel the Lord has called us to do."

Violet's heart warmed at his words. He and his mother would be here for those in need no matter what the objections from others.

"And it is very noble of you to want to help. But —"

"Lila, you're fortunate you've never been in the position some of the young women who come to us have found themselves in. Mother has her reasons for opening her home to regular boarders like you and they are as important as her reasons for taking in those who need help immediately. But if you are unhappy here with what we do . . ."

It was no surprise to Violet to hear Lila backtracking. "Oh, no, of course I'm not. Who wouldn't love living here?"

"Good," Michael said. "I'm glad that is settled."

Conversation quickly turned to small talk as if everyone wanted to change the subject, and Michael turned to Violet, speaking in a voice meant only for her ears. "It's been a beautiful day and I wondered if you would like to take a walk later. There's something I'd like to show you I think you'll enjoy."

At this moment she wanted nothing more than to get away from Lila and her sulky silence and resentful stares. "I'd like that very much."

"Good. But I'd like not to have to go with the others. We'll head out once everyone has gathered in the parlor, if that's all right with you?"

Violet nodded as her heart flooded with warmth that he wanted to spend some time with just her. But when she took a sip of water, her eyes met Lila's over the rim of her goblet and she knew the other woman wanted to know what they'd said to each other.

It was doubtful they'd ever become friends, but Violet was determined to keep trying — if for no other reason than for the Heatons' sake. She wondered what it was Michael wanted to show her but wasn't sure it mattered. It would be good to get out of the house for a bit.

Once dinner was over, she hurried up to her room to freshen up and have a reason not to join the others in the parlor without a lot of questions. When she came back downstairs, she was pleased to see that the parlor doors were closed and Michael was waiting for her at the front door. She felt like a child slipping out of the house with him, but she knew she was safe in his company. He'd never harm her.

He pulled her hand through his arm and they headed down the street. "I don't know why we haven't shown you Gramercy Park yet, but it dawned on me today that you might want to know we have a park nearby for those days when you feel you must be outdoors. Mother's garden is wonderful, but it is small. It was she who suggested that you might need an outing."

"Your mother reads people very well. I love being at Heaton House, but I must admit that there are times when it's —"

"Too much noise — too many people?"

"Considering it was just Mother and I for the last few years, at times it does seem a little overwhelming. I'm sure I'll get used to it, though."

"I hope so. Mother would be very upset if you left us."

Violet couldn't help but wonder how he would feel, but couldn't bring herself to ask, so she changed the subject. "Is Gramercy Park large?"

"Nowhere near as large as Central Park and only residents can get in." He flashed his dimples at her. "I feel the same way you do — I'm glad that everyone in the city can go to Central Park and I feel they should. But it's nice to have an oasis in the middle of this neighborhood we live in."

They turned a corner and Violet didn't need Michael to point out the park to her. She could tell from the trees and the iron gate that surrounded it. As they neared the entrance she could smell the roses and see all manner of blooming flowers. "Oh, Michael, it's lovely."

"It is. Come see it all." He pulled out a key and unlocked the gate, leading her through to a walking path. "See, it's not really large enough for the whole city to visit, but it's —"

"Wonderful." As they strolled around the paths, Violet felt herself relax. She'd always loved being outdoors and, much as she liked the city, she'd missed just walking outside to lean against the porch rail to hear the birds sing and watch the squirrels at play. "Thank you for bringing me here."

"You're welcome. Would you like to sit awhile?" He pointed at a nearby bench.

"I'd love to." She sat down and sighed at the beauty around her.

Instead of sitting, Michael stood and propped a foot up beside her. He looked down into her eyes. "You've seemed a bit somber this evening. Are you all right?"

"I'm fine. I've just been wondering about the temporary boarder and praying that things are better for her today."

"You have a heart like my mother, Violet. There is no way of knowing about the young woman, but our prayers are joining yours. We had to accept that we wouldn't be able to help everyone who came to us a long time ago."

"Oh, I realize there is no way you could. I just admire what you do. I'd like to be able to help people in that way."

"You are helping."

Violet shook her head. She wasn't doing anything. Michael's touch on her chin as he lifted it to look into his eyes stilled her thinking and sent her pulse racing. "As I said before, just having you here has helped my mother more than I can tell you."

"But it's not the same. Besides, I'm the one being helped."

"It's helping another person, Violet. In whatever way we do it. I can't thank you enough for what your presence in our home has done for my mother." His thumb grazed her cheek and then he suddenly dropped it. "Would you like to walk some more?"

Violet gave a quick nod and swallowed hard. She might not be quite as safe in Michael's presence as she first thought. Oh, he'd never harm her, of that she was sure. But she wasn't so sure of her heart. That could be another matter entirely. And she couldn't allow herself to have feelings other than friendship for him. Besides the fact that she was disillusioned with men in general. Violet was beginning to like feeling independent and making her own way. For now, falling in love simply wasn't in her plans.

# CHAPTER TEN

By the time Violet and Lila got home from work on Friday, it was apparent Lila was only going to talk to Violet when she felt she had to and that seemed to be whenever Michael or his mother were around or when one of the supervisors at Butterick was nearby.

Violet tried not to let it bother her. Surely Lila would get over her anger one day. The only thing she could think of to do was to offer to help Lila to learn to sew, and that only if she could get her sewing machine shipped there.

She was sure Mrs. Heaton would loan her sewing machine to her for that purpose, but Violet didn't want to tie it up if she didn't have to. Besides, she could make her own clothing if she had her own machine here.

So, she'd written to Beth on Wednesday evening to let her know about her position at Butterick, to tell her all about what she'd seen of the city and to ask if she could have her papa crate up the sewing machine and have it shipped to her. She'd inquired as to the amount it would cost to send it before-hand and sent the money to Beth, as well. Hopefully, she'd hear from her friend soon and once she knew the machine was on its way, she'd see if Lila wanted to learn to sew. Other than that, she didn't know how she could help their relationship.

It was wonderful to have two days off to look forward to, and when Elizabeth knocked on her room before supper to ask if she was going to Central Park with the rest of them the next day, she was pleased she was included even if Lila might not want her to go.

"I would love to! I didn't know you were all going."

"Oh, I'm sorry. Didn't Lila mention it to you? We decided on it last night after you went upstairs, but she said she'd tell you today."

"No, Lila didn't say anything about it." But she hadn't said more than a few words to her since Tuesday.

Elizabeth closed her eyes and blew out a breath. "I'm sorry, Violet. I'll be sure to let you know when we plan something from now on. Anyway, we're going to leave here around eleven and take a picnic. I told Mrs. Heaton about it this morning, and she said she and Michael might join us."

They headed down to the parlor together. "What should I wear tomorrow?" Violet asked.

"It's getting really warm out, but of course it's cooler in the park than anywhere but on the water this time of year. Just wear what you'd wear to work and as cool a material as you have."

"I can't wait. I only saw Central Park driving through that one time and now we'll get to picnic there."

"Mrs. Heaton said she'd have fried chicken prepared and lemonade, and I'm sure there will be a cake. There always is when we picnic. I can't wait for you to go skating with us in the winter. It's so much fun," Elizabeth said.

"What's so much fun?" Michael asked as they entered the parlor. He walked over to them with a smile.

"Skating in the winter. Sledding, too, for that matter."

"Don't forget sleighing. I love it most of all," Mrs. Heaton added as she came into the room.

Lila still hadn't shown up when Mrs.

189

Heaton called them to dinner, but she slipped into her seat across from Violet right before Michael said the blessing. She barely got her head bowed before Michael began praying.

"Father, we thank You for this day and for our many blessings. We ask You to be with all around this table and keep each one safe, and we ask You to bless this food, Father. In Jesus' name we pray. Amen."

Michael began carving the ham his mother had set in front of him and passing plates down before Gretchen began passing side dishes around.

"Just in case some of you have not heard the news, we're all planning on going to Central Park tomorrow and taking a picnic, as well. Please be ready to leave by eleven o'clock," Michael said.

"I can't wait," Violet said. "I've been looking forward to going again."

"I forgot to tell you about the outing, didn't I?" Lila acknowledged with a shrug. "Oh, well, I was sure someone here would tell you. It appears I was right."

Michael found he was looking forward to showing Violet more of Central Park. She'd get to see and experience it so much better on foot. So many of them were going, they'd arranged for an omnibus to pick them up. As everyone gathered and got in the vehicle, he was a little put out to see that Luke had taken a seat next to Violet before he had a chance to.

He really was taken aback a bit by the quick surge of jealousy that rose up inside him. He'd never had quite this kind of reaction to any woman, not even Amanda, and that fact alone told him he'd begun to care more about Violet than he'd intended to.

But as she answered his smile with one of her own, taking her attention away from Luke for at least a moment or two, his heart quickened and he realized he'd begun to look for her smile, to try to elicit it.

"Michael," Lila said as she sat down beside him, sitting a little closer than he was comfortable with. "It's a beautiful day for a picnic, isn't it?"

"Yes, it is." He scooted over to put some space between them but Lila moved even closer, keeping only a pencil's width of room between them. She leaned nearer. "Violet seems to be fitting in at Butterick very well."

"Oh? Do you see much of each other?"

"Not as much as we would have if she'd stayed in the pattern room. But she seems happy." She nudged him and motioned to where Violet was laughing at something Luke had said to her. "She does look happy."

Yes, she did. But was it because of working at Butterick or was it Luke making her look that way? Just then she looked over and caught him staring at her and he watched a warm color steal up her neck and cheeks as she smiled back at him. For that one moment he felt it was only the two of them in the bus. Lila and Luke both seemed to fade into the background. Then Lila spoke his name and Violet broke eye contact and looked down before Luke claimed her attention once more.

Lila grabbed Michael's arm, but before she could gain his attention fully, John nudged him from the seat behind them. "Michael, have you had a chance to find out any more about the matter we discussed the other night?" John asked. "Remember, the break-in on Irving Place?"

"A little," Michael said, glad to have someone other than Lila to talk to. "I'm not sure there's a story there."

"There might be." John shrugged. "You never know."

"That's true. And one day, you're going to get that big story, my friend. Of that I have no doubt."

"Thank you, Michael. It helps to know someone believes in me."

"I'm not the only one who does, John. It'll happen. You try to stay on top of everything and you care about this city and the job you do. It'll happen when the timing is right."

"Timing has a lot to do with it. Part of my problem is that there are so many of us out there trying to get a story. And whoever gets the scoop first is the one that breaks in. My goal is to be the one who will break a big story first one of these days."

"I understand." And he did. Michael knew what it was to hunt for something so hard you were sure you had it — only to find that you didn't. He'd followed more leads than he wanted to think about trying to find his sister. He knew his mother had almost given up on them ever finding her.

And from the amount of leads he received now, perhaps they should. But every once in a while he'd get a new tip and there was no way he couldn't follow it, even if he was sure it would lead to another dead end. He knew he'd follow any lead he found for as long as it took to find Becca, or for as long as he was alive. He couldn't stop trying to find his sister.

■ ■ ■ ■

Violet hadn't expected such a strong reaction to seeing Michael and Lila sitting so
close. Nor had she ever had her heart feel
as if a knife had punctured it, but that's
exactly how it felt to see Lila leaning so
close to him.

To Michael's credit, however, he had tried
to put some space between them, but if
Violet had learned one thing about Lila, it
was that she was very persistent, especially
when it came to Michael.

She'd tried to ignore them and pay attention to what Luke was saying to her, but
when she looked up it was to find Michael's
gaze on her. She could feel the flush of color
flooding her cheeks, but she found she
couldn't tear what she had intended to be a
quick glance away. At least, not until Lila
called his name and grabbed his arm again.

And then she couldn't keep from looking
over again when she heard Michael talking.
She saw that it was John he was speaking to
and not Lila. Lila didn't seem the least bit
happy with that turn of events, and it was
written all over her face.

The omnibus came to a stop and she was
relieved that they were at Central Park. Her

attention certainly hadn't been on the ride over. The park was even prettier than she remembered. A few days made a big difference this time of year, and it seemed there were twice as many flowers in bloom as last time.

She was so busy looking around she didn't realize that Michael was walking beside her, holding a huge basket. He smiled when she looked up and those dimples seemed deeper than ever, causing her heart to skip a beat or two.

"Michael, I didn't know —"

"Whom you are walking beside? Or even quite where you are." He grinned, bringing out those dimples again. "That's why I fell into step beside you. I didn't want you getting lost."

His dimples were definitely playing a game of hide-and-seek today, and Violet's heartbeat was having a hard time keeping up with them. "And you do know where we are going?"

He led her through a hedge and followed some of the others, who seemed to know where they were going. "I believe we are going to claim a spot for our picnic and then everyone will take off in different directions. Some will go to the lake to canoe. Others will rent a bicycle, and others will just take a stroll through the gardens. Think about what you want to do, okay?"

"It all sounds good to me, but I suppose I can't do it all in one day."

"Well, you could, but you wouldn't get to enjoy any of it to its fullest. Remember that you live here now. We can always come back, you know."

She did live there now, and the city was beginning to feel like home to her. Michael had said they could come back . . . did that mean he wanted to come back with her? Maybe his sitting by Lila meant nothing. After all, Luke sat down beside her before Michael got on the omnibus. And it was Lila who'd sat down by him.

"Michael, Violet, we're over here," Mrs. Heaton called, waving to them.

Violet saw that she'd found a grassy spot under a nice-size tree that would give shade for the time they were there. She followed Michael over and helped his mother spread a huge quilt over the ground. There were several baskets to be unloaded, and everyone helped. By the time it was all laid out, Violet wondered how they could possibly eat it all.

She wondered how many chickens had been fried early that morning so that it would be ready for the picnic. There were also sandwiches made with minced ham mixed with a touch of mustard on thin white buttered bread. They also had potato salad and boiled eggs along with pickles and olives and pickled peppers. There were two cakes, chocolate and a yellow pound cake, to round out the meal.

Violet thought that maybe she should decide to go for a stroll after eating. She was pleased when Michael followed her to a spot under the tree beside his mother. It was cool under the tree's branches, and Violet couldn't remember a prettier setting for a picnic.

"I'm so glad we've had such a beautiful day for our picnic," Mrs. Heaton said. "I love this time of year. We come out here quite often in the spring and summertime. But it is truly beautiful in the fall and winter, too."

"I can't wait to see it then," Violet said. She tried to picture the trees with no leaves, the bushes bare and snow all over everything. But today the sun was bright, the sky blue and a light breeze made a perfect day for a picnic. She'd have to take Mrs. Heaton's word for the other seasons until she could see it for herself.

The park was a wonderful place to just sit under a shade tree and watch people —

much different from Grand Central Depot. Instead of looking harried, these people looked relaxed and eager to enjoy the day.

There were people dressed in their Sunday best and others more casual, as Mrs. Heaton's group was. Others were dressed in what was most likely the best they had. But all seemed to be having a wonderful time.

"What is that language those people next to us are speaking, Michael?" Violet had never heard it spoken before.

He leaned his head to the side and listened. "It's Italian."

"Mmm." Violet smiled as she watched the family. There was a lot of gesturing and laughter and she'd love to know what they were talking about.

Just a few trees away, there seemed to be a group that could well have come from any of the homes she'd seen on Fifth Avenue. She could tell the walking costumes the ladies had on were of the finest materials and custom-made. The gentlemen were dressed much the same as the men in her group, but again, their clothing seemed to be custom-made. They appeared to be having a good time, but no better than the Italian family to their left.

A couple bicycled by them and then another. It looked like such fun. She'd only been on a bicycle one time and for few wobbly moments and she'd enjoyed it very much. She couldn't help but notice that one of the women was wearing a bicycling costume. She wondered if that pattern was one Butterick made. She'd like to make one for herself one day.

Out in the middle of the grassy area, children were playing, flying kites and chasing one another. Violet could have sat there and watched those around her for the rest of the day, but Michael stood just then and held a hand out to her. "Come on. There's a lot to see and do. Have you decided what you'd like to try first?"

"I'm not sure. What are your recommendations?" Violet turned to look down at Mrs. Heaton. "Would you like to go with us?"

"No, dear, thank you. You'll be able to go much faster without me. I think I'll just sit here and enjoy watching people."

"I think I'll join you, Mrs. Heaton," Elizabeth said.

Lila seemed to have appeared out of nowhere. "Why don't you come canoeing with me and Julia, Violet?"

"I'm going to show Violet around some, Lila," Michael said. "Then if she wants to go canoeing or bicycling, we'll do that."

"Thank you for inviting me, Lila," Violet said.

Lila only shrugged and walked away.

Julia smiled. "We'll have plenty of time to bicycle together. There is a lot to choose from. You have a nice walk."

Violet sighed. She knew Julia wasn't upset with her, but Lila obviously was. "Perhaps I should have gone with Lila. That's the first time she's asked me to do anything with her."

She didn't think for one moment it was because the other girl wanted her company. Lila's motive was much more personal than that. Violet had come to realize Lila didn't like it at all when Michael was giving his attention to anyone besides her.

"Sorry if I misspoke, Violet. If you wish to go —"

"Oh, no, Michael, I didn't mean I'd rather go with her. It's just —" she shrugged her shoulders "— I don't think she likes me very much."

"And you have very good manners and wouldn't want to disappoint me." Michael grinned down at her.

"Well, there is that." Violet smiled back at him and took the arm he offered. She didn't want to disappoint him in any way. And she would much rather see Central Park with

200

Michael than spend the afternoon with Lila anytime. "Let's go."

# CHAPTER ELEVEN

Michael had never enjoyed Central Park more than he was right then, with Violet. She loved watching people out on the lake. There were all sizes of rowboats, from those for two people to the kind that held Julia, Lila, John and Ben. They waved when they passed by and he was glad when Violet didn't seem disappointed not to be with them.

"I believe I'd like to be rowing my own boat, although I've never done it before," Violet said.

"It's quite fun. Of course, it does take some strength."

"Are you saying I'm weak, Michael Heaton?" Her eyebrow shot up, daring him to do so. Oh, how he'd missed that look. She'd always been a bit feisty as a child and he was glad to see she still had some feistiness left in her.

He laughed. "Oh, no. I wouldn't dare do

that. But I'd love to take you rowing. You can even have your own oar."

"All right then, let's do that."

"Let's do." It would be nice to have her out on the water, just the two of them. He loved his mother's home, but sometimes it was very hard to find a quiet place for two people to talk without someone barging in on the conversation.

In only a few minutes, he'd helped Violet into her seat and taken his own. He explained how to hold the oar and what to do, going from one side to the other, although he'd be the one doing most of the rowing.

As he lowered his oar, she did the same. Mimicking his movements, she held her own as they floated over the water and into the middle of the lake. They passed the larger canoe that held their friends and waved once more as they headed across to the other side of the lake. People were standing or sitting all around the edge watching the boats glide over the water.

"Oh, this is fun. And it's so much cooler on the water, too."

"The light breeze is helping today. You're doing very good."

"Thank you. I must admit, however, that my arms are getting a bit tired. Guess I'm not quite as strong as you." She grinned and dipped her oar in the water again.

"I think that's how the Lord wanted it to be, don't you?"

"I suppose it is. I really don't want to be as strong as a man — not physically, anyway."

"You are a strong woman in every other way, Violet. You've been through a lot."

"So have you and your mother."

"Want to stop for a while? I can row us or we can sit still for a bit and float."

"That would be nice."

They pulled their oars in. "I should warn you that you may be very sore tomorrow. The first time works muscles you might not have used in a while."

"Or ever?"

"Now, that only you would know." Michael chuckled and looked a little closer at her. He grinned and reached out to touch the tip of her nose. "Your freckles are back."

Violet giggled and rubbed her nose. "Must be this time out in the sun. I don't think I'll ever be rid of them."

"I hope not. I've missed them — I'm glad to see them again." Her smile warmed his heart.

"Thank you. I'm not sure I feel the same way, but I'm so glad we came today. I love this park, the lake, all of it." She looked around and sighed.

"I think all New Yorkers feel the same way."

"It is so quiet and peaceful, as if the city has disappeared and yet it's right there." She raised her arm and pointed all around them. She didn't mention that her arm was already beginning to hurt, but he saw the slight wince as she put it back down.

Michael hoped she wasn't too sore tomorrow. "And that's what draws everyone. It is a wonderful place to relax and think, knowing that there is more to life than the hustle and bustle of the city."

"Do you think you'll ever move back to Virginia?" Violet asked.

"No. Our lives are here now. What about you?"

"Oh, I don't know. I want to keep my family home because it is my inheritance, I suppose. But I must admit that I like it here. And I know I haven't had my fill of this city."

Michael breathed an inward sigh of relief. "I'm glad you like it here. And I'm glad you don't plan on leaving anytime soon. Mother and I would both miss you. We're just getting to know you again."

"Thank you, Michael. I can't begin to tell

you what it's meant to me to have your mother's and your support at this time. I do have some friends in Ashland, but no family now, and it will never be quite the same to me there. When Harlan made it impossible for me to stay there unless I married him, I felt I had no choice but to leave."

"Black is a cad of the first degree. I'm glad you didn't accept his terms, Violet." For more reasons than he wanted to go into at present. Michael wondered if it was time to tell her he was looking into Black's business dealings with her mother. He just wasn't sure what to do. He'd not heard back from his agent yet and there really wasn't anything to report.

He picked up his oar and Violet started to do the same. "You don't need to help, you know. These canoes are fine for only one to row."

"Then I'm going to plead female weakness and let you do it."

"Thank you for making me feel stronger."

"You're welcome."

He rowed them around the lake. As they got closer to the bank they'd left from, he saw Elizabeth waving them in. When they got close enough to hear her, she said, "Hurry! There is a family fight going on right next to where we had our picnic. Luke is there, but —"

The boatman held the canoe steady while Michael helped Violet out. They all took off in a run toward the picnic spot. By the time they got there, a brawl was in progress. Violet and Elizabeth hurried to Mrs. Heaton's side. Michael stepped into the fight just as two policemen showed up and pulled the man who'd evidently been causing all the problems off Luke.

"What's going on here? Heaton, what started this?"

Michael knew both officers from working with them on cases in the past. They were good men and would get to the bottom of things.

"I don't know. I just arrived."

"I can tell you, Officers. This man tried to harm that young lady and his wife tried to pull him away." Michael's mother pointed from one to another of the women as she spoke. "He tossed his wife aside and the other gentleman was coming to the women's defense."

"Is this true, miss?" O'Malley, the officer Michael knew best, asked.

"This is a family affair, Officer," the man that Luke had been fighting with said as he was being handcuffed. It was obvious they were Irish from his accent. "It's not your business."

" 'Tis our business when it's out here in public," O'Malley said. He turned to the two women and Michael's mother. "We need to ask you a few questions, ladies. We can do it here or at the station."

"Oh, please, here, Officer," the woman with the man said. From the looks of her she was expecting a child.

"I can tell you what it's about," the man yelled. "My wife's sister owes me rent money, is what this is all about."

"Ma'am —" Officer O'Malley broke into the conversation. "Do ya owe rent to this man?"

"No, she doesn't," the man's wife said.

"Ma'am, do you be wishin' to press charges against this man?" Officer O'Malley asked the sister.

The man's wife shook her head and said, "Please, no, Kathleen."

The woman she'd called Kathleen looked at the two little boys who'd come running up and hidden behind their mother's skirts.

"Aunt Kathleen, please don't let them take Papa to jail." The boy peeked out from behind his mother and added his plea to hers.

Michael knew what she was going to say. He'd seen it happen too often not to.

"Ma'am?" Officer O'Malley prodded.

"No, Officer. I won't press charges — at least not this time." She looked at her brother-in-law, who'd turned a hateful glance her way.

"You give either of these woman cause to call us and they won't have to press charges. We'll have you in the clinker before they have a chance to decide," the officer said as he took the cuffs off the man. His wife hurried over to him, pulling him off in the opposite direction as the officers, her young boys following.

"Thank you, Officers," Michael said.

"Yes," Luke said, rubbing his jaw with one hand and shaking each officer's hand with the other. "I'm certainly glad you all showed up when you did."

The younger woman, who'd begun to follow her sister's family, turned and ran back to where they were. "I thank you for comin' to our aid."

"You get in touch if he roughs you or your sister up again," Officer O'Malley said.

"I will." The young woman turned to Mrs. Heaton. "I'm sorry we ruined your day."

His mother handed the woman one of the cards she'd had printed up for anyone she felt might need a safe place. "You keep this. If you ever need to, you come to us again."

The young woman looked down at the card and nodded. She slipped it in her pocket. "Thank you. I will."

Michael looked at Violet, who had tears in her eyes as she watched the young woman leave.

"Those little boys . . . they're the ones we saw in the street that day. Aren't they, Michael?" she asked, a tear escaping and running down her cheek.

Michael wanted to pull her into his arms to comfort her, but pulled a handkerchief from his pocket and handed it to her instead. "I'm sorry to say, I believe they are, Violet, and their aunt is our last temporary boarder. The one who stayed only one night."

The ride back to Heaton House was a somber one. Violet couldn't get the image of those little boys out of her mind. That they'd had to witness their father acting in such a way as Mrs. Heaton had described and beg their aunt not to send him to jail. And what about once they got out of sight? How did he treat those women — or his children, for that matter?

The question was still in her mind late that afternoon as she sat in Mrs. Heaton's garden and enjoyed the air sweetened by her roses. Her mother had loved roses, anything flowering. She missed her so much. But she thought it might be even harder if she'd stayed in Virginia around so many memories of the last few months when her mother was in so much pain. Violet's sigh was ragged as she wondered if the ache ever went away.

She heard the back door shut and wiped at her eyes. Tears weren't going to bring her mother back, and she reminded herself of her admonition to live her life and not to grieve. But she was finding that it was much harder to do than to say.

"Violet? Are you out here?" Michael's voice found her at the back of the garden.

"I'm here." She headed toward the house.

They met in the middle and she found that he'd brought her a glass of iced lemonade. "Gretchen said she thought you were out here. We thought you might like this about now."

"How thoughtful of you, Michael. Thank you." Violet hoped he couldn't tell she'd been crying as she reached out for the glass he held out to her.

Michael led her back to the bench, and they both sat down to enjoy their lemonade.

"Is your mother resting?"

"She's napping. Something she doesn't

do very often. I think this afternoon bothered her more than she let on."

"I'm sure it did. It was very hard to see those little boys so upset. I pray things get better for that family soon."

"So do I. There is so much hurt out there. . . ." He looked up at the sky and sighed.

"Michael, do all of the boarders know about Becca and why your mother decided to open her boardinghouse?"

"Some do, but not everyone."

"Do you still have hope that you'll find her?"

"Some days I wake up hopeful and others . . ." He shrugged and sighed. "But I try to let Mother only see the hope."

"Do you get many leads anymore?"

"Not near as many as I'd like, and none in a while. I don't know. It would help if I knew what she'd been doing before, who she was with, what made her leave in the first place."

His voice sounded raw with sorrow and Violet felt to blame. "I'm sorry, Michael. I shouldn't have brought it up. I didn't mean to bring you painful memories."

"No, Violet. Don't be sorry. Actually, it feels good to talk about Becca. Mother and I don't talk about her disappearance much anymore. I think we're both afraid to bring each other sorrow. But the need to talk about it is sometimes still there, even after all this time."

"I must admit that I don't know why Becca decided to leave and come here in the first place. I've always wondered about that."

"That's our problem. We don't really know why either. Oh, she'd always been independent and more than a little feisty and it was no surprise that she wanted to be in charge of her life. But her decision to move seemed to come out of the blue. Mother and I both tried to talk her out of it, but she seemed almost desperate to get away."

"And once she was here? Did she keep in contact?"

"She wrote, giving us an address where she was going to be living, and said she would write more soon. But days went by, then weeks. Finally, Mother insisted that we come here and make sure she was all right."

Michael rubbed his temples as if he had a headache, and Violet waited for him to continue. "But as you know, she'd left the boardinghouse."

Tears sprang to Violet's eyes. How devastating that must have been for both him and his mother. Wanting to comfort him, Violet reached out and touched his hand. "I'm so sorry, Michael. I wish I knew something that could help you."

He turned his hand and squeezed hers. "Thank you, Violet. I wish you did, too. But knowing I can talk to you about this helps more than you know."

"I'm glad." His words touched her heart and his touch sent her pulse racing.

"I suppose we should go inside. It's about dinnertime and Mother likes us to be on time," Michael said.

Violet moved to stand and Michael stood, too, pulling her up with him. She slipped her hand from his. "Please feel you can talk to me anytime."

"Thank you. I can't tell you how much good this has done me. Just going over it all from the beginning again has helped."

As they headed toward the house, Violet thought she'd seen a side of Michael very few others did, and she felt they'd created a bond she would cherish always.

They entered the foyer just as Lila and Elizabeth came down from upstairs. Not wanting to hear what Lila might have to say about them being in the garden together, Violet quickly took Michael's glass from him. "I'll just take these to the kitchen."

"Coward," Michael whispered. He grinned down at her and gave her a wink no one could see but her. It was as if he had read her mind and understood, and her heart turned to mush.

# Chapter Twelve

After supper the next evening, Violet was surprised when Gretchen handed her a letter from Beth. "This came in the mail for you today."

"Thank you, Gretchen." Violet hurried to her room and slit the envelope open with her mother's letter opener. She unfolded the stationery and dropped down onto the settee to read it.

Dear Violet,
It was so good to receive your letter! I miss you so much, but I'm so happy you found a good position at Butterick and you are happy at Mrs. Heaton's boardinghouse. Is Michael still as handsome as ever?

Oh, yes, he was.

Papa and I have already crated up the

sewing machine and he'll put it on the train tomorrow. I'll be making your payment soon. Papa is going to go with me just to make sure Harlan Black doesn't give me any problems. He's been asking about you everywhere. Wants to know where you are and everything. But don't worry. We aren't going to tell him.

The very thought of Harlan still made Violet nauseous, even this far away.

I've sent you a long letter in with the sewing machine. You answer back soon, okay? Just don't put your name on the outside of anything. I'll be sending things to you addressed to Mrs. Heaton, so be sure and tell her. The postal clerk, Mr. Tyler, is a friend of Papa's and he said Harlan was in there asking if we'd had anything from you. Take care of yourself, Violet. Much as I miss you, I'm relieved you aren't here. That man seems obsessed with finding you. He wants more than your home, Violet. He wants you.

Violet shuddered.

Now don't you start liking the city so much you don't ever want to come home. If you have to stay gone too long, I just might have to come see that city for myself.

Violet hated that her friend had to deal with Harlan Black. Maybe after Beth made the next payment, he'd realize she was going to pay off the loan and accept that he wasn't going to get her home or her.

In the meantime, she needed to let Mrs. Heaton know about the sewing machine coming to her and any letters that might follow.

She found her in her study having a cup of tea. "Why, Violet, dear, how nice to see you. Sit down." She motioned for Violet to take the other chair in front of the fireplace. "Would you join me for some tea?"

"I'd love to, if you have enough."

"I always have a big pot and extra cups brought in this time of night. Sometimes Michael joins me and once in a while one of the other boarders." She poured a cup and handed it to Violet.

"Did you come to chat or is there something on your mind?"

"Well, I just received a letter from Beth Edwards, my best friend back home," Violet said. "Do you remember her?"

"I remember the Edwardses. They are very

218

good people. What did Beth have to say? I hope she and her family are doing well."

"They are. She wanted to let me know that she's sent my sewing machine, and I wanted to let you know to expect it."

"Oh, good. I'll be looking for it."

"She also told me Harlan Black is trying to find out where I am, and that she would be sending things for me addressed to you. I'm glad that when I sent the letter to Beth, I just put your name and address on it and sent it to her mother."

"That was very clever of you, Violet," Michael said from the doorway. "I'm sorry. I wasn't trying to eavesdrop, but I didn't want to interrupt you."

"It's fine, Michael. You might as well know, too."

"So Black is trying to find out where you are?"

"It appears so. Beth thinks he's obsessed with finding me now."

"He has that type of personality."

"I thought I should let you know in case he shows up here one day," Violet said.

Michael shut the study door and leaned against it. "I guess it's time I told you I sent one of my men to Ashland trying to find out what we can about what your family finances were when your mother passed away."

"Oh?" Violet wasn't sure what she thought of that. "Why?"

"Mother has some concerns about your property, and they made sense to me."

"What concerns, Mrs. Heaton?"

"Violet, dear, I remembered that when your papa died, your mother said you two were fine. That he'd left you with a home paid for and with enough money to live in the manner you'd been accustomed to. And I can't understand why your mother would have needed to put your home up as collateral for a loan when it sounded as if she had a nice bank account."

"And we both know how Harlan works. We became concerned he's been up to something unethical. We just don't know what yet," Michael said.

"You know, I wondered the same thing, but then Harlan showed me the papers after Mama passed away."

"You only then found out about the house being mortgaged — when your mother died? Is that when Harlan came to you about the loan?"

"Yes. And as I told you, he offered to forget it if I would —"

"Marry him." Michael nodded. "Something isn't right here, Violet, and I'm going to get to the bottom of it. Hopefully before too long. Isn't Mr. Atwood your family's attorney?"

"He is, but he's been ill and I think he went to Arizona because of his asthma." Violet blew an errant strand of hair off her forehead. "I tried to get an address before I left, but his office was closed and his wife went with him. I should have asked around more, but I was afraid word would get back to Harlan and I didn't want him to know what I was doing."

"It's all right, Violet," Michael said. "We'll get to the bottom of it all. My agent is there now. I'll let him know what you've told us and he can go from there and try to get an address for Atwood."

"I hope you aren't upset we've taken it on our own to find out what is going on, Violet," Mrs. Heaton said. "It's just that your mother was my dear friend, and I can't get rid of the feeling Harlan is up to no good."

"Oh, no, ma'am. I'm thankful you care and relieved you know what is going on."

"Good. I'm glad you know what we've done," Michael said. "I didn't want to tell you because I didn't want you worrying about Harlan without reason. Now I want you to be on guard at all times. Should Harlan learn where you are, he could well show up here."

Violet closed her eyes at the very thought. She heard movement in the room and opened them to find Michael sitting on the footstool in front of her. He reached out and touched her chin.

"Violet, rest assured I will *not* let Harlan Black harm you. I won't."

She released a shaky sigh. "I don't want him to bring harm to anyone here. Perhaps I shouldn't have come to New York."

"This is exactly where you should be, and it's where you belong now," Mrs. Heaton said. "You're family to us and you're safe here."

"I'm glad this is all in the open. I'll let you know when I hear anything. You be sure to let us know whatever you find out from your friend back home. Agreed?" Michael smiled, bringing out those wonderful dimples.

"Agreed."

"Good. Now let's finish this pot of tea and talk about happier things. How are you liking your job?"

By the time the teapot was empty, Violet felt much better. It was a relief to know Michael was aware of what was going on in

Virginia. And that he cared enough to send someone there to try to find out what Black was up to. She tried not to think about the fact that Harlan was trying to find her. But she had to admit she felt safer now that Michael knew, too.

She said her good-nights and took her leave, nearly running over Lila just outside the door. "Oh! I'm sorry, Lila. I didn't see you. Were you waiting to speak to Mrs. Heaton or Michael? They are both still there."

"No. I, ah, I was just on my way to the kitchen to see if there was any dessert left over from dinner," Lila said. "Want to come with me?"

Violet tried not to show how surprised she was at the invitation. "No, thank you. I just had tea with Mrs. Heaton. I think I'll call it a night."

"All right. See you tomorrow."

"Good night." Violet headed to the staircase, but when she looked back, it was to see Lila still outside the study. Was she waiting for a chance to talk to Michael alone? Was there something going on between the two of them?

Later that evening, Michael knocked on Luke's door. He was thankful he had an agent living in the house, even if he worked for him part-time. Just the fact that he was here gave Michael a peace of mind, knowing that his mother could call on him anytime Michael wasn't around.

"Yes? Who is it?" Luke called out.

"It's Michael, Luke."

"Come on in."

Michael opened the door to find his friend seated at his desk in front of his typewriter. "Looks like you're writing. I'm sorry to interrupt, but I need to talk to you."

"No, it's fine. I'm at a good stopping place." Luke pecked a couple of keys and turned around. He motioned for Michael to take a seat. "You have my undivided attention."

Michael quickly explained about Violet and the letter about Harlan Black. "I wanted you to know, in case he should show up here looking for Violet."

"I'm glad you told me. I've always wondered why she couldn't find work in Ashville. It makes sense now. This Black guy sounds a little . . ."

"Obsessed?"

Luke nodded. "Yes, that's the word."

"I think he is. And that's what worries me. I'm going to send Jim to Ashland to see what he can find out. I'd send you if it were any other case, but I need you here more. I certainly don't want to leave Violet and my mother vulnerable at home, where they feel the safest."

"No, of course you don't. I wouldn't either. And you know you can count on me."

"I do. And I'm thankful for it."

"But, as far as we know now, Black doesn't know where Violet is, does he?" Luke asked.

"Not yet. But it may only be a matter of time until he does. He's asking questions everywhere."

"Sounds as if he's determined to find her. I hope Jim can find out more for you soon, and if there is anything else I can do, let me know."

"You know I will." Michael stood. "I'll let you get back to it. What's this story about?"

"Oddly enough, it's about a banker, a woman and dirty dealings."

"Doesn't take place in Ashland, does it?"

Luke laughed. "No, it takes place down in Texas. The sheriff saves the day and gets the girl."

Both men chuckled.

"That's the way it should be," Michael said. "I'm glad it has a good ending."

"All this will, too. You'll see."

"I hope so. Good night."

"Good night, Michael."

■ ■ ■ ■

Violet's sewing machine arrived on Thursday and was waiting in the foyer when she and Lila got home from work. As usual, Lila had barely spoken five words to her that day, but one look at the crate and curiosity got the better of her. "My goodness, whatever did you order, Violet?"

Mrs. Heaton joined them in the foyer. "I'll have Michael or one of the men bring it up soon as one of them gets home, Violet."

"Thank you, Mrs. Heaton." She turned to Lila. "I had my sewing machine sent to me."

"Whatever for? Don't you sew enough all day at Butterick?"

"Well, I can't sew for myself there. And . . . I thought that you might want to let me teach you to sew so that if another opening comes up in the sewing room, you could apply."

For once, Lila seemed speechless.

"You don't have to. Some of the others may want to learn —"

"You'd do that for me?" Lila asked as if she couldn't believe Violet's offer.

"Why, of course. But you don't have to decide right this minute. You can think about it."

"I will. I . . . Thank you," Lila said.

As she went on up the stairs, Mrs. Heaton and Violet both stood there watching her. This time, it was Violet who felt speechless. They were still staring up when Michael came in the door.

"Mother, Violet, is something wrong?"

Mrs. Heaton chuckled and Violet giggled.

"I don't think so. Something out of the ordinary just happened, and I think we're both wondering if we imagined it," his mother said.

"Well, if you both witnessed the same thing, then it probably happened. What was it?"

Mrs. Heaton stood on tiptoe to whisper, "Lila thanked Violet for something."

"She actually said the words?"

"She did," Violet said.

"What for?"

"Violet has offered to teach her how to sew so that the next time an opening comes up, she'll be qualified."

"That is very nice of you, Violet. Especially considering the cold shoulder she's been turning to you ever since you moved in."

"Thank you. But I really don't mind at all. I'll ask the others if they'd like to learn, too."

"Can you get the crate upstairs by yourself, Michael? Or would it be easier for you if it were in the little parlor, Violet? That way if someone wants to be sewing they wouldn't always have to use your room."

"Oh, that would work better, if you are sure you don't mind."

"I don't mind at all. It isn't used that much, and when it is, it's mostly by you girls. Go ahead and put it back there, Michael. I know just the spot for it."

Ben walked into the foyer just then and heard the last of the conversation. "Need some help?"

"I wouldn't turn it down."

Together, they uncrated the sewing machine, and Violet was pleased to see that there wasn't a scratch on it. The two men easily picked it up and took it to the back parlor where Mrs. Heaton instructed them to put it under a south-facing window where there was plenty of light.

"That is a perfect place for it, Mrs. Heaton. Thank you."

"You are quite welcome. If you have many wanting to learn, we'll bring mine in here, too."

"Do you need anything else?" Michael asked.

"No. Thank you for your help, Michael and Ben," Violet said.

"You're quite welcome," Michael said. "I'll go get rid of the crate. It'll make good kindling for the winter."

"Glad to help. See you at dinner," Ben said, giving a wave as he walked out the door.

"And speaking of that, I'd best go check on our meal," Mrs. Heaton said.

Violet stayed in the room for a few minutes. Seeing the machine her mother had taught her to sew on, the one she'd made many of Violet's clothes with, brought warmth to her heart. Of all her mother's possessions, it was this sewing machine that held many of Violet's best memories — it and the sewing box she'd always had with her. She'd kept her pins and buttons and all kinds of trims in it. Violet could remember reading to her mother while she mended a tear or did the hand sewing of trims on her outfits. She wished she'd asked Beth to send it, too.

She sat down on the tapestry-covered stool that had been packed with the sewing machine and rubbed her hand across the shiny black machine. Somehow, just having it there gave her some peace.

Violet remembered many of the frocks she'd made on that machine in the past few years. Then of the ones her mother had made for her, the last being a gown for her senior commencement. And . . . she remembered her papa standing in the doorway smiling as her mother talked and sewed at the same time. That was back before he'd died from influenza.

Odd, she hadn't thought about her papa's smiles in a long time, but now she remembered how he'd looked at Mama. How had she missed the look of love in his eyes at the time? She was glad to have the sewing machine here. It brought back long-forgotten memories of a happier time.

Michael hoped Lila learned to sew soon. Evenings were getting a little boring for him. He didn't know exactly when or how it had happened, but he'd come to realize that he looked forward to seeing Violet first thing at breakfast each day and at dinnertime and after, more each day. But the "after" had been cut short by the sewing lessons.

The past few weeks had been a whirl of activity, with the women disappearing into what had become the sewing parlor after dinner Monday through Thursday. Violet said they'd picked those days so that they could be free on the weekends. The women had all decided to keep each other company, with those who didn't have a desire to learn to sew reading or just chatting with each other. But that meant the men had only themselves for company.

They'd taken to reading, playing chess and talking politics after dinner, waiting for the ladies to join them, if only for a little while. But they were all getting just a bit tired of each other's company. It was music to Michael's ears to hear the ladies coming down the hall that Thursday evening, and particularly to hear Violet's voice. He could recognize her from anywhere in the house now — and it never failed to lift his spirits.

"It's about time," John said. "Are you ladies ever going to get through with these lessons?"

"Actually, we just about are," Violet said. "At least I'm nearly through teaching. The girls have made several outfits now and they know how to follow Butterick's directions very well. The rest is just practice."

"Oh, I know I need more help, if I'm ever to get promoted, Violet," Lila said. "Please help me with at least one more gown."

"I'll be here whenever you need help. But now it's time for you to gain confidence without me standing over your shoulder."

Michael was proud of the firm way Violet handled Lila. She'd gone out of her way to help the woman, but she shouldn't have to give up all her free time.

"Violet's right," his mother added. "You girls will learn more from just sewing on your own than anything. We know you know how to read the directions and to do as they say. You know how to adjust the patterns, how to do about anything that will come up in the patterns' instructions. And both of us are here if you have any questions."

It appeared that Lila had no choice but to accept that she'd be responsible for how adept she became at the sewing machine, and she didn't look very happy about it. But there really wasn't a lot new about that.

Although in the past few weeks, she had seemed easier to be around. She was nice to Violet, nicer to everyone in fact, but Michael couldn't shake the feeling that it was a ruse. He just wasn't sure why. Violet was trying to help Lila out of the kindness of her heart, and she'd done nothing to hurt the woman. Still he didn't really know what Lila was thinking so maybe he was jumping to conclusions. He hoped that was the case and that Lila truly did want to be Violet's friend.

Nevertheless, he was quite happy that Violet wouldn't be spending all her evenings in the back parlor. He'd missed her company more than he wanted to admit.

"Well," Luke said, "I, for one, am glad to hear we'll have you ladies as company again."

"So am I," Ben added. "We're getting a little sick of each other, to tell the truth."

"Yes, we are. We've missed your company," Michael said, his gaze resting on Violet.

"Well, it's good to know we've been missed, isn't it, girls?" his mother asked. "Let's celebrate by going to get an ice cream soda."

# CHAPTER THIRTEEN

Violet loved charades and was having a great time watching Luke try to get his idea across to everyone on Friday evening when Mrs. Heaton came and whispered, "I hate to interrupt your fun, but Michael asked if you would come to the study. He needs to talk to you about something he's found out."

Michael had been called to the telephone just as dinner ended and hadn't been seen since. Much as Violet was enjoying herself, she'd wanted Michael to join the game and was disappointed when he didn't. Besides just wanting to spend time with him, Violet realized it must be important for him to say he was working and then ask to see her.

"Of course. I'll go now." Everyone was having such a good time; she didn't think anyone noticed when she left with Mrs. Heaton. They entered the study to find Michael sipping a cup of tea from the pot he'd had Gretchen bring them.

"Please get a cup of tea first and then we'll talk." Violet and his mother did as he suggested and took seats in the two chairs in front of the fireplace. Michael made sure the door was closed and took a seat at his mother's desk.

"I have news for you."

"News? About Harlan?"

"Yes. Just as your friend said, he is trying every way he can think of to find you, and, apparently, now he's got some idea you're here in the city. He's already thinking about sending someone to find you."

Violet's breath caught in her throat. "But why? I've kept up my payments and —"

"He doesn't want your payments, Violet. He wants your property. Mostly, though, from what you've told us and from what your friend has said, I think he wants you. But try not to worry. The man he's thinking of sending is the agent I sent to find out what he was up to. He went into town as a former Pinkerton agent who was interested in opening his own agency. Black went to him a few days ago and hired him to try to find you. But with my man working for him, it gives us time to come up with a plan to prove Black is up to no good."

"But how are we going to prove anything? Mr. Atwood isn't there and —"

"The good news is my man gave me an address for Mr. Atwood. And I'm sending another man out West to meet with him."

"Wonderful, Michael. I'm sure Mr. Atwood can shed some light on all of this," Mrs. Heaton said. "He must know what is going on."

"I am so glad you know where he is." Violet breathed a sigh of relief. "Surely he'll know how our finances were before he left."

"I believe he will. I just need your approval to talk to him about your situation."

"Of course you have it, Michael. Do you really think he can help us?"

"I do. I think he's the only one who really knows what your mother's finances were before he left town. And I believe he might know what Black is up to and why."

"Thank you for trying to get to the bottom of it all."

"I think it's very good news," Mrs. Heaton said. "And I believe the Lord is at work in that Black hired Michael's man to find you."

Violet was sure it must be. She prayed it was.

"I'm going to leave you two to talk it over. Thank you for including me and letting me know what's going on. I've got to talk to Gretchen about tomorrow's menu, but I'll peek in on the charade game so our boarders won't become too curious about my calling Violet out."

Michael took her place in the chair next to Violet. He took one of her hands in his. "I'm sure this news has upset you, Violet, and I'm sorry. But I felt you needed to know the latest developments."

"I'm glad you told me, Michael. My only worry is, what if you can't find Mr. Atwood? What if he's gone somewhere else?"

Michael looked her in the eye. "Violet, please try not to worry. I am not going to let Black get to you. I'm not going to let him hurt you. I just wanted you to know what's going on and assure you we are going to get to the bottom of it all."

She took a deep breath and let it out. "Thank you, Michael. I'll try not to worry, and I will pray about it. I know you'll do all you can to help me. But I don't want you or any of your men hurt either. Harlan Black has always given me the shivers. I don't like him, I don't trust him and I —"

Michael's fingertips on her lips silenced her. His touch was light and gentle. Her breath seemed to be lodged in her throat. "Don't worry, Violet. I won't let Black hurt you. I promise."

His touch had her wanting him to pull her into his arms, and Violet forced herself to put some distance between them. She got up from her chair and walked over to the window. "I'm not so afraid of him as I am sickened by him, Michael." She could still see the look in Harlan's eyes when he'd grabbed her arm and pulled her close, demanding that she marry him. The repulsion she felt was as strong now as it had been then. She shook her head to get rid of the vision. "I just hope we can settle things so he won't foreclose on the loan Mama took out."

Michael came to stand beside her. He tipped her face up toward him and looked into her eyes. Violet couldn't help but compare the two men. While one left her cold, this one took her breath away with his nearness.

Michael's large hand cupped her cheek. "Oh, he's not going to foreclose, Violet. We'll come up with something. Don't worry. Harlan Black isn't taking your home away. He's not taking anything that belongs to you. I'll see to it."

Michael's gaze settled on her lips, and Violet found herself wishing he would kiss her. The thought alone shocked her. She'd never felt that way about any man, but right now, at this moment, she wanted to feel his lips on hers.

As if he had read her mind, his head dipped down and his lips captured hers, softly, gently . . . and she responded. . . .

A soft knock came at the door but Violet reacted as if a cannon had gone off, jumping back and putting a hand to her lips. Had he really kissed her or had she imagined it?

The door opened before Michael got to it and when his mother entered, Violet breathed a sigh of relief it was only her and not Lila or one of the other boarders.

"The boarders asked for hot chocolate of all things this time of year. Gretchen is making it now, but I thought I'd see if you two might want some, too."

"I don't," Michael said. "Isn't it a little warm for cocoa?"

"I think so, but that's what they asked for. What about you, Violet?"

"No, thank you. I think I'll pass this time. I'm going to turn in. I'll see you both in the morning." She turned back to Michael. "Thank you for letting me know what you found out."

"You're welcome. I'll update you again after I've met with Jim Moore. Sleep well."

"Thank you. Good night." The intensity in his eyes when their gaze met sent another warm flush up her neck as she hurried out the door.

If Mrs. Heaton noticed anything different about her, she didn't say anything. But Violet knew something had changed in the past few moments, and she was certain it was written all over her face.

"Violet seemed a bit flustered, son. Is she all right?"

Michael didn't think she could be any more flustered than he was and he hoped his mother didn't pick up on that fact. "I think so."

He hoped so — if he hadn't put panic in her heart by kissing her. But she had responded, he was sure of it.

"Are you all right, Michael?"

His mother looked at him closely. The last thing he wanted was for her to start asking questions he didn't want to answer. "I just want to make sure she's safe from Black. I'm going to put a man out to follow her, just to make sure she is."

"Did you tell her?"

"No, not yet. I've got to write Atwood and get someone on the earliest train I can tomorrow. I hope he'll have some answers for us."

"So do I. I am certain Violet's father had provided for them. I just don't see how it could be possible a mortgage would have

240

had to be taken out on the house. It doesn't make any sense to me. I do hope once everything is settled in her favor, as I'm sure it will be, Violet will decide not to go back."

Michael's heart twisted at the very thought she might decide to and he knew he'd do whatever he could to keep her in New York now.

"She seems happy here, Mother." At least she had — if he hadn't ruined things tonight. "Surely she won't want to go back. But if she thinks she does, we'll just have to persuade her to stay."

His mother smiled at him. "I was hoping that's what you were going to say. You know, Michael, it's about time you thought about starting a family of your own. I wouldn't object if you made Violet part of this family one day."

"Mother —"

"Oh, dear, I think I hear Lila calling me," his mother said as she hurried out the door.

Michael had a feeling she didn't want to hear what he'd been about to say and he was relieved he didn't have to say anything at the moment. Because if he hadn't been thinking about marriage before, he certainly was now.

Violet's goal was to get her home back free and clear and then go back to Virginia.

And he couldn't go back there to live. The only hope he had of finding his sister was here in the city. Amanda hadn't understood his need to be here — he wasn't sure any woman could — and he didn't need any more heartache. So any thoughts of marriage needed to be done away with. His life was here now.

He'd go find Luke. He needed to fill him in on what was happening with Harlan Black. Michael was glad he'd let Luke in on what was going on. With Black, one never knew what he might decide to do next. It helped to have Luke around to talk to and know he could count on, should Black show up here. Michael would sure like to have all of this settled as soon as possible — for all kinds of reasons.

Violet hurried up the stairs, hoping not to run into Lila or any of the boarders. She needed time to herself — time to think about what Michael had told her about Harlan Black and what might happen because of it.

But first and foremost in her mind was what had happened in those last few minutes in the study. The kiss they'd shared. And how she felt about it. Her heart was beating so hard she could feel it in her ears, and her fingers were trembling so badly she could barely unlock her door. Once inside, her legs seemed to turn to jelly before she reached her settee and sank down on it.

She leaned her head back and let out a sigh. Michael had taken her by surprise. Now she didn't know what, if anything, to do about it. She'd never thought to have strong feelings for Michael or any other man at this point in her life. Her goal was to get her home back, not give her heart away. After Nick and Harlan, she'd had enough disillusionment. The best thing for her to do was to concentrate on the reason she'd come to the city in the first place. And it wasn't to fall in love. And in fact she was enjoying the feeling of independence living here in New York City gave her. But somehow this man she'd known all her life as a friend seemed to be quickly working his way right into her heart as something more.

How did it happen? Violet forced herself off the settee and hurried into the bathroom to get ready for bed before Elizabeth came up and needed it. She tried to put the earlier events out of her mind, but as she looked in the mirror, the pink of her cheeks and the glow in her eyes brought the touch of his lips to mind once more and she splashed her face with water, trying to erase the telltale signs of how much she'd been affected by those few moments.

All she did know was the last few minutes in the study had become much more important to her than what Michael had called her into the study to talk about. She wasn't really worried about Harlan Black. Not after Michael's promise to protect her.

But she was concerned that somehow she'd never get her home back, and that remained of utmost importance to her. Her father had worked hard for what they had . . . sometimes to the extent of leaving too much for her mother to take care of, to Violet's way of thinking. Still, they had a nice home and her mother had loved every inch of it. The last person she wanted to have it was Harlan Black.

Violet finished her toilette and went back to her room. She turned her bed down, thinking about her home. While Mrs. Heaton's house now felt like home to her, the one she was raised in was full of her childhood memories.

After her mother had passed away and Violet found her mother had taken a mortgage out on it, she'd blamed her father, wondering what he'd done with the money. But if what Mrs. Heaton thought was true, then maybe he *had* provided well for them.

If so, Violet had been wrong to blame him.

Her head still reeling from the events of the evening, Violet sighed and opened her Bible to Proverbs. Tonight it seemed to speak to her confusion. In chapter three, verses five through six, it said, "Trust in the Lord with all thine heart; and lean not unto thine own understanding. In all thy ways acknowledge him and he shall direct thy paths."

Well, she understood nothing tonight. Not how it happened that Michael had kissed her. Not what would happen if Harlan Black came to New York, nor if she'd ever return to her family home. And she was beginning to wonder if she'd misjudged her own father.

Violet slid to her knees and prayed. "Dear Father, please help me to understand what is or isn't happening between Michael and me. To know what You would have me do about my family home. Please direct my path and help me to do only Your will. In Jesus's name, I pray. Amen."

She put her Bible up and slipped beneath the covers, feeling at peace. She might not know what the next day would bring, but the Lord did and she'd rely on Him to guide her through it.

■ ■ ■ ■

With thoughts of the kiss he and Violet had shared fresh in his mind, Michael lost no time writing a letter to Mr. Atwood the very next morning and assigning a man to get it to him. It was imperative that he contact the attorney as soon as possible because they'd only be able to put Harlan Black off for so long.

If Black was sending someone to find Violet, he must be afraid Atwood knew things Violet didn't. At least Michael was hoping that was it and that her home really was free and clear of debt.

Once that was done, he went to Grand Central to meet Jim's train. At some point, Jim would have to let Black know he'd found Violet, and when he did, Michael was sure Black would act on the news. It was entirely possible he would show up at the boardinghouse.

When the younger man got off the train, they shook hands and went to pick up his luggage.

"It's good to be home," Jim said. "I don't think I like small-town living much. And I don't like working for a man like Harlan Black, even if I'm only pretending to. Half the town seems to owe him something and he doesn't let them forget it. He's not a good man, Michael."

"I know. Thankfully I didn't have any dealings with him, but I know many of the people in town think he should be run out of the state."

They stopped for lunch at a café just down from Michael's office so Jim could go into more detail about what he'd found out. The restaurant was full of men who worked in the area. After they'd given their order for the day's special of beef and fried potatoes, Jim filled him in. "The man seems to make a practice of keeping his clients in debt in one way or another. Once they're late on a payment, he adds so much interest over time that it becomes near impossible for them to catch up. And he uses the fact that they owe him to get them to do things for him, tell him things about other clients."

"You think that's how he found out Miss Burton might be here?"

"I only know it could be."

"Any idea why he hadn't already hired someone to come find Violet?"

Jim shook his head. "He tries very hard to act as if he is a benefactor instead of a crooked banker, and even though most people know what he is, they don't know exactly what he's up to. He appears to be an upstanding citizen and makes sure he's in church every Sunday, but I think it's all for show. You should hear the language he uses when he is angry. Just as we figured, he didn't want to go to anyone in town and that's why he came to me."

"Did he give you any timetable to get back to him?"

"He wants results as quickly as possible."

"And you are to collect money from Miss Burton?"

"No. He just wants me to make sure she is here. In fact he told me not to let her know anything. He just wants to know her whereabouts for now. He seems almost obsessed with finding her."

"From what I know of him, I'm not surprised."

"I didn't figure you wanted me to argue with him, boss."

"You're right. I don't want him getting suspicious of you. How did you come up with an address for Mr. Atwood?"

"It was pretty easy. I asked around town for the names of good lawyers and was told Atwood was the best and that even though his office is closed now, he will be returning in a few months. One of his good friends said I could write him if it was important and gave me the address." Jim grinned at him. "Don't worry, boss. Harlan Black doesn't know I was asking about him."

Michael certainly hoped not. The last thing they needed was for Black to get suspicious. "That's good to know. I'll keep you here as long as I can, but I'm assuming Black is wanting you to telegraph him with what you find out."

"Yes, he does. I'll try to put him off as long as I can."

"We'll figure out what to do. Where are you staying?"

"He thinks I'm staying in some fleabag hotel, if the traveling money he gave me is any indication. But I'm staying at my apartment."

"Good," Michael said. "I'll know where to find you."

"I'm glad I don't have to work for Black . . . not for real anyway and not much longer, I hope."

"I'll get you back here to stay soon as I can." Michael wanted things with Black settled. The sooner the better.

Violet was glad to see Monday come. She hoped keeping busy would take her mind off Michael and what to do about her growing feelings for him. If she could quit thinking about him and his kiss, that would be even better, Violet thought as she worked the pedal on the sewing machine. He'd only meant to comfort her, she was sure of it. The kiss wasn't because he cared for her in any romantic way. And she couldn't let herself begin to think that he might. It would only lead to heartache.

She sighed in exasperation and tried to put all thoughts of him out of her mind as she worked on one of the bicycling costumes. If it turned out well, she might make one for herself. It'd be nice to go cycling in Central Park one day.

"Violet," Harriet, the girl working on her left, called to her. "Did you hear?"

"Hear what?"

"One of the girls just got engaged!"

Apparently it was true, because by midmorning all the talk at Butterick was about another seamstress who had announced her engagement and impending marriage. As soon as Violet heard the news, she hurried to talk to Mrs. Waters about Lila having learned to sew.

"But do you think she's talented enough to work in the sewing room, Violet?"

"Well, I think so. I taught her, and while I wouldn't say she loves it, she is quite adept at it. I believe she would love to work up here."

"She has been with us for a while. I suppose we could promote her and see how she does, since you recommend her. I'll talk to Mr. Wilder and Mr. Pollard about it."

"Thank you." Violet was glad to have the decision out of her hands. She'd taught Lila to sew and asked Mrs. Waters to give her a chance. Now it was all in the Lord's hands and whatever happened, she hoped she could quit feeling guilty that Lila hadn't been promoted before.

By midafternoon, Lila was being shown around the sewing room and told to think about whether or not she wanted to make the move.

"One does have more freedom to talk in the pattern-making room," Mrs. Waters said. "Up here, it's mostly the sound of the sewing machines you'll be hearing. But there's a feeling of accomplishment in seeing a beautifully finished garment."

"Yes, ma'am, I know there is. And folding patterns can get quite boring after a while," Lila said. "I really don't think I need time to think about it. I would love to work up here."

Mrs. Waters smiled. "I'm sure you will. We all do. Still, I'll give you this evening to think

251

about it. If you are still sure about it tomorrow morning, the position is yours and you'll start this coming Monday."

"Oh, thank you, ma'am," Lila said.

"It is Violet you need to thank. She's the one who recommended you."

Lila turned to Violet and her smile looked almost genuine. "Thank you, Violet."

"You're welcome. I think you'll like working up here."

"Oh, I'm sure I will."

Violet had no doubt that Lila would like the pay and being out of the pattern room. What she wasn't so sure of was how they'd both like working in such close proximity to one another. She wasn't sure about that at all.

The next night, as she did for all her boarders, Mrs. Heaton had a special meal prepared for Lila in honor of her promotion. She'd made her favorite meal of ham and mashed potatoes and peas, along with coconut cream pie for dessert.

Lila seemed genuinely happy for the first time since Violet had come to stay. For once everyone's attention was on her.

"We're all so happy for you, Lila. I hope you like it in the sewing room," Julia said.

"I like the pay much better, I know that

much. And truthfully, folding patterns is a very boring job."

"I imagine it would be. It was so nice of Violet to teach you how to sew so that you could qualify for this new position," Elizabeth said.

Lila glanced over at Violet and smiled. "Yes, it was. I can't thank Violet enough for recommending me for the position."

"You are welcome, Lila. It helped that you wanted to learn. And I think Butterick likes to promote from within, if they can. I'm just glad that you wanted to learn so that you could apply for the position when it came along."

"All the women down in pattern folding are very envious that I was promoted," Lila said. "I'll miss a few of them, but I won't miss that position at all."

"Maybe you could teach one or two of them to sew, like Violet taught you," Mrs. Heaton suggested.

"Perhaps," Lila said, but she didn't seem very enthused to Violet.

"That would be nice." Michael smiled at her. "I'm sure it is very rewarding to help someone move up at their workplace."

Violet was glad that Lila had been moved up, but she still wasn't sure how well she would like having her in the same department. Hopefully it would all work out fine.

She had a feeling that while Lila was thankful that she'd learned to sew, she wished anyone but Violet had taught her. Oh, she'd thanked her on the way home and again at dinner, but her manner had been a bit stiff and forced.

Other than that, they hadn't talked any more about it. Lila had burst into the house and announced to one and all that she had finally been promoted to seamstress, as if it were a position she'd been qualified to have for a very long time.

Of course, anyone living at Mrs. Heaton's boardinghouse knew that it'd only been a short while since she'd learned to sew, but Lila seemed to have forgotten that part of it all. No matter — Violet could quit feeling guilty because she'd been given the seamstress position right off. She'd done what she could to help Lila and now that they were both on equal footing at Butterick, hopefully, Lila would be easier to be around from now on.

She had been nicer overall since Violet had taught her to sew, but that wasn't saying a lot. Still, anything was an improvement on the outright distaste she'd shown to Violet since she'd first come to live at Mrs. Heaton's.

Violet was still convinced that Lila's dislike of her was because she was an old friend of Michael's. As she watched Lila trying to capture his attention this evening, she was even more certain that the woman wanted Michael for herself. And deep down, Violet knew that what bothered her most of all was not really knowing how Michael felt about Lila.

# CHAPTER FOURTEEN

Once dinner was over, Michael knew he'd need to move quickly before Violet went upstairs or joined the others in the parlor. "Violet, may I speak to you a moment?"

"Of course," Violet answered.

Michael could see that Lila wanted to hang back, but he turned his back to her so that she wouldn't hear what he was saying and bent down to whisper in Violet's ear. "Would you like to take a walk in Gramercy Park?"

Her eyes seemed to light up as she smiled at him. "That would be very nice. Thank you."

"I'll let Mother know where we're going and meet you back here in ten minutes, all right?"

She nodded and hurried up the staircase while he went in search of his mother. He made it back to the foyer just as Violet came back down, and he swept her out the door

256

fast as he could so as not to draw notice that they were leaving.

"I feel like a kid trying to slip out of the house without letting anyone know," he said as he took Violet's elbow and steered her down the walk. It wouldn't surprise him if Lila called out the door for them to wait for her. She was getting increasingly hard to avoid.

"Has something happened with Harlan that you need to talk to me about?" Violet asked as he unlocked the gate to the park.

"No. You just looked a little frazzled and I thought you might enjoy some quiet time in the park."

"You read me almost as well as your mother does, Michael. This is just what I need."

"Good." He drew her hand through his arm as they strolled through the garden. He loved coming here. There were always others from the neighborhood, but not too many at one time, and there were areas where one could find a quiet spot and sit and relax. Being here with Violet, knowing she loved it as much as he did, made it even more special, and he knew he'd never be able to come by himself again without thinking about her. He led her to the bench they'd sat on when he'd shown her the park for the first time.

"It's beautiful out this evening," Violet said. "I love the way lights in the houses around the park come on one at a time here and there this time of day. The lights shining down make me feel safe."

Michael wanted to be the one who made her feel safe. Had he failed in that respect? "Violet, are you worried about Harlan coming after you?"

"Not really. But I don't know what he's going to do as time goes on."

Michael turned to her and tipped her chin up with his thumb and forefinger. "I'm not going to let him get to you here. We're going to get to the bottom of everything and take care of Harlan for you."

"I know. I just wish we could get word soon."

"So do I. And I feel that we will but I know the waiting isn't easy."

"At least my job keeps me busy."

"How do you think it will be working with Lila in the same department?"

Violet gave a little chuckle and shook her head. "That I don't know. But at least I don't feel guilty for being given a seamstress job before her."

"You had no reason to feel guilty. And you taught her to sew so that she'd get this job."

"I'm glad she did. Hopefully it will make life easier on all of us."

Michael didn't have the heart to tell her that their home had been full of tension from Lila for one reason or another ever since she'd moved in. He didn't have much hope that it would change just because she got promoted. Maybe for a day or two, but then it would be something else she'd be upset about.

"Well, if it doesn't, it won't be your fault. It seems that Lila brings a lot of her distress on herself."

"That's sad."

"It is. I just don't want you worrying about her. You've done a lot for her even if she doesn't appreciate it."

"Thank you, Michael. And thank you for bringing me here tonight. It's just what I needed."

Michael was glad, but not only for Violet's sake. Sitting here with her made him realize just how much he'd needed to have even a few minutes with her just to himself. He was beginning to think of this park as their special place.

On Wednesday morning, Michael was pleased to have a letter from Mr. Atwood, saying he wanted to meet with Michael at his earliest convenience to discuss Violet's predicament with Harlan Black and discuss what could be done about him. He planned on coming to New York City before going home to Virginia for that very purpose and would be arriving on Friday.

At last it seemed that they'd be able to find out what Black was up to. From reading between the lines of Mr. Atwood's letter, Michael was pretty sure his opinion of Black wasn't much better than Michael's.

He met with Jim Moore that afternoon and found that Black was pressing to know what he'd found out.

"I've tried to stall as much as I can. I told Black that I haven't been able to see Miss Burton going in or coming out of the boardinghouse and finally had to remind him that he had told me to make certain that I didn't make anyone suspicious about his trying to find her."

"What did he say to that?"

"He gave me more time."

Michael nodded. "Good. Hopefully, he won't insist that you return to Virginia until after we've heard what Mr. Atwood has to say. I'm counting on whatever information Atwood has will help us come up with a plan to help Miss Burton keep her home."

"She's very well thought of in Ashland.

I've met her neighbors and they all want her to come home."

"How'd you find that out?"

"I said I was interested in her house — asked if they knew if it was for sale or not. Every one of them said they hoped she came home soon."

Violet going back home was the last thing Michael wanted, and he prayed that she felt the same way. Oh, maybe she'd want to go home for visits, but he hoped that she thought of New York as her home now. At least he knew she did love some things about the city. The thought of living in this city without Violet here too was almost enough to make him think of moving back to Virginia. But he couldn't just up and leave his mother here to do the work she did by herself either.

And that was another problem. Violet had given his mother a new outlook on life. It was as if she'd helped to fill that hole in her heart from the loss of Becca. Not that Violet would ever take his sister's place in his mother's heart. But she'd made a place of her own there and his mother would miss her terribly if she left.

"Miss Burton is a wonderful woman. I can see how they would feel that way. She's been a real boost for my mother. I hope she decides to make the city her home and just keep the place in Virginia for visits or maybe even sell it."

"Maybe after this is all settled, she'll be free to make a decision," Jim said.

"Hopefully so." Who was he trying to fool? There was only one decision Michael wanted Violet to make — and that was to stay here. And it had nothing to do with the good she could do in the city, or even how much his mother cared for her. Deep down, Michael knew that wanting Violet to stay here had much more to do with the place she was claiming in *his* heart than anything else.

Over the next couple days, Violet tried not to think about Harlan Black or what might happen if he showed up. That was the last thing she wanted. If anything bad happened to Michael or his mother or anyone else in this house because of her, she wouldn't be able to forgive herself.

"Why don't we plan a visit to the Ladies' Mile this weekend?" Julia asked as she passed the breadbasket.

Her idea was a welcome interruption of Violet's thoughts. "Oh, I'd love to. I've been wanting to see more of the shops."

"We haven't been back down there, have

we?" Mrs. Heaton asked. "We've been quite busy, though."

"Yes, we have." Violet could hardly believe she'd been living in the city for over two months now. Time had sped by, with learning a new job, teaching the girls to sew and trying to learn her way around.

"Well, let's go this Saturday. We can go right after breakfast and have lunch at one of the restaurants down there," Mrs. Heaton said.

"What are we doing to do?" Ben asked. "I don't think I want to go shopping."

"Ben, you men can surely entertain yourselves for a day," Julia said. "I mean, we do know you don't always consult us when you want to do 'men' things."

"That is true. I've wanted to check out a new exhibit at the Museum of Natural History. Any of you want to go with me?" Luke asked.

"I might," Ben said.

"I'm not sure what my plans are yet," Michael said. "I'm hoping to meet with someone from out of town on Friday, but I don't know exactly when we'll finish our business."

Violet wondered if it could be Mr. Atwood that Michael was meeting with. Oh, she hoped that was the case. And if it was, she was sure that he would let her know. The thought that he might ask for her to come to his mother's study again brought thoughts of the last time they were together there and the breath caught in her throat. She had to stop thinking about that night and the kiss they'd shared. She had to. He'd only meant to comfort her, she was sure of that. But he'd done much more. He'd made her want him to kiss her again, and she didn't have any idea what to do about it.

"You men can do whatever you wish," Mrs. Heaton said. "We'll be back for dinner, but we're going to have a great time showing Violet all that the Ladies' Mile has to offer."

Luke gave a mock shiver. "How you can all stand to spend hours looking at the latest frippery is beyond me, but I hope you all enjoy the day."

"Oh, never fear. We'll enjoy ourselves," Elizabeth said. "It's been quite a while since we had an outing like this. And it will be even more fun showing it all to Violet."

"I can't wait. Michael and I only went to Macy's the day we celebrated my getting hired at Butterick."

"We won't get to see it all even in a whole day," Mrs. Heaton said. "But you'll certainly find out why there is such an attraction of the mile."

Violet remembered so many things about the day she and Michael celebrated her new job at Butterick. The lunch and getting to know each other better were highlights of the day. But what she remembered most was running upon the tenements and those two little boys who looked at them so wistfully — the same ones they'd seen at the park. To go shopping after that had been a stark reminder of the differences in society, and it'd been almost overwhelming to Violet.

She hoped she could enjoy the outing on Saturday, but after all that had happened at the park, she thought those differences might be more glaring than ever.

Michael was glad everyone had plans for the day, for he was to meet with Mr. Atwood at noontime. He'd arrived the evening before, but asked to have a good night's sleep before they met — unless the need was urgent. Michael was relieved to be able to tell him that as far as he knew nothing was urgent at the moment.

Now, as he picked up the older man at his hotel and they took a rented hack back to the boardinghouse, Michael could tell that his illness and the trip had been hard on him. "Mr. Atwood, sir, I can't tell you how much I appreciate your willingness to help Miss Burton out."

The man might look frail, but his handshake was that of a much younger man, firm and strong. "No need to thank me, Michael — if I may call you by your first name. And, please, call me Nigel. I've felt guilty for getting sick and not being there to take care of the Burtons' business when I heard Mrs. Burton passed away. I didn't even know she had until a month or so ago. It was then that I knew I needed to get back to work."

"Still, I know it wasn't easy to go out of your way to come up here."

"Better than for Black to see us together. He'd be sure to put two and two together and I fear that could cause even more problems for Miss Burton."

"That is the last thing I want for Violet."

"I feel the same way. How is your mother doing?"

"She's doing quite well. She'll be pleased to have you to dinner this evening. She and the women boarders have gone on an outing — which worked out very well for us today. The men took off in different directions and we won't have to worry about interruptions. I think you'll be more comfortable at my home than you would be in my office."

"I've learned to try to be comfortable in most situations and places, Michael. But I'll take you up on your hospitality."

"Good. I've asked our housekeeper to make us a nice lunch and my agent, Jim Moore, will be joining us. That way, we'll all have the same information to assimilate."

"That makes good sense," Mr. Atwood said. "I'm sure we can come up with a plan to put an end to Black's dishonest dealings. It's about time he was found out."

"That is what I think, too."

They'd no more arrived at the boarding-house than Jim Moore showed up. Michael made introductions as he led them to the dining room where Maida had set the table for three and was ready to serve them as soon as they were seated.

Michael waited until she served them lunch before getting down to business. "So, you have knowledge of Black's underhand-edness?"

"I believe I do. At least where it concerns the Burtons. I know that there should have been no reason at all for Mrs. Burton to take out a loan on her home."

"Then my mother was right. She said she was certain that Mr. Burton left Violet and her mother well enough off to live the life they'd been accustomed to. Not that it was one of luxury, but they should have been able to live debt free."

"Your mother is exactly right. Mr. Burton worked long and hard to provide for his family, and he was very determined to leave them a good inheritance. His place had been paid for long ago. And there was ample money in the bank to take care of their needs and more. Even Mrs. Burton's illness."

"Then what do you think happened? How could things have turned so bad?"

"I don't believe they did. I think that Harlan Black saw an opportunity to pull the wool over their eyes, and once I was gone and Mrs. Burton got sick, he did just that."

"So how do we prove it?" Michael handed a basket of crusty rolls to Mr. Atwood.

"I know a judge that will make sure we can go through the bank records, once I give him my records and documentation." He took a roll and buttered it as he continued, "Mrs. Burton's doctor will help, too. I know there is no way Doc Malone would have charged her so much that she'd have had to put her place up for a loan. Did Violet say if she asked the doctor about his charges?"

"No. I'm not sure she thought to. Violet is a very trusting person. I think she just believed Black."

"Yes, she is that. I don't know how Black got to her mother, but I do have an idea why he's after that property and possibly even Violet herself."

Michael sat up straighter in his chair and took a drink of water to wet a throat that had suddenly gone dry. "What would that be?"

"Back in the day when I was young, Harlan Black's father had it bad for Violet's mother. She'd have nothing to do with him and he couldn't stand it. When Burton won Grace's heart and married her, Harlan Senior went on a drinking binge that lasted over a week."

Atwood popped a piece of bread in his mouth and Michael waited until he'd chewed and swallowed for him to continue.

"Once he found out that Burton was going to build his new bride a home where it stands today, Harlan Senior tried to overbid him. The seller didn't like Harlan any more than anyone else in town did and wouldn't change his mind to sell to Burton. Harlan Senior went on another drinking binge and ended up married to Harlan Junior's mother. She was a good woman. Didn't deserve a man like Black."

"How would Harlan Junior know about

all of that?"

"Oh, the whole town knew his papa still carried a torch for Grace. I think somehow Harlan Junior thinks that if he can get the land and Violet, he will have somehow won the prize for his father."

"Is his father still alive?"

"Oh, yes, he is. I'd have thought he would have drunk himself to death by now, but he's still with us. Wouldn't surprise me if he put the whole idea into his son's mind."

"From being around him, I wonder if he was warped by his papa's obsessions? He seems to have a lot of his own," Jim Moore said.

"I'm sure he does. He's just like his father was when he was that age. I'm glad Violet got away from him when she did. Now we just have to make sure he doesn't get to her."

That had become Michael's worst nightmare, and he had no intention of letting it become a reality.

Maida cleared the table and brought in dessert. Michael didn't feel much like eating anymore, but he waited until the other men finished before suggesting, "Let's have coffee in my mother's study. I don't want to take a chance of anyone overhearing our plans should the boarders return sooner than expected."

"Don't worry, Michael. We'll come up with a plan and put a stop to Black's best-laid ones. He's not going to get away with his scheme."

As they made their way to the study, Michael could only pray that Mr. Atwood was right.

Violet had never had a day quite like the Ladies' Mile outing. She'd forgotten just how congested it'd been the day Michael and Mrs. Heaton had driven her around. That had been bad, but today the crush of women on the streets and in the stores was almost unbelievable. Of course, she was in the crowd instead of a hack and found that made a huge difference.

Once one got past the women window-shopping outside the stores, it was even worse inside. The clerks couldn't seem to move fast enough for their customers and there were women lined up to make purchases, ten deep in some places.

The first store they went in was Macy's, and although she'd been there before with Michael, Violet was glad to go again. They'd made such a quick trip that day and she'd still been reeling from seeing the tenements and from excitement over finding employment, she hadn't really had her mind on shopping. Not that she planned to buy anything today, but it was fun to see what was on display. It appeared that everything a woman could think of, and more, was offered in these stores.

They looked at ready-made clothing from bicycle dresses, which seemed all the rage at the moment, to ball gowns that most only hoped to one day have reason to wear.

To be sure, Ladies' Mile was an accurate name for the area. The only men Violet saw were a few clerks and the many drivers of the various vehicles waiting for their owners to return. It was not hard to tell the very rich from everyone else, for they seemed to have someone by their side to hold their packages, to do their bidding. They were dressed in the most fashionable gowns of the day, custom-made in the best materials and trims, and wearing jewels that Violet had only seen the likes of behind cases in the jewelry store back home. And those were nothing like the diamonds, emeralds and rubies she saw on the necks of some of the women in this store.

From one department to another, then one store to another — Hearns Department Store, Le Boutellier down the street from Macy's — women coming from all walks of life shopped together. If one of the not so wealthy had to wait for one who was to be waited on, no one seemed to mind, being a bit awestruck by the wealthier woman.

But it wasn't until Violet returned from purchasing a lacy handkerchief in Le Boutellier, so delicate she couldn't resist, that she realized she'd been standing next to one of the Vanderbilts.

"Violet, do you have any idea who you were standing next to?"

She turned to look at the woman who was still being waited on. She was elegantly dressed, bejeweled and wearing a hat Violet was sure Mrs. Heaton would love. She turned back to Elizabeth and shrugged. "Should I?"

Julia laughed. "No, there is no reason you would. At least not until you live here a little longer and know all the Vanderbilts." She leaned closer and whispered, "That is Edith Vanderbilt Shepard, Margaret's middle daughter."

"Oh!" Violet turned to look at the woman once more. The woman turned just then and saw Violet looking at her. She gave a short nod and a small smile as she swept by the group. For a moment Violet wondered if she was expected to curtsy, and then chided herself for the thought. This was America, which didn't have royalty. But, the way people got out of Miss Vanderbilt's way it was hard to tell.

"Violet, the look on your face is priceless!" Lila pointed at her and laughed.

"I'm sure you looked the same the first time you came to the Mile," Elizabeth said. "It's very intimidating to visit the first few times. And even more daunting to run into American royalty."

"You are joking, right?" Violet said.

Elizabeth laughed. "Of course I am. But here in New York, many consider the Vanderbilts and others of their wealth in that way."

"They set the style for the elite in the city. So it never hurts to keep up with what they are wearing so one can stay in fashion," Lila said. "I'm sure even the people at Butterick stay abreast of what the wealthy are wearing here in the city."

"Oh, I'm sure they do," Mrs. Heaton agreed. "They are in the fashion business, after all. In fact, I would imagine they know what is in style even before the Vanderbilts show up in a designer gown. They have people at all the European fashion shows."

"No wonder the clerks take such a long time with them. They've probably been told to. The longer they stay in one store, the more others want what they buy," Violet said.

"Well, I'm ready to move on," Mrs. Heaton said. "Let's go get some lunch before we shop any more."

"Yes, we must make sure we have enough energy to make it through the afternoon," Julia said. "We've barely started."

Violet's feet were hurting already, and she wasn't sure what they could possibly find in any other store different from what they'd already seen, but she was going to enjoy the outing with the others even if she had to soak her feet for hours just to be able to get them in her boots for church the next day.

By the end of the day, they'd seen more ladies' clothing and adornments than Violet would be able to remember, much less where she'd seen an item, if she should recall it. All she really wanted was to get out of her shoes and soak her feet — providing she could get them off. But she felt like patting herself on the back for she'd only thought of Michael about once every half hour today — wondering what he'd been doing and how his meeting had gone. She couldn't wait to get home and find out.

# CHAPTER FIFTEEN

When they arrived back to the Heatons', Violet was more than pleased to learn that Mr. Atwood was there and would be taking dinner with them. They got back just in time to freshen up before dinner, and she hurried down to the parlor to greet him, only to find he wasn't there.

But Michael had sent word by Maida asking Violet to come to his mother's study to meet with an old friend and she hurried down the hall and gave a light knock on the door.

Mr. Atwood greeted her before she could say a word, coming to take her hands in his. "Violet, dear, I am so sorry about your mother. I didn't get word about her until a month ago. Had I known, I would have contacted you with the details of your father's will immediately."

His sincerity brought tears to her eyes. She was so happy to see that while it was apparent that he'd been ill recently, as he'd lost weight since the last time she saw him, he seemed on the road to recovery. "I should have made more effort to find you. I was just so confused that there was a mortgage on the house, and then I couldn't find a job."

Mr. Atwood patted her hand. "I assure you that I am much healthier than I appear, Violet, and I'm determined to get back to Ashland and get to the bottom of whatever it is that Harlan Black has been scheming."

"Then you think he has not been telling the truth, as Mrs. Heaton does?"

"Oh, I am certain of it. And I'm very glad that Michael contacted me about Black. Don't you worry. We are going to get to the bottom of this and put an end to his dirty dealings as soon as possible."

"I knew I was right. And I can't wait to hear more about it," Mrs. Heaton said. "But we need to continue this later. The boarders are waiting for me to call them to dinner and I don't want to stir up their curiosity any more than necessary."

"We'll talk later, Violet. Mr. Atwood has helped us form a plan, but we want to get your opinion before we put it in action," Michael said, taking her arm to escort her to the dining room.

They headed down the hall as Mrs. Heaton called everyone to dinner. She'd had Maida prepare roast chicken and dressing in honor of their guest. She introduced him as a friend of her and Violet's families from back home, and everyone was very cordial to him.

Mr. Atwood had been given a seat adjacent to Michael's mother, and he turned to her after the introduction. "Mrs. Heaton, I can tell you that you are missed greatly by my wife and the ladies in the Ashland Women's Club. Edith said to tell you so."

"Thank you, Mr. Atwood. Please let Edith and the others know that I miss them, too. I'd love it if you'd bring her back for a visit sometime. There is much to see and do in the city and I'd love to show you both around."

"I'll tell her. Don't be surprised if she writes you accepting your invitation."

"That would be wonderful."

Dinner conversation revolved around the ladies' outing and Luke and Ben's trip to the Museum of Natural History. John had missed out on that because he'd been covering a fund-raiser that the Carnegies were holding that afternoon.

"Nigel, you should hear some of the stories John can tell," Mrs. Heaton said.

"He covers their parties and fund-raisers and all manner of things the rich do in this town."

"Is that right?" Mr. Atwood said. "Please tell me a few stories to take home to my wife. There aren't a lot of high-society doings where we live."

John obliged and entertained them through dinner and dessert with tales of the events he'd been to and covered for the newspaper.

Mr. Atwood was still chuckling when they excused themselves to have a private chat in the back parlor. "I hope to get to visit with you all more on my next trip, but for now I hope you will forgive me if I take these old friends off to myself for the evening."

He'd quickly gained favor with the boarders and they were all quite gracious in being left to their own devices for the rest of the evening.

Violet breathed a sigh of relief that finally she might find out if there was a way to keep Harlan Black from trying to take her family home.

Out of hearing of the others, Michael had asked Luke to join them in his office, too. While he waited for him to show up, he finally let Violet know that he'd told Luke

279

about Black in case he came looking for her.

"Luke works for you?" she asked.

"He is a writer, just like he told you. But sometimes he does work for me and right now it makes me feel much better just knowing that he's here when I can't be."

"I see." She nodded but still looked a little confused when Luke slipped in the door.

Luke looked at Violet and then at Michael. "Does Violet know you've told me —"

"About Black and that you sometimes work for me?"

"Yes, I do, now," Violet said.

"Good." Luke nodded. "I'm glad."

"So am I." Michael let out a huge breath and smiled at Violet. He was relieved she finally knew about Luke. "I didn't like keeping it from you, Violet. But I didn't want you to start worrying about Black any more than necessary."

"I understand, Michael. But since you've told me, does that mean I might have reason to worry more now?"

"I hope not. We're going to do all we can to see that you are safe. You know that, don't you?"

"I do."

Michael nodded. He hoped he was worthy of her trust in him. "Now, I want to update you on what's going on while Mr. Atwood is still here and can fill in anything I might forget. That way everyone will know our plan." He watched Violet closely as he and Mr. Atwood explained everything and how they hoped it would pan out.

Michael could see the hope in Violet's eyes and he prayed that it all would work out the way they hoped it would. "We'll let you know what we need you to do, should he show up here, Violet. And I'm sure he will come to the city once Jim lets him know that you are here."

"When I get back home and talk to the judge and we get our part of the plan together, I'll let you know," Mr. Atwood said. "I feel I let you down by not being there with you when your mother passed away, Violet. Rest assured I will be here for you from now on."

"Oh, Mr. Atwood, I don't blame you. You couldn't help getting sick any more than my mother could."

"Her illness came on very fast, didn't it? I know she was fine when I left."

Violet nodded. "Yes. One day she seemed perfectly all right, and the next she was having horrible stomach pains. Even Doc Malone didn't know what the problem was but he did all he could to help. And then, a few weeks later, she had the stroke."

"I'm so sorry, Violet. Before the stroke, did your mother tell you she'd taken out a mortgage on the house?"

"No, sir." Violet shook her head. "I didn't know that until after her funeral. Harlan came by to offer his condolences and tell me what she'd done."

"Hmm." Mr. Atwood rubbed his chin and let out a sigh. "None of it makes any sense and I'm going to find out what he's been up to."

"Thank you. But why would he say such a thing if it wasn't true?"

Mr. Atwood explained the past to her as he had done to Michael. "I believe he somehow thinks that if he can win you and gain the land, he will be avenging his father for past hurts."

"But why would it matter to him, especially after all these years?"

"Well, that I don't know."

"And when did he decide to do it?" Violet asked.

"Did he ever make any advances to you before your mother died?" Michael asked.

"Well, yes, he did. He asked me to a church picnic a year or so ago. I told him no. And then he asked me again a month or so before Mama became ill."

"I wonder if maybe he told his father and

282

that brought up his past with your mother?" Mrs. Heaton asked.

"And he was bound and determined not to lose you like his father lost your mother," Michael suggested.

"But why would anyone want a life with someone who didn't feel the same way about them?" Violet asked. "That just doesn't make any sense to me."

"Nor to any of us in this room. But the Blacks don't like to lose at anything," Mr. Atwood said. "And it appears that Harlan Junior is determined not to lose you."

"How can you lose something you never had? I never gave him any encouragement."

"And that is probably what made him even more determined to win you." The thought of Harlan getting anywhere near Violet made Michael sick. He thanked the Lord that she'd had sense enough to spurn his attentions and get out of town.

"Well, that will never happen," Violet said, her gaze resting on him as if she was trying to reassure him in some way. "I'd never marry the likes of Harlan. I must take after my mother when it comes to the Blacks. He makes my skin crawl."

"Yes, well, I'm sure you do take after your mother in more ways than that. And I'm certainly glad you do," Michael said. "Your instincts are very good, Violet. Trust them."

He watched Violet flush the most delectable shade of pink. He wanted this thing with Harlan Black settled. There were other things he wanted to take up with Violet, and her feeling about another man wasn't one of them.

On Sunday, Mr. Atwood had joined them for church and the sermon seemed one meant for them all. It was about how one should not worry about tomorrow, that today had enough worry of its own, that had her turning it all over to the Lord and asking Him to protect Michael and Mr. Atwood as they tried to discover what Harlan Black was up to.

As they'd left church, Violet felt more peace about the situation with Harlan Black than she ever had. Both Michael and Mr. Atwood had assured her they were on top of it all and that had helped, but it was knowing that the Lord was in control of it all that really calmed her. She'd been able to fully enjoy going to lunch with Michael and his mother and Mr. Atwood before they took him to catch his train back to Virginia.

At quitting time on Monday, Violet was surprised when Lila told her she'd be coming home later.

"I made plans with an old friend who used to work for Butterick. He started up his own pattern company several months ago and he asked if I'd have an early dinner with him since we both have something to celebrate. He's probably going to try to get me to work for him."

"You wouldn't quit Butterick after just getting a promotion, would you?"

"No, of course not. At least not until I know how his company is coming along."

The man showed up just then, but Lila didn't make any introductions. She simply said, "Please let Mrs. Heaton know that I'll have an escort to get me home if I'm not there before dark."

"Yes, I will."

"Bye!" Lila waved and took the arm of the gentleman as they headed in the opposite direction Violet was going.

It seemed odd that Lila had never mentioned her friend before now. Violet didn't think she was romantically interested in the man — not the way she acted around Michael. But truthfully, she knew very little about Lila. From what she'd heard from the others, no one else knew much about her either.

Violet headed toward the trolley, thinking it would get her home faster and she was more familiar with its stops, since that was the way she and Lila traveled back and forth to work, most days.

She looked in her reticule, just in case, to make sure she still had the map and directions Michael had given her weeks before. As long as she had it, she wasn't overly worried about getting back to the boarding-house.

Once on the trolley, she felt a new kind of independence. It was the first time she'd ever traveled anywhere in the city alone. She knew she wouldn't want to go anywhere alone after dark, but it was a relief not to have to put up with Lila's up-and-down emotions. Or her total silence.

Violet took a deep breath and expelled it. It was quite nice to relax on the way home. She looked around and noticed that many of the people on the trolley were the ones she traveled with most days. A new gentleman had begun to ride the same trolley a few days earlier and she'd wondered about where he worked and lived. He nearly always got on the trolley when she and Lila did, and he got off at the same stop in the mornings. But afternoons, when the trolley stopped just down from Mrs. Heaton's, he stayed on it. She couldn't help but wonder if he had a second job somewhere. Not that it mattered, really. It was just something to think about as she and Lila traveled back and forth. Only today, she couldn't help but wonder if he was one of Michael's men. The thought that he might be, did make her feel safer.

She felt a sense of accomplishment when the trolley stopped and she got off and walked home. She almost wished Lila would have somewhere to go every afternoon. This had been the most peaceful ride home she'd had since beginning work at Butterick.

They were just finishing up dinner when Lila came home. Her eyes were bright with excitement, and Violet couldn't help but wonder what had brought that about.

Nor, it seemed, could anyone else.

"Good evening, everyone," Lila said, slipping into her seat at the table just as Mrs. Heaton began cutting into the chocolate cake that was a favorite of the boarders. "I see I'm right on time for dessert. I was hoping I'd make it."

"We're glad you made it, dear," Mrs. Heaton said. "You should have asked your escort to join us."

"Oh, I've been with him long enough today."

"You look as if you enjoyed yourself.

287

Where did you go for dinner?"

"We went to that new little café down the street from Butterick. The food was pretty good. Mostly we were celebrating my new position and his new company. Of course he's trying to get me to come work for him, but I only told him I would think about it."

"But Lila, you just got a promotion. Surely you aren't going to quit Butterick now," Elizabeth said.

"I'm not planning on it, but you never know." Lila took a bite of cake and chewed before continuing, "At this time it probably wouldn't be the smartest thing to do. But he's got some great ideas and I'd like to help him if I can. The day may come when I do go to work for him."

Violet bit the inside of her mouth to keep from saying anything. Part of her wanted to let Lila know what she thought of her even considering changing companies after she'd just been promoted. But there was another part of her that would be almost relieved if she quit Butterick. She knew she needed to pray about her attitude, but as time went on, Violet wasn't sure she liked Lila any better than Lila liked her. So maybe she'd better reserve judgment and leave it all in the Lord's hands.

"He also asked me to keep an eye out on

others who might be willing to change companies. His starting pay is more than Butterick —"

"But he's only been in business a short time. How can he possibly compete with Butterick and the other large pattern companies?" Luke asked. "That doesn't make sense unless he came into some kind of inheritance to start up his business."

Lila shrugged. "I didn't ask. But it is a growing business and there should be plenty of room for new pattern companies, don't you think?"

"Quite possibly," Julia said. "Still, I would much rather work for a well-known company than one just starting out. But it will be your decision to make, Lila."

"True. And I'll let you all know if and when the time comes that I make it."

"My goodness, Lila, one would think you were talking about being a department manager instead of a seamstress position."

"Well, maybe I am." Lila smiled and looked over at Violet. "You might think on it, too, Violet. Being a department manager would pay really well."

"I like what I'm doing a lot, Lila. I don't think I'll be going anywhere else for employment. I like the people at Butterick. Why would I want to leave?"

"Well, that will be your decision eventually, I suppose. But you might want to keep an open mind."

"Thank you for your advice, Lila. I will keep an open mind, I can assure you."

# Chapter Sixteen

The next day, no one was more surprised than Violet when she was called into the offices of Mr. Wilder and Mr. Pollard and offered the position of assistant supervisor of the sewing department.

"But, Mrs. Waters does such a wonderful job."

"And it is for that reason that we want an assistant for her. She works very hard and has said that she is thinking of turning the reins over to a younger woman with more energy," Mr. Pollard said.

"Why, Mrs. Waters has more energy than anyone in the sewing room," Violet said.

"She certainly expends much energy. We think it may be that she is just tired, and we don't want her to leave. We've discussed it with her and she's said she would stay if we get her an assistant and she can have a little more time off. She also recommended you for the position."

"Oh, but I'm so new to the company — and, well, I'm sure there are several women in the department that have much more experience than I do and have been here longer."

"Not really," Mr. Wilder said. "And those who do have the experience aren't much younger than Mrs. Waters. According to her, the others don't show the same regard for the work they do that you do."

Violet was touched by the other woman's high opinion of her. But, oh, how she dreaded Lila's reaction to her getting yet another position higher than hers. She would be livid. And they lived in the same boardinghouse. Violet began to shake her head. "I'm not —"

"Please think it over, Miss Burton. I know there will be some resentment from some of the younger women," Mr. Pollard said. "They are going to try to make your job very difficult. But you are the one we want and the only one Mrs. Waters is willing to stay on and train, as she says. Should things get too bad, I expect you to come to us so that we can take care of it. Just think about it and let us know tomorrow. Agreed?"

"Yes, sir." Violet couldn't help but smile. She worked for some very nice people and they'd been good to her. She owed them the courtesy of thinking it over. "I'll let you know my decision tomorrow."

"Good, we hope you decide to take the position, Miss Burton," Mr. Wilder said. "You are the kind of person we like working for us. We look forward to talking to you tomorrow."

"Thank you, Mr. Wilder, Mr. Pollard."

Violet left their offices unsure of what to do next, other than to think on their offer and pray hard about it. It was a wonderful opportunity and she knew it. She didn't want to turn it down, but she knew Mr. Pollard was right. It wouldn't be easy. Still, it hadn't been easy to leave her home and move to New York City either. But she'd done it. It wasn't easy to think that she might lose her home, but she was doing all she could to be able to make those payments — unless it was proved that Harlan Black was a crook and her mother hadn't needed to take out that loan. Until then, she had loan payments to pay and this promotion would make that much easier.

"Where have you been? Are you in trouble?" Lila asked when Violet got back to the sewing room.

"No. I'm not in trouble. I —"

"Violet, could you come here, please?" Mrs. Waters called from her glass-enclosed office doorway.

"Well, if you weren't before, I'm sure you are now," Lila whispered. "Mrs. Waters isn't going to be happy you were gone so long from your machine."

Violet didn't miss the smirk on Lila's face as she got up and hurried over to her supervisor's office, thankful for the interruption.

"Yes, Mrs. Waters?"

"I just wanted to see if you accepted the position I know you were offered. I'm hoping that you did."

"Oh, Mrs. Waters, I am so grateful for your recommendation, but I don't know what to do. I don't have near the experience I feel I'd need to be an assistant to you."

"Violet, you have all the experience you need. I'll be training you to be a supervisor while you take a great deal of pressure off me. I can't think of a better arrangement — at least for me. You didn't turn it down outright, did you?"

"No, ma'am. I am to give an answer tomorrow."

Mrs. Water sighed. "Oh, I'm glad. Please say yes, Violet. I'm not quite ready to retire yet, but I can't keep going at the pace I have been. I truly need help, and you are the only one in the department that is young enough, trustworthy enough and that I like well enough to work with in that capacity."

"I promise you I will truly think about it and pray on it. I do want the position, Mrs. Waters. I just am not sure . . ." Violet hesitated. "There are women out there who are going to be very upset and —"

"Oh, I know. I remember well when I was given this position. I had some trouble from some of the other girls. That is to be expected anytime one is promoted over another, I suppose. And some will try to make things hard for you. But it is a good promotion, Violet. Look at it this way. If you take the assistant job, you will one day be qualified for my position. And even should we both leave at some point, another position has been created. You will have helped with that."

That was something to think about. "Thank you, Mrs. Waters. It has helped to talk to you."

"Good. Just know that I'll be praying that you take the position." She looked at the clock on the wall. "Looks like it's quitting time. You go do that thinking and praying and I'll see you in the morning."

"Yes, ma'am. Thank you." Violet felt like hugging the woman for wanting her to take the position and for recommending her. But

she was sure Lila and all the other seamstresses were curious enough about their
meeting and she didn't want to make it
worse. She didn't have a clue what she was
going to tell Lila as it was, but from the look
on her face, Violet knew she'd better figure
something out quickly.

As soon as the quitting bell rang, Lila ran
up to her and asked, "Did you get in
trouble?"

"No, Lila. Why would I? I didn't do
anything wrong."

"Well, I certainly wouldn't get away with
being gone as long as you were this afternoon. Is someone getting fired or quitting?"

"Lila, I really can't say."

"Violet, I thought we were becoming good
friends. Why won't you tell me why you
were gone so long today and what you and
Mrs. Waters were talking about?"

Somehow, Violet had a hard time believ-
ing that Lila considered them good friends.
She'd never given any indication before that
she wanted to be friends at all. "Thank you
for your concern, Lila, but I'm not at liberty
to say what our talk was about."

"I see," Lila said. "Well, I'm not going to
be riding home with you today. I'm meeting
my friend again. Will you tell Mrs. Heaton?"

"I'll be glad to. Have a good time."

Lila only gave a brief wave and hurried off.

Violet breathed a sigh of relief that she would have a peaceful trip home. She needed some time to herself for she had much to think about.

After dinner Violet went in search of Mrs. Heaton. She knocked on the door of the study and said, "Mrs. Heaton, do you have a minute?"

She was surprised to hear Michael's voice. "Come in, Violet."

She entered and looked around, but Mrs. Heaton wasn't there. "I'm looking for your mother. Do you know where I might find her?"

"She said she was very tired and went on up to bed. Is there something I can do for you?"

He was sitting in one of the chairs by the fireplace, an open Bible in his lap.

"Oh, I'm sorry. No, that's all right. I don't want to interrupt your Bible reading."

"You aren't. I've just finished my reading for tonight. Come join me for some tea." He didn't wait for Violet to accept, but poured her a cup and handed it to her instead.

"Thank you." Violet took the cup and sat

down in the other chair.

"What can I do for you? Is something wrong?"

"No, not really. I just need some advice and I know your mother will tell me what she really thinks." That was one of the things she loved about Mrs. Heaton. She felt she could come to her about anything — with the exception of her growing feelings for her son.

"I'd be glad to listen, if it's something you can talk to me about. What is it that's happened?"

"Well, it's nothing bad. It's quite the opposite, in fact. I've been offered a promotion —"

"Another one? That's great news, Violet. Mother has always said Butterick was the best place for you. What is it they want you to do?"

"They want me to be the assistant supervisor of the sewing department."

"Oh, that is quite a step up. But you don't seem terribly excited or happy about it."

"Oh, I am, or at least I want to be. But I know that I'm going to have some resentment in the department. I can't blame anyone. I might feel the same way if I'd been at a business for as long as some have and a new person came in and got promoted over me. I don't imagine I'd like it either."

"Well, I suppose there might be some who won't be happy about it, but it is that way in any business, Violet. You aren't thinking of turning it down, are you?"

"I'm not sure. I want to take it, but, oh, Lila is going to be so upset."

Michael shook his head. "You taught her to sew so that she could get the promotion to the sewing department, Violet. You can't live your life worrying about Lila's reaction to your good news."

"I know. And Mrs. Waters has said she needs me. Mr. Wilder and Mr. Pollard seem to think she will resign if she doesn't get some help soon. And from what she said, I believe she might."

"Well, then, if you are considering feelings, you might want to think about what it would mean to her if you don't take the position."

"Oh, I have. She's been so good to me, and as far as I can tell, everyone in the department thinks highly of her. But she did say that when she got promoted, she had some who resented her, too."

"It didn't stop her from taking the position, did it?"

"No, it didn't. I suppose it shouldn't stop me either." Violet took a sip of tea and made her decision. "I'll let them know I'll be happy to accept the promotion first thing tomorrow."

"Good. I think that's exactly what you should do and I'm sure my mother would tell you the very same thing."

Violet smiled. "I think you're right. Thank you, Michael." Her heart slammed against her ribs at the smile he gave her and her pulse began to race at the sight of those dimples.

"Still, I don't want to make it hard on everyone living here," Violet said, giving a small smile. "I feel the tension between Lila and me pours over to everyone."

Michael shook his head. "Well, you're wrong. Everyone living here knows Lila and her moods. No one is going to blame you for those. Enjoy your good news, Violet. Lila can get another migraine if she doesn't want to celebrate with us. You do know Mother is going to want another celebration dinner, don't you?"

"I'm sure she will, but it's not necessary."

"It is to her. Thank you for giving Mother something to look forward to, once more."

"Oh, Michael, thank you. She's a very special lady and I can see why my mother counted her as her best friend. She's become very dear to me, too."

*And you've become very dear to me.* If he thought about Violet once a day, he thought of her a thousand. In fact, she was on his mind from morning 'til night and beyond. He had only to get a glimpse of her to begin thinking about the near kiss they'd shared. He was sure that Violet only thought he'd been trying to comfort and assure her that he wouldn't let Black get to her, and he'd told himself that was the reason he'd kissed her. But he knew that his yearning to kiss her now had nothing to do with comforting her. It went much deeper than that.

"I have some news for you." Michael dropped into his mother's vacant seat and took it on himself to pour Violet another cup of tea. He wanted to keep her there as long as he could. It seemed way too long since they'd had any private time together.

"What is it? Has Mr. Atwood found out anything?"

"Not yet, but he's getting closer. He says it won't be long now." He filled her in on what Atwood had passed on to him. "Just pray that our suspicions turn out to be right. I'll let you know as soon as I know more."

"Thank you, Michael. I appreciate all you are doing to try to find out the truth of my family's finances."

"No need to thank me, Violet. I hate to

see someone taken advantage of. Speaking of which, Lila has taken advantage of your good nature. She got her promotion only because of you. Don't you let her take the joy out of yours."

"I'll try not to. I've got to give them an answer tomorrow. She knows something is up and she wanted me to tell her, because we're good friends and all."

Michael's laughter startled her and she felt her lips twitch in response. Finally, she couldn't contain her giggles as he continued to laugh.

"It is funny, I suppose," Violet said when she got her giggles under control.

"You could say that. Anyone who's sat at the same table with the two of you would think so, too. No one in this household would ever think that you and Lila were good friends. Through no fault of yours, Violet. It's very hard to think of Lila being good friends with anyone."

"Perhaps. But maybe it is a good friend she needs." That thought had just come to her and she couldn't help but wonder if that was part of Lila's problem. Maybe she simply didn't know how to be a friend because she'd never really had one.

Michael looked thoughtful. "Maybe you are right. But she doesn't make it easy for anyone to be good friends with her. She's too busy thinking about herself."

What he said was very true. Lila didn't seem to care enough about anyone else to be interested in what was going on in their lives. Violet wondered if maybe that was because Lila hadn't had anyone care about what was going on in hers. Maybe she'd been too hard on her.

As if he read her thoughts, Michael said, "Violet, are you trying to blame yourself for all of Lila's problems now? You know, Lila hasn't changed into what she is just since you moved in. She's been the way she is for at least as long as she's been here."

"Not so much blaming myself, but wondering if there is something I can do to help her. I suppose all I can do is try to be a friend to her."

"I hope your efforts aren't for nothing, Violet. You have the biggest heart of anyone I know besides my mother."

Violet shook her head. "There is no way I compare to your mother, although I would love to help others as she does. And don't for a moment think that Lila's attitude doesn't get as tiresome to me as it does to you."

"And yet you still want to help her."

"I feel sorry for her at times. I can't help

it. It's just hard for me to believe that anyone would want to be moody and hard to get along with, and —"

"Hard to like? I'm sorry, Violet. I don't mean to hinder your willingness to try to be her friend."

"I know you don't."

Michael wanted to explain. He had a bad feeling about Lila's intentions. He couldn't believe that she really wanted to be friends with Violet — much less good friends. He'd seen the way she looked at Violet when she thought no one was watching. "I just don't want you to get hurt."

Color flooded her cheeks as his gaze locked on hers. "Thank you, Michael. It means a lot to know that you want the best for me. I don't really expect to be great friends with Lila. If I'm honest, I don't want to be. We don't have much in common. But I do feel the Lord wants me to try to get along with her, to try to be a friend. We'll see if she truly wants to be friends or not. The first test will be when I tell her I've been offered a new position."

"We'll see if she will celebrate with you or not."

"Yes. We will."

Michael stood in his mother's study waiting

for Violet and Lila to return home from work the next afternoon. He hoped she'd had a good day because he had some disappointing news to report to her. Earlier in the day, he'd received a long-distance call from Atwood that it was taking a little longer than they'd expected to get access to the records he and the judge needed. Plus he was trying not to let Black know he was even back in town. Michael sighed. He wanted this to be over with for Violet's sake — and for his own.

He heard the front door open and several of the boarders arriving back home at the same time. Michael hurried out of the study and down the hall to the foyer just as the door opened once more and Violet and Lila entered. He could see the storm clouds in Lila's eyes, but she managed a smile to all who were in the foyer.

"Guess what, everyone? We have another celebration to look forward to. Violet received another promotion! She's been made assistant supervisor over the sewing room. It's a brand-new position made just for her!"

Her voice sounded loud and a little brittle to Michael's ears, but at least she didn't run upstairs claiming to have a migraine like the last time. Of course, she'd taken the moment from Violet, but Violet didn't seem to mind. In fact, he was sure she didn't. Violet didn't feel as comfortable being the center of attention as Lila did.

"Congratulations, Violet. Mother has dinner going as we speak."

"I love celebrations." Julia gave Violet a hug. "I am so happy for you! I know you will make a wonderful supervisor."

Michael wished he felt free to give Violet a hug. It'd been much too long since he'd held her close, and he wondered if she even remembered that he had. But as her eyes met his, color flooded her cheeks and his chest tightened. Maybe she did. Of course that could be wishful thinking on his part, but he hoped he was right.

Violet was swept upstairs with the other girls wanting to know all about her new position and he was left to go let his mother know that Violet had officially been promoted. He'd tell her about the conversation from Atwood later when he could talk to her privately. The prospect of having a few minutes alone with Violet put a spring in his step as he went to find his mother.

# CHAPTER SEVENTEEN

Lila did join them for dinner, but Violet couldn't say she celebrated with her. Still it was more than she'd expected and everyone else made up for Lila's broodiness.

When dinner was over and everyone went their own way — Lila heading up to her room for a change — Violet thanked Mrs. Heaton for the trouble she'd gone to.

"I loved doing it, dear," she said. "I can't tell you how happy I am about your promotion and that you've given me so many things to celebrate since you've been with us."

Violet leaned over and kissed her cheek. "You are so dear to me. I will never be able to thank you enough for all you've done for me. I can't think of anyone my mother would want me to have turned to than you."

"Oh, my —"

"Excuse me, ladies," Michael interrupted. "But, Violet, I've heard from Atwood today and I've been hoping for a chance to talk to you without fear of interruption."

"Of course. Where would you like to talk?"

"Why don't we go to the park?"

"I'd love to."

"You children go on. Enjoy the evening. It's a beautiful one," his mother said, waving them away and heading toward the kitchen.

They slipped out the door unnoticed and with relief on Violet's part that Lila wasn't watching every move they made.

Once at Gramercy Park, they strolled to the bench she'd secretly come to think of as "theirs." Michael waited until Violet sat down before joining her. She missed his hand when he removed it from her elbow as she sat down, but when he joined her on the bench, she caught her breath at his nearness.

Trying to ignore the rapid beating of her heart, she asked, "What did Mr. Atwood have to say? Have they been able to find any records that could free up my property?"

"No, not yet. Evidently, it's been a little harder than they thought it would be to get in without Black finding out. And it's not been easy for Atwood to keep undercover so that Black doesn't know he's in town."

"I can see how that would be a problem. I'm sure that Mr. Atwood has clients who want to speak to him as much as I did."

"Well, it's going to take a bit longer that he thought, but he says it will get done. He's staying with the judge — that's where he telephoned me from. His wife and the judge's are good friends and so no one is the wiser when she comes to visit him. She came in early to get the house and office cleaned and ready for him while he came here. Now everyone is asking when he'll be home and she's had to tell them that they'll know when she does. So far everyone seems to accept that he'll be there before long."

"That's good, I suppose?" Violet asked.

Michael nodded. "We hope so. But evidently Mrs. Atwood has had several visits from Black wondering when Mr. Atwood will be home and that tells them that they need to come up with the records as soon as possible before he does something with them. My agent has heard from Black, too, and he wants an immediate accounting of what he's found out about you. Things will be happening fairly fast once Mr. Atwood and the judge get hold of the bank records, but until then, all we can do is wait."

"Well, if not for your quick work in finding Mr. Atwood, we still wouldn't be this

far along. I'll just need to pray for patience,"
Violet said. But, oh, how she wanted it all
settled.

The bells on a nearby church rang the
hour, and Michael stood up and gave her
his hand. "I suppose we should be getting
back to the house."

"I suppose we should." Although she
hated to go back — she really had begun to
think of Gramercy Park as *their* place and
she loved being there with Michael. Violet
rose a bit too fast and lost her balance. Michael's arms circled her to try to steady her
and she caught her breath at his closeness.
"Thank you. I —"

"I must have tugged you too hard. I'm
sorry." Michael took the blame for her clum-
siness.

"No, I just —"

He reached out and tucked an errant
strand of hair behind her ear, looked into
her eyes and smiled. "One day soon, Violet,
we're going to talk about something other
than Harlan Black or Lila. One day soon
we're going to talk about us."

Violet's pulse quickened at the tender look
in his eyes, but she was caught off guard by
his words and didn't know what to say. She
only knew that she couldn't wait for that
day to come. She managed a nod and Mi-

chael pulled her hand through his arm once more, covered it with his own and escorted her home.

The boarders decided to continue celebrating Violet's promotion by going to Central Park on Sunday. This time they were taking the trolley and Michael intended to sit by Violet, if one of the other men didn't beat him to it, and he was going to make sure they didn't. It had taken all the willpower he had not to kiss her the other night in the park. And it was getting increasingly hard not to tell her how he was feeling, what he was thinking. Ever since his mother had mentioned it was time he made a life of his own he'd been thinking about what it would be like to be married to Violet, to call her his wife.

Since Amanda, he'd never thought that way about any other woman. Never let himself because he wasn't sure he could trust his heart to another one — not after his failed relationship with Amanda. And yet Michael knew Violet was nothing like his ex-fiancée. He'd come to realize that his relationship with Amanda wasn't what it should have been from the beginning. Neither of them had loved each other enough. Truth was, he hadn't been the same since he kissed Violet. And what had been meant to comfort her — at least that's what he'd told himself — had brought him nothing but turmoil. Every time he saw her, he thought of the kiss and how it had felt to hold her.

"Are you ready?" Violet asked, interrupting his thoughts as she came down the stairs.

"I am. Did you sleep well?" Michael held his arm out to her and they joined the others as they headed out the door to catch the trolley.

"I did, thank you."

As the group made their way to the trolley stop, Michael was glad he'd made sure that he would be sitting beside Violet. He'd not been quick enough last time, but this time he dropped right down beside her and felt a cocky sense of pleasure when Luke frowned in his direction before grinning, shrugging his shoulders and taking a seat beside Julia.

Michael had a feeling Luke suspected he cared a lot for Violet from some of the remarks he'd made lately, and he saw no reason to let him think otherwise.

John sat by Elizabeth and Ben had no choice but to sit beside Lila. It was just the eight of them today. His mother had decided to stay home and rest after her busy day on

Saturday, promising them a good meal when they got back.

It promised to be a beautiful day, with the sun high in the sky and a light breeze to cool the heat. Once at the park they all discussed what they wanted to do. Michael only knew he wanted to be able to talk to Violet in private and rowing on the lake seemed to be the best way to accomplish that.

"Our boating time got interrupted last time. Want to go out again?" he asked Violet. She looked beautiful in her summery outfit of yellow-and-white lawn.

"I'd love that."

"Well, I want to go cycling," Lila said. "Anyone up for that?"

The rest of the group agreed to rent bicycles and they set a time to meet back up before heading home. Michael caught the look Lila gave him and Violet before she linked arms with Ben and he hoped that Violet didn't see it. Lila was not happy and her anger seemed aimed at Violet.

Oh, he had a feeling it was partly because of him. He'd have to be blind not to know that Lila had hoped he cared about her — even before Violet got there. But he'd made sure not to give her, or any of the other women boarding with his mother, any indication that he was interested in them. More for his mother's sake than his, but he truly hadn't been interested in any woman romantically . . . until recently. And in spite of his determination not to care about another woman, Violet had captivated him from the beginning and he could no longer deny that his feelings for her had been growing since the day she came to stay with them.

He felt bad that he hadn't been able to hide his attraction for Violet as well as he'd thought he had and had caused Lila to dislike Violet. And yet, he didn't think Violet had any idea how he felt about her. And he certainly didn't know how she felt about him. But it was becoming more important each day for him to find out. Only he didn't know how to go about it.

For now, he'd enjoy his time with Violet and hope that by the end of the afternoon, he'd have an inkling of how she felt about him. She seemed happy that he'd sat beside her and pleased that he asked to take her rowing.

Now, as they headed out to the middle of the lake, she looked more relaxed than he'd seen her since the last time they were out on the lake together. He loved looking at her watching the people on the shore, those who gathered at the plaza, those who were strolling along the lake and others out on the lake just as they were.

"You seem deep in thought." Michael smiled as he dipped the oars in the water. "What are you thinking?"

"Oh, about how nice it is out here in the middle of the lake. It's so beautiful and peaceful."

"What else?" He smiled as he rowed the boat across the water.

"How glad I am I accepted your mother's invitation to come to the city. I can't think of anywhere better to be than here, today. To see the sky and feel the space. I do love coming to Central Park."

So did he. And he could think of nowhere he'd rather be than in that rowboat with Violet.

"I'm glad you like something about the city." He was more than glad. If she could begin to think of New York City as home, perhaps she'd want to stay even after she got her house back.

"Oh, I like many things about it. In fact it sometimes surprises me how I've come to love this city — in spite of how much I wish there wasn't a need for the tenements and that life wasn't so hard for the people living in them."

"I know that feeling well," Michael agreed. "I hope that one day we'll see life get better for those who are living in the tenements. I know there are many trying to make life better for the poor. I pray that we'll see the children there now grow up to become respectable citizens helping things get better for those less fortunate than they are and that it will continue that way."

"Oh, Michael, that would be wonderful. But do you really think —"

"Sadly, no. I know better. There will always be tenements here. There will always be the destitute among us. I just hope there are less of them in time."

"Yes, so do I. And I pray about it. I just wish there was something more I could do to help."

As she'd actually admitted that she loved the city he thought maybe now he might add one more thing. "You know, I realize that your goal is to get your home back free and clear, but I hope you consider keeping it as a summer home and staying here in New York. Mother is going to feel lost without you."

Violet looked sad, and Michael changed the subject as he picked up the oars and dipped them in the water, down, up and down again. "Enough talk about things we don't have control over. We can pray about all that and do what we can to help. But for now, let's enjoy the rest of the afternoon. Fall will be here before we know it. I think you will like it here then, too. And after that there is winter and ice-skating and sledding and sleigh rides."

"It all sounds wonderful. I can't wait to see the seasons change. There is still so much of the city I haven't seen yet, but every day I seem to find out something new."

"I was thinking you might enjoy going to Carnegie Hall to a concert one night. Would you like to?" He felt the need to introduce her to other things to love in the city.

"I've never been — we talked about it, remember? But we never planned anything. I'd love to go, Michael."

"Good. I'll find out who's performing and when and we'll try to set a date." He could think of nothing he'd enjoy more than to spend an evening out in Violet's company.

"Wonderful. I look forward to it." Her smile dove right into Michael's heart. He cared about this woman. Could she begin to have feelings for him, too?

Violet's heart did a funny little dive and she tried to ignore her racing pulse at the knowledge that Michael seemed to want to spend more time with her. Could she begin to hope that he had feelings for her, too?

When he'd said he was glad there were some things she liked in the city, she'd realized that there was much she liked about the city and that there were people she'd come to care deeply about. Mrs. Heaton was like family to her, and she was so thankful the Lord had nudged her to suggest Violet to come to New York after her mother passed away.

She also had come to care about most of the boarders and she liked being around them. She hadn't really realized how lonely she was and how much she could enjoy being in others' company until she'd moved here. Life was never boring at Heaton House.

But what she'd also come to realize she could no longer deny to herself was that she cared deeply for Michael Heaton. And that caused her some amount of turmoil. He'd never found anyone after Amanda. Did that mean he'd never gotten over her? They had shared a kiss, but she was sure it was only to comfort her, and there'd not been another.

And he'd only told her that his mother would be lost without her here. Nothing about how he might feel. Maybe he only felt brotherly toward her?

And that was the last thing she wanted. Yet he'd said they needed to talk about them one day soon. Could he care for her the way she cared for him? And even if he did — after her experiences with Nick and Harlan, she still wasn't sure she could trust her heart to him or any other man. But she wanted to. With all her heart.

She told herself she couldn't even think about it until after things were settled with Harlan Black. When she'd come to New York, her goal had been to get the mortgage paid off on her home and get it back free and clear. And she'd intended to go back to Virginia.

And do what? Get a job, if she could find one? Hope for a beau to come along — although he'd have to be a stranger moving to town for she knew the others and most were already married and starting families. And those that weren't, well, she couldn't see herself with any of them.

Then she'd be watching her friends marry and start their own families and she'd become the town spinster. No, that wasn't the life she wanted. She wanted more. So much more.

But if Michael didn't feel the same way

about her that she felt about him, she wasn't sure she could stay here. She was almost certain she could not.

# CHAPTER EIGHTEEN

The next few weeks seemed to drag as they waited to hear from Atwood. The longer it went with no news, the deeper Violet's spirits seemed to sink, and Michael wanted nothing more than to take her in his arms and tell her how he felt about her. But he held off, wanting things settled about her home and Harlan Black before he did. Only then would she know what she truly wanted to do — go back home to Virginia or stay in New York City. And only then would he feel he could find out for sure if there was a chance that she cared for him the way he did her.

In an effort to raise Violet's spirits, Michael suggested that they all take in a concert at Carnegie Hall. He would have preferred it be only him and Violet, but at this point he didn't trust himself to keep how he felt about her to himself if they were alone for any length of time.

Everyone seemed up for the outing, and Michael made sure he sat beside Violet.

Violet was quite impressed with the music hall. "Oh, Michael, it's lovely." She looked all around at the tiered seating, the red plush seats and the private boxes at the top of the hall as the Philharmonic Society began to tune their instruments. "Thank you for suggesting we come here this evening."

He leaned close to her ear, taking in the sweet scent of her hair. "*You* look lovely tonight, and you're welcome. After all that's happened lately, I felt you needed an outing." He smiled and made a little motion for her to look at his mother and the others. Their excitement was obvious as they looked in every direction and chattered about the people they recognized from the society pages of the newspaper.

"Look at that box up there, Violet," his mother whispered and gave a little nod in the direction she was talking about. "It's the Vanderbilt box. And over there is the Astors'."

Michael chuckled at his mother's excitement. "Actually, I think we all needed this."

Violet nodded and turned back to him. "I think you're right."

Their faces were so close it took his breath

away and he could hear Violet's quick intake of breath and see a delicate flush of color flow to her cheeks.

Being so near to Violet sent Michael's heart soaring — just as the notes being played soared to the top of the ceiling. From that moment on, Michael couldn't distinguish his heartbeat from the instruments being played, until the last note sounded and he looked into Violet's eyes. The look in them had his heart flying higher than any note he'd heard that night.

It was a magical evening, sitting together, enjoying another first for Violet in this city, and Michael hoped there would be many more — some he and Violet could enjoy without the company of others. What was he thinking? More time with Violet wasn't what he needed. He cared about her too much already and once she got her home back free and clear, she could easily decide to go back to Ashland and take his heart with her. Not to mention what her leaving would do to his mother.

His chest constricted at the thought of Violet going back to Virginia. But the choice had to be hers, and he couldn't pursue a relationship with her until he knew her decision. And even if she decided to stay in the city, he needed to pray for direction.

■ ■ ■ ■

Michael was getting more impatient by the hour, but finally on Friday morning the telegram he'd been waiting on from Atwood was delivered. Thankfully, Violet hadn't left for Butterick yet, and he sent Gretchen to find both her and his mother and ask them to meet him in the study.

Once they were both there, Michael wasted no time. "It appears we are about to get to the bottom of Harlan Black's shady dealings."

"Finally!" His mother sank into her chair and looked up at him expectantly while Violet stood speechless.

"I had this telegram from Mr. Atwood first thing this morning. This is what he says. 'We have the goods. Put plan into action. Rumor has it Black is leaving for the city in a few days. Must work fast, but make sure you get in after dark. Will meet you at the Edwardses' home tonight.' "

"Tonight?" Violet and his mother asked at the same time.

"Yes. I'm going to send Jim and another agent on ahead of us so that they'll be in place before we get there. It looks as if your worries about keeping your home will soon be over with, Violet."

"Really?"

"Yes, really." Her smile lit his heart and he truly was happy that things would soon be settled for her. He only hoped she wouldn't decide to move back once everything was cleared up — especially after being back home again. But it would be much easier to get Black behind bars there, on his turf, than here in the city.

"I don't know what to say," Violet said. "I'll be so glad to get to the truth and have this behind me. I can't thank you enough."

"So will we all, Violet," Michael said. He was more than ready to get it behind them for personal reasons of his own. Until things were truly settled, he didn't feel free to tell Violet how he felt about her.

"When do we leave?" his mother asked.

"Mother, there is no need for you to go with us. It might get dangerous, and I don't want you in harm's way. It's bad enough that Violet has to be there. If I could take care of it all myself, I would."

"I'm going, too. I don't want to wait here worrying about the two of you. As you always tell me, Maida and Gretchen can take care of the boarders, and it's not like there won't be men in the house to protect them all. Besides, I think I'd like to see some of my old friends and invite them personally to come for a visit."

"But, Mrs. Heaton, if it's dangerous —"

Michael's mother's hand went up and he and Violet exchanged a glance. They both knew not to argue with her when she did that. She'd made up her mind and she wasn't going to change it.

"All right then. We'll leave as soon as Violet gets home from work and can get packed. I'll make arrangements for the first evening train. That way it will be dark when we get there as Mr. Atwood instructed. If everything goes according to our plan, by tomorrow evening we should be celebrating."

Michael prayed as he went to find Luke and let him know what they were doing.

Violet was happily surprised when the train pulled into the station to find Beth and her father waiting for them.

Beth hurried up to her and hugged her. "Oh, Violet! I'm so glad you are back!"

Michael and his mother got off from the next car and were quickly taken to a surrey where Mr. Atwood's wife was waiting. "Oh, Martha, it's about time you paid us a visit, I can't tell you how much I've missed you!"

Evidently Mr. Atwood and the judge had

coached the two women on how to act and what to say to throw any suspicion their arrival might cause.

Violet went in through the front door of the Edwardses' home and was greeted like a long-lost daughter by Beth's mother, just before Michael and his mother were escorted down the alleyway and into the house by the back door. Once they were all inside the Edwardses' home, where the shades were drawn tight, there was a collective sigh and some nervous laughter.

Both Mr. Atwood and the man Violet presumed to be the judge greeted her as a dear friend and granddaughter.

"Violet, Michael and Mrs. Heaton, this is Judge Bancroft. Do you remember him?" Mr. Atwood asked.

"Of course, I do," Mrs. Heaton said.

"I know I've heard the name, but I don't believe I've had the pleasure. I'm pleased to meet you, Judge," Michael said, holding out a hand to the older man. "Thank you for being willing to help with this case."

The judge shook his hand. "You're welcome, son. When I heard what Atwood thought Black was up to, I was determined to see if we could put together an airtight case against the scoundrel." He turned to Violet. "And you, young woman, do you remember me?"

"I do. Mama thought very highly of you, Judge."

"Thank you for letting me know that, Miss Burton. Your parents were well-thought-of in this town. I'm sorry that scoundrel Black has caused you even more grief after the loss of your mother."

"As you can see, the judge is as determined to put a stop to Black's shenanigans as we are," Atwood said. "And we have all the proof we need, right in here." He patted a briefcase. "Violet will have her land free and clear by tomorrow this time."

Violet prayed that was so. She'd done a lot of thinking about what she would do if they could prove that Harlan had been lying and there was no mortgage on her home. She still wasn't sure exactly which way she would go with it, but she did know that if she had money once all was said and done, she wanted some of it to help those in need someway. But things were still up in the air, and she was afraid to make a solid plan until she knew for sure her home was hers — and after that, she hoped she'd find out how Michael felt about her.

After the wonderful meal Mrs. Edwards had prepared for them, they went into the parlor to discuss the final plans. Everyone would have a part to play. Mrs. Heaton would be spending the night with Violet in her home because Michael and his men would also be staying there — in case Black showed up that night or first thing the next morning before Mr. Atwood and the judge got there. If that happened the alternate plan could go forward.

The judge and Mr. Atwood had even involved the police, and the chief informed them that they had a patrolman watching Mr. Black to make sure he was nowhere around when they went over to the Burton home. A policeman would also take Jim's place first thing in the morning when he went to let Black know that Violet was back in town.

Michael had a feeling Black would know long before that, but at least they seemed to have all possibilities covered. Mrs. Edwards and her daughter had stocked the kitchen for the next few days. Once Violet showed them around so that Michael could decide where to place his men, they all adjourned to the kitchen for coffee and the three-layer chocolate cake that Mrs. Edwards had provided. They went over the plan one more time.

And while Michael couldn't wait for it all

to be over with, he prayed that once Violet knew she didn't have a mortgage to pay off, that she really didn't have to work for a living, she'd still want to stay in the city. He didn't want to lose her. Not now — not ever. She'd stolen his heart without lifting a finger to do so.

However, Michael wasn't sure his heart was what she wanted, and he hadn't been able to tell her how he felt yet. Just as soon as this was all settled, he intended to. He wasn't going to lose her without a fight. But first he had to make sure she stayed safe, to make sure that Black didn't get to her.

When Violet awoke the next morning, she lay in her bed listening to the sounds of the house she'd grown up in, just as she'd done numerous times before. But something was different. The house she'd been born in, grown up in, no longer felt like home to her. Thinking back, she realized it hadn't felt the same since her mother had passed away. There had been a different feel to it as soon as her mother had been laid to rest.

And now, after living in New York City, Violet wasn't sure she would ever really feel at home here again. Wasn't sure she wanted to. New York and Mrs. Heaton's boarding-house had become home to her. Oh, she knew that if she moved back here, she would eventually feel differently, but more and more she realized that just as her home felt different, so did the town.

It was wonderful to see Beth and her parents again, but Violet couldn't really think of anyone else here that she was eager to see, to spend time with or even that she missed. And yet, she knew she would miss most everyone at the boardinghouse if she came back. Being an only child, she felt as if she almost had siblings now, with the family atmosphere of Mrs. Heaton's home. Not to mention that there was so much more to do and see in the city.

Violet flung her covers off and got out of bed. She could find many more reasons not to leave New York City, but deep down she knew that the real reason she didn't want to move home was Michael. He'd become so much a part of her life, so much a part of her heart, that she couldn't imagine even a day without seeing him. Didn't even want to. But did he feel the same way about her? *Dear Lord, I pray he does and that I'll know for sure soon.*

She hurried to get ready for what the day would bring and prayed again that it would bring truth out into the open and that it would all be settled soon so that she could move forward with her life.

Mrs. Heaton had slept in Violet's mother's room, and Violet tiptoed past her door so as not to waken her. Violet had planned to cook breakfast for everyone, but as she got closer to the kitchen, she smelled coffee and her heart melted at the sight of Michael standing at her mother's range, frying bacon. He must have heard her footsteps for he turned and smiled, those dimples deep and captivating.

"Good morning, Violet, I hope you slept well."

"Good morning, Michael. Actually, I did sleep pretty well. I didn't know you could cook."

"My mother insisted I learn years ago. It's been a long time since I have, but I don't think I've lost my knack for it, if I do say so myself." He forked the bacon that was done just the way Violet liked it onto a plate. "I don't think my biscuits will be as good as Maida's or Gretchen's, but I think they'll be edible."

Mrs. Heaton entered the kitchen just as Michael took the biscuits out of the oven. "I am so glad I taught you to cook, son." She kissed him on the cheek and turned to Violet.

"Violet, dear, didn't you say you hoped to

find your mother's sewing box? When I got into bed last night, I kicked my slipper under the bed and when I went to retrieve it, I found the sewing box under the bed."

"Under the bed?" That was odd. "I can't imagine why Mother would have put it there, but I am so glad you found it. Of course, she hadn't felt like using it for weeks before she passed away. Maybe she put it beside the bed thinking she could get to it when she felt up to it."

"I'm sure that was it. Anyway, I just wanted to let you know it is here."

"Thank you so much." Violet fought the urge to go get it and look through all the things her mother kept there. To bring back good memories. Maybe she'd feel more at home here if she could.

"We can't tarry long over this wonderful breakfast I made," Michael said. He grinned as he put the biscuits and bacon on the table. "Simple but good, I hope. Anyway, I sent Jim to get breakfast out. Didn't want him teasing me if this was bad and I wanted Jim to be able to contact Harlan first thing to keep him from showing up here before we're ready for him."

"I don't think I'll ever be ready for him. But I so want all of this settled." Violet opened her biscuit and spread butter on it.

She took a bite and closed her eyes. "Mmm, you do know how to cook, Michael! These are as every bit as good as Gretchen's and Maida's."

"Thank you." Michael grinned as he handed her the plate of bacon.

"Yes, it's always been quite a relief to me to know that if the girls couldn't come into work, Michael could help me in the kitchen," Mrs. Heaton said. "He always loved helping me when he was young. And I don't think it hurts any man to know how to feed himself."

A knock on the back door startled them all. When Violet started to get up to go see who was there, Michael waved her aside, letting her know that he'd go. But it was only Mr. Atwood and the judge showing up as planned.

"Looks like we got here just in time, Judge," Mr. Atwood said. He put his briefcase down and helped himself to a biscuit.

"We just ate breakfast, but those do smell mighty good. I think I'll have one, too," the judge said. "Must be a case of anticipation of closing a case that has us so hungry."

"Soon as we finish here, I guess we'd better take our places, just in case Harlan decides to come calling on Miss Burton earlier than is deemed appropriate."

"Well, he'd better not, but I wouldn't put it past him," Mrs. Heaton said.

Violet took a deep breath. This was real. They'd talked and planned the best they could, and now it was time to put those plans into action. A shiver of apprehension slid down Violet's spine and for the first time she felt nervous. She sent up a silent prayer that it would all work right, and hopefully, Harlan Black would be behind bars before nightfall.

# CHAPTER NINETEEN

Violet found it hard to keep still as they waited for Harlan to show up. The judge and Mr. Atwood were playing a game of chess in the front parlor; Mrs. Heaton was trying to keep to the kitchen in the back — although she'd already been up front several times to check on everyone and see if they needed anything. And Michael was just inside the front door, out of sight, but a reassuring presence to her. His men and the local police chief were hidden around the sides of the house.

"Violet, if you keep pacing back and forth you are going to make Black think you are waiting for him when he shows up," Michael said softly. "Why don't I have Mother make you some tea? Is there a magazine or paper around you can read while we're waiting?"

Violet stopped in her tracks. Michael was right. Harlan might think something was brewing if she were out here pacing when he arrived. "I'm sorry. I'm just so nervous."

"That's understandable, Vi, but it's going to be all right."

Did he realize that he'd called her Vi? Or how it warmed her heart? She'd never had a nickname before and no one had ever called her Vi. That Michael was the only one made it sound even more special to her.

"The Lord is with us. Never forget that, Vi." Michael continued to try to calm her.

"Thank you, Michael. I needed that reminder. I really did."

"Violet, dear," Mrs. Heaton whispered from over her son's shoulder. "Why don't you sit down and look through your mother's sewing box? Maybe there's something in there to mend and you can keep your hands busy, instead of your feet, while we wait." She handed the white wicker sewing box to Michael and he handed it to Violet. "You are making us all nervous, dear."

Violet took the box. "Thank you."

"Yes, thank you, Mother," Michael said. "But please go back to the kitchen and make something. *You* are making me nervous."

Everyone chuckled as his mother smiled and patted him on the cheek before heading back to the kitchen.

Violet took the sewing box and went to sit

in the porch swing her father had put up for her mother.

She opened the basket and looked inside. There were spools and spools of thread, packets of needles, a pattern — Butterick, of course — and as she dug down to the bottom she found a packet. Violet opened it and found cards and notes . . . sweet loving ones from her father to her mother.

Violet pulled out one more envelope. It was crumpled, and Violet smoothed it out to find it addressed to . . . Mrs. Heaton, in her mother's handwriting. But the flap wasn't sealed.

"Violet, stay there and try to stay calm." Michael's voice came to her softly from behind the screen door. "Black is coming up the street now. Don't worry. I've got you covered from all sides. Just be yourself."

Violet's mouth went dry as she swallowed, and all she could manage was a nod. She stuffed the packet into the box and put the lid back on. Only then did she look to the street to see that Harlan Black was almost at the front walk.

She stood, smoothed out her skirts and waited for him.

Harlan reached the front walk and stopped. He took off his hat and waved it. "Miss Burton, you *are* back. I'd heard you were and came to see if it was true."

"As you can see, it is, Mr. Black."

"I'm glad. Will you be staying?" He hurried up the walk to the porch, but stopped at the first step.

"For a few days, at least."

Harlan came up the steps. "And what brings you back to town? Did you get homesick?"

"I just wanted to come home and check on things and take care of some business."

"Oh? What kind of business?"

Violet wanted to tell him it was none of his, but that wouldn't get them where they needed to be. "Well, I was coming to see you later this morning."

"Oh?" Black leaned against the porch railing and smiled. "Why did you want to see me? Have you —"

Violet couldn't bear to have him ask if she'd changed her mind. "I want to see the paper my mother supposedly signed putting our home up for collateral on the loan."

Black pushed away from the rail and moved a little nearer to her. "I showed it to you. Don't you remember? Why do you want to see it now?"

"I was mourning my mother at that time and you know it. I didn't look at it that closely and I'd just like to see it again."

"You don't believe her signature is real?" He took a step closer.

"I just want to make sure it is hers. I can't understand why she would have put our home up when my father left us enough —"

"No. He didn't."

"I believe he did."

"Well, you're wrong."

"No, she isn't, Black." Mr. Atwood appeared at the door. "I know for a fact that Mr. Burton left this family well-off. Why don't you come in, Mr. Black?" He held the door wide. "We have some things to straighten out."

"Mr. Atwood! The rumor mill said you'd be back soon. Glad you are better, but I don't believe we have a thing to discuss. Mrs. Burton asked me to take care of things since you were gone."

"I think you are lying, Black," Mr. Atwood said.

Harlan turned to leave, but by then Michael's men had come around the side of the house and stood ready to stop him. Jim Moore was one of them.

"What is going on, Moore? Have you set me up?" The hatred in Black's eyes was evident for anyone to see as he looked for an escape route.

"You could say that," Michael said, coming out of the house and standing right behind Violet. "But I'm the one he works for."

Violet could see the fear on Harlan's face. "Heaton. I should have known you'd be mixed up in all of this. I'll have you all arrested!" Harlan's eyes looked wild and Violet wasn't sure what he was going to do.

"I don't think so," Judge Bancroft said, slipping out the door and moving to stand beside Michael and Mr. Atwood. "Mr. Black, why don't you come in and talk this over with us? It's not going to do you much good to run at this point."

"What have you got in there? A whole army?" Harlan yelled.

"We just want to ask you a few questions, Mr. Black. It appears you've been doing some creative bookkeeping. Come on inside. Or, if you'd rather, we can do this down at the police station."

Violet was fearful for everyone as Harlan made to slip a hand to the inside of his jacket. Did he have a gun?

"I wouldn't try that if I was you, Black," Michael said.

"It's not worth it, son," Mr. Atwood said. "You can't change the past. You are in enough trouble. No need to make it worse."

Harlan looked from one man to the other

for several minutes before he slipped his hand inside his jacket and pulled out a gun, pointing it straight at Violet. "I don't think you want to pressure me just now."

But Michael quickly pushed her behind him and then dived for Harlan, pushing his arm away and wrestling him down, managing to knock the gun from his hand. Harlan dived after it and Michael grabbed him before he could get to it. Michael threw the gun to Jim Moore just before Harlan's fist caught him in the eye.

Michael gave as good as he got and it took Jim and the other agent to pull them apart. Then everything seemed a blur as Jim Moore stopped Michael's fist from crashing into Harlan's face once more. "It's done, Michael."

By then the chief of police and the other agent had handcuffs on Harlan and had yanked him to his feet. Michael looked at Violet, and she could see that his eye was turning black already. But there was a gleam in his eye as he looked at her and smiled. She smiled back and his dimples deepened as he winked at her. He was all right. Her heart slammed against her chest. Only then did Violet feel that she could breathe again. *Thank You, Lord.*

"Let's talk," the judge said, opening the

door wide.

"Maybe it will help you to hear what we know," Mr. Atwood said once everyone was seated in the parlor. "I know what Mr. Burton left his wife and daughter, and it was a home and land, free and clear of debt, and a tidy sum in the bank. But somehow you left Mrs. Burton, and then Violet, under the impression that they were near penniless."

"I never —"

"Yes, you did. You went so far as to convince Mrs. Burton that she needed to put her home up as collateral so that there was enough money in her account to pay for her medicine and the doctor."

"You are making this all up."

"No. I'm not. We've checked your records and we know what Doc charged."

Harlan laughed. "You're bluffing."

"He's not bluffing," the judge said. "I was with him. We've seen all your records."

"You broke in and —"

"We had a search warrant. It was all legal and above-board. Your actions, however, have not been."

Mr. Atwood drew out papers showing that the bank account in Violet's mother's name was still intact and in fact had money in it. "What were you planning on doing? Persuading Miss Burton to marry you, get her house, land and bank account for yourself? And for what reason? To show your papa that you were a better man?"

It was at that moment that Harlan Black broke. "He never loved my mother. Always wanted Violet's mother, right up until she died. He never stopped loving her. And he never loved me. Never wanted me. I wanted to show him that I could have it all. But Mrs. Burton didn't want me to come around and try to court Violet. Didn't want to give me a chance because of him! I knew I had to do something. When she got sick, well, I tried to convince her that she had money troubles and the only way out was for me to give her a loan, putting up the house for collateral. I knew she wasn't long for this world, so I even promised to leave Violet alone."

He looked at Violet. "But she yelled at me and told me to get out of the house. She was real agitated. And then she collapsed. She wasn't ever the same after that. Couldn't talk or anything." He looked at Violet and then down at the floor.

Did he have any remorse at all? He'd probably helped cause her mother's stroke. Violet closed her eyes and willed herself not to throw up. The pity she'd begun to feel for him changed to repulsion.

"So you forged her name on the papers and told Violet she'd signed them?"

Harlan raised his head and grinned. "She believed me."

"Because she was in mourning, not thinking straight, and I wasn't here to tell her different and to look into it for her," Mr. Atwood said.

"And if you'd waited to come back, you old coot, I probably could have convinced her to marry me by now. Especially now I have someone in the Heaton House working for me."

"What are you talking about? Who is working for you?" Michael asked.

"Not your agent, if that's what you think. No. It appears there is someone who wants Violet away from you as much as I do."

"Lila," Violet whispered. "But how —"

"Miss Lila Miller got in touch with me a few weeks ago. Let me know right where you were. I bought a train ticket and was going to leave on Monday. We had everything set up so when you came out of Butterick she could say she'd met a friend and leave you to catch the trolley on your own. And I'd be there waiting for you." Black grinned at Michael. "And you'd never see her again. But you ruined all my plans by coming here before I could leave town."

His arrogance had Michael on his feet and grabbing his collar. "You are scum, Black. You always have been and it doesn't have anything do to with your father."

There was loathing in Black's eyes when he looked at Michael and sneered. "Your sister didn't think so, though. No, she didn't think I was scum at all. I remember one night —"

Michael drew back his fist and only the fast action of his men stopped him from giving Harlan Black exactly what he had coming to him.

It had been a long day, both heartrending and happy. By nightfall, Violet had seen Harlan Black arrested for fraud and the inheritance she'd never realized she had reinstated to her. Her home was really hers, and she had money in the bank and never had to worry about paying Black one more cent. She even had the means to be able to help some less fortunate than her.

They'd had dinner with the Edwardses that evening, and afterward Violet, Michael and his mother relaxed on her front porch before going in to pack for the trip back to the city. She and Mrs. Heaton shared the swing and Michael was in one of the wicker chairs.

He looked pitiful, his eye swollen, black-and-blue and looking worse by the minute. Her heart swelled with love for this man who'd fought for her today. He'd won — though he looked a bit worse for it. But it could have turned out so differently. He could have been shot and killed. She shuddered at the very thought.

Just thinking about how close he'd come to losing his life on her account made Violet tremble.

"I'm so glad this is all over and we're headed home," Mrs. Heaton said. "I loved Ashland when we lived here, but I don't want to move back. I might feel differently if your mother was still alive, Violet, but not now."

At the mention of her mother, Violet finally remembered the letter her mother had written and never mailed. She reached into the sewing box she'd left on the swing, dug out the letter and handed it to Mrs. Heaton.

"I have something for you. I found it when I was out here earlier today, but it was about the time Harlan showed up and so much has happened since then, I forgot until now." She handed it to Mrs. Heaton.

Mrs. Heaton took the packet from her and turned it over. She opened the flap that had never been sealed and pulled out another envelope with a letter wrapped around it. Her quick intake of breath told them that she was surprised. She swallowed hard. "This envelope is addressed to your mother and it is from . . ." She sighed deeply and her eyes were full of tears as she continued, her voice shaky, "It's from Becca!"

She ran trembling fingers over the writing before opening the letter from Violet's mother and reading out loud. " 'Dear Martha, I received this from Rebecca a few days ago. I don't know that anything in it will help you and Michael to find her, but I pray it does. I have a suspicion that Harlan Black had something to do with her disappearance, but I have no proof of anything. Just that he makes the hair on the back of my neck stand on end. He's made it known that he wants to court Violet and I'm going to let him know just how I feel about that — in no uncertain terms. Please let me know you received this, I —' "

Mrs. Heaton turned the paper over and looked at Michael and Violet. "That's it. She stopped in midsentence." She handed the letter to Violet.

"Maybe she got interrupted or just didn't

have the energy to finish right then. She never told me about it and it's dated only a few days before her stroke." Violet handed the short note to Michael. His mother opened the envelope containing Becca's letter and began to read. " 'Dear Mrs. Burton, I know I've been gone a long time without being in contact. But I wanted to write and ask you to let my mother know that I am all right. I've heard she and Michael moved, but I don't know where they are. I hope that you do, so that you can forward this to her. But I do not want her to know where I am because she never wanted me to move away, and, well, I fear seeing me now would bring her more heartache. I just want her to know that I am all right. Please tell her I love her. Sincerely, Rebecca Heaton.' "

Michael's mother looked up at him, her eyes swimming in tears. "Oh, Michael, this means our Becca is alive. She's really alive."

Violet brushed at her own eyes as she watched Michael hug his mother, unshed tears making his eyes bright.

"I know this doesn't mean we'll ever find her, Michael, but —"

"I'll try to renew the search, Mother, I —"

Mrs. Heaton shook her head. "No, son. You've done all you can to that end. Follow leads if you get them, but I don't want you to feel you can't have a life until you find Becca. I can rest easier just knowing she's alive, and I know that if we're meant to find your sister, the Lord will see to it that we do."

Michael nodded. "I'll continue to pray that we do, Mother. And you know I'll never give up looking for her."

"I do. But I want you to have a life of your own. You gave that up once. I don't want to see you do it again." Mrs. Heaton held the letter close to her heart. "I believe I'll turn in now. I'm ready to go home."

# CHAPTER TWENTY

Michael opened the door for his mother to go back inside and then turned to Violet. "I can't begin to tell you how much the letter you found means to Mother and me. It's given us hope that Becca is alive and that one day we *will* find her. Or she'll find us."

"You really aren't going to give up just because that letter said she didn't want to be found, are you?" Violet asked.

"No, of course not. But —"

"But what?"

"I won't let the search for her turn into the obsession it was at the beginning. Mother is right. I did do that once, although I know now that it worked out for the best."

"What do you mean? Are you talking about your engagement to Amanda?"

"I am. She wasn't willing to support my search for my sister in any way and she called off the engagement when I decided to move to New York City."

"I knew the wedding had been called off, but I didn't know why. I'm sorry, Michael."

"I'm not. At least not now." He'd never loved Amanda the way he loved Violet. What he'd felt for Amanda had been more of an infatuation, until he'd realized what kind of woman she was. "I decided a long time ago that if I ever gave my heart to another woman, it would be one who supported my need to try to find my sister. But it would also be someone I loved so much that I would make sure that whatever I was working on would come second to her needs. I didn't feel that way about Amanda and she didn't feel that way about me, or what I had to do. Maybe I was too fixated with finding Becca, but —"

"She's your sister. I can't believe that Amanda couldn't understand that you had to search for Becca. I'd do anything I could to help you find her."

And she would. Michael knew it as sure as he knew he loved her. This was the one woman who could and would stand by his side no matter what — if he was blessed to have her return the love he felt for her. But this was her home and she just had it returned to her. He had to ask.

"Violet, now that you have your home free and clear and an inheritance — do you know what you're going to do? Are you going to move back here?"

"I don't know what I'm going to do. But I can't leave my position at Butterick without giving notice so that they can name someone to replace me. And I'm just not sure . . ." She shook her head. "I've got a lot of thinking and praying to do, Michael."

He joined her on the swing and put it into motion. "The decision must be yours. But just so you know —" he reached out and cupped the side of her face with his hand "— while you're praying, I hope you stay in the city."

He heard her catch her breath and he dipped his head, his lips touching hers for a brief moment — only until she responded and then he deepened the kiss. He loved this woman. *Please, dear Lord, let her decide to stay in New York City.*

He raised his head and looked into her eyes, wanting to tell her how he felt, wanting to ask her to marry him. But she looked exhausted and his head had begun to throb. Now wasn't the time to press. It could wait until they got back home. Maybe that was the place to tell her how he felt. At least she was going back with them. He'd be thankful for that.

"Please just think about it, and we'll talk

when we get back to the city?"

She nodded. "It's been a long day and you need to get some rest. Can I get you some ice or a cool rag to put on your eye?"

"No, I'll get it when I go in. I'm just going to sit here for a while, though."

She got up from the swing. "All right. I'll see you in the morning, then."

"Night, Violet."

"Good night, Michael."

Violet tossed and turned most of the night. What was she going to do? Move back here or stay in the city? She loved Michael with all her heart — and he'd fought Harlan for her. But did that mean he loved her, too? He'd kissed her and said he wanted her to stay, but was it for his mother's sake or his own?

She pounded her pillow and turned over. *Dear Lord, please help me to know what to do. Help me to know how he feels about me. I don't know if I can stay in the city only for Mrs. Heaton's sake, much as I love her. If Michael doesn't love me, I don't think I'd be able to continue living at Heaton House. Please show me what to do.*

Finally, once she heard Michael come inside and shut the door, she drifted off to sleep.

The next morning they joined the Edwardses at church. Michael seemed to sport his black eye with pride. All Violet knew was that she was extremely proud of him.

Then, after a wonderful dinner with Beth and her family, Mr. and Mrs. Atwood, the judge and his family, Violet waved goodbye to her friends as she and Michael and Mrs. Heaton boarded the train to go back to New York City.

They took their seats on the train, Michael beside her, and Mrs. Heaton sitting across from them, talking to an old friend across the aisle who was going to visit her son's family in the city.

Now, as the locomotive began to move, Michael smiled down at her and said quietly, "Are you all right? Sure you want to return to the city?"

"I'm fine now. And I'm happy to be going back. I have a job to return to. And I've realized that with no family in Ashland, there really is nothing holding me here now. Beth will be more than happy to come visit me in the city."

Michael's dimples deepened. "I'm glad. I wasn't sure if you were feeling sad to leave."

"No. I'm better than I've been in months. I know that what I suspected about Harlan was true and I'm relieved to know that he's going to pay for his deeds. I can't thank you enough for being the reason for that, Michael." His eye was black and blue and purple now. Just looking at it made her hurt for him. She wanted to say so much more, but now wasn't the time or place.

Mrs. Heaton's conversation with her friend ended and she turned her attention back to them.

"I still can't believe Lila was working with Black, giving him information about Violet. How did she know about him anyway?"

"I don't know." Michael rubbed his temple.

"I ran into her in the hall coming out of your study one night. I have to admit I wondered if she might be eavesdropping, then I felt bad for thinking it. But it was the night we talked about Harlan."

"Now that you mention it, I caught her coming out of your room one night. She said she'd been returning a shirtwaist you'd loaned her. I believe it was right after your sewing machine arrived."

Violet inhaled quickly. "The letter Beth sent — when I went up to read it later that night, it was on the floor. I just assumed I'd knocked it off the bedside table, but —"

"Most probably, at least at one or the other time, and maybe in both instances,

Lila found out enough to contact Black. I knew she was a scheming young woman, but I never thought she'd turn on someone living in our home," Michael said.

"I am so sorry, Violet. I knew she was jealous of you, but she was always envious of anyone getting more attention than she was." Mrs. Heaton shook her head. "If I'd had any idea that she would turn on you, try to put you in harm's way, I would have told her to leave."

"Oh, Mrs. Heaton, please don't blame yourself. I knew Lila didn't like me, but I never suspected she'd go to such lengths to get rid of me." Her heart filled with love for Michael and his mother. "I'm sorry I've caused you so much trouble."

"You've given us much joy, Violet. The only ones who've caused problems are Black and Lila. We've taken care of one, and the other will be taken care of as soon as we get home. It's time Lila learned her actions have consequences," Michael said.

Violet looked at Michael's bruised face and shuddered. He could have been killed. He was right. She just wished Lila had taken a different path in her life.

Violet could feel the tension radiating off Michael as he opened the door of his mother's home that afternoon. Gretchen met them just inside, as if she'd been on the lookout for them. She opened her mouth to speak, but before she could say anything, Michael said, "Gretchen, please tell Lila I want to see her in Mother's study right away."

Gretchen began wringing her hands and shaking her head. "She's not here, Mr. Heaton. She's gone."

"Where is she, do you know? Is she with some of the other boarders?"

"No, sir. She must have moved out all of her things in the middle of the night. When she didn't come down for Sunday dinner, Elizabeth went to check on her and there was nothing in her room except for a letter to Mrs. Heaton and one addressed to Butterick. Nothing else. We don't know where she went."

By then Elizabeth, Julia, Luke and John had joined them in the foyer.

"I'm so glad you're home, Mrs. Heaton." Elizabeth had several letters in her hand and handed them to the older woman. "Lila started acting odd as soon as she found out you all had gone to Virginia on Friday, and she was jumpy as a cat all day yesterday, but we couldn't get her to tell us what was wrong and she went to bed early last night."

"We don't know when she left," Luke added. "Our best guess is that it was after everyone went to bed last night or first thing this morning before anyone was up."

"Let me read her letter," Mrs. Heaton said. "Maybe it will shed some light on why she left. If not, I believe we can. Let's go into the parlor."

Violet sat down on one side of Mrs. Heaton and Michael sat on the other while she silently skimmed Lila's script. Then she handed it to Michael. "You tell them, son."

Michael nodded and began to read: " 'Dear Mrs. Heaton. I've been called home suddenly and couldn't wait until you returned from your trip. I don't know when I will be able to return, so I must resign from Butterick. Please have Violet give them the letter I've addressed to them. I thank you for your kindness to me and I ask you to give Michael my regards. Please tell everyone else goodbye for me. Lila' "

Michael sighed and looked at Violet. "Obviously she had a feeling we'd find out what she'd done and got out of town before we could confront her with it. I think I'll send one of my men to her hometown, but I don't think she's been called home suddenly."

"No, neither do I," Luke said.

"What is it? What has Lila done?" Elizabeth asked.

By the time they'd explained everything to the boarders, Gretchen was there to tell them dinner was ready and they moved from the parlor to the dining room.

Violet could understand that Elizabeth and the other women might miss Lila, but when she voiced as much, Elizabeth put that thought to rest.

"Well, much as I hate to admit it, it took a lot of energy to be polite to Lila most days. It wasn't easy to be a friend to her," Elizabeth said. "I'm sorry she betrayed you after all you've tried to do for her, Violet. I can't say I'm sorry to see her go."

"True," Julia added. "I knew she resented Violet, but I never thought she would go so far as to try to put her in danger. I admit I'm glad she's gone, too."

"It will be a lot more peaceful around here," Luke said. "Lila liked to stir things up on a daily basis. It's a shame she couldn't appreciate the friendship you ladies tried to show her."

Angry as Violet was at Lila, she pitied her at the same time. Now she could only pray that the woman would find the Lord and turn her life around.

■ ■ ■ ■

It was later that evening before Violet and Michael had a chance to talk to one another in private. So much had happened so quickly that Violet's head was still spinning. Coming home to the city was part of it. Violet had known that she was glad to be coming back, but when she had walked through the doors of Mrs. Heaton's boardinghouse, there was no longer any feeling as if it was *almost* home. Now it *was* home to her, and when the boarders welcomed them back she knew that she was in New York City to stay. She might not stay in this house, depending on how Michael felt about her, but she didn't want to move back to Ashland.

Michael had asked if he could speak to her after dinner and visiting with the boarders, telling them about all that had happened and Lila's part in it. Violet was more than happy to oblige. She had much to thank him for. And she secretly hoped that they might have that talk about them, the one that Michael had said they would have "one day."

When the gathering began to break up, Violet went to Mrs. Heaton's study where

Michael had asked to meet her. She was a little surprised to see Luke there, too. But Michael smiled at her and motioned her to come in.

"Luke is blaming himself for not keeping Lila here."

"I'm so sorry about Lila's part in all this, Violet," Luke said. "If I'd had any idea I would have watched her closer."

"Why, Luke, it's not your fault. None of us suspected she even knew who Harlan was."

"Still —"

"Luke, I should have called home that night. It's my fault that she left before we got here," Michael said. "I thought she'd be here when we returned."

"Well, if you haven't decided who to send to her hometown, I'd sure like to go," Luke said. "Maybe she'd just think I came looking for her as a friend. She doesn't know I work for you."

"I was going to ask you to do just that. But I don't think she went home."

"I'm sure she didn't. But I'd like the chance to find out what I can."

Michael nodded. "You have it."

"Just be careful, Luke," Violet said. "She's not to be trusted."

"I know. I'll be careful. Now, a bit of

advice to the two of you."

"Oh? What advice is that?" Michael asked.

"Quit wasting time and tell each other what everyone else in this house already knows."

Michael raised an eyebrow and smiled. "And that would be?"

"That you are in love with each other. It's pretty obvious to everyone but the two of you."

Violet could feel her face flush as she and Michael glanced at each other.

"I'll leave you to do that in private," Luke said.

"That'd be nice of you." Michael grinned.

Luke chuckled on his way out the door, and Michael's arms encircled Violet before it clicked shut.

His cheek had been changing colors by the hour and Violet couldn't stop herself from reaching out to touch his face now that they were alone. But, afraid that her touch would hurt, she quickly pulled her hand back. "I'm so sorry you got hurt. But you saved my life, you know, in more ways than one."

Michael waved his hand to dismiss her thanks and then brought it down to grasp the fingers she'd lowered. "I'm glad it all turned out well. After Mother voiced her fears, I knew something wasn't right, and there was only one thing to do and that was to get to the bottom of it all. But as for saving a life . . ." He paused before bringing Violet's fingers to his lips and then laying them against his cheek. He looked deep into her eyes and released a deep breath. "I think it was my life I saved, for if anything had happened to you, Vi, I don't think I would have been able to forgive myself."

"Michael, no. Don't even talk like that."

Michael pulled her into his arms and put his head against hers. "Violet, it is well past time that we talk about us. I can't begin to tell you how I felt when Black pulled that gun on you. I thought for sure my heart would never beat again."

"Oh, Michael —"

His fingertips sealed her lips as he shook his head. "Please let me finish."

Violet nodded and he removed his hand to pull her closer. "I know I'm probably doing this badly, but after coming so close to losing you, I don't want to wait one more minute before telling you how I feel about you, Violet. Luke is right. It's time. I love you with all that I am and I can't tell you how relieved I am that you don't want to go back to Ashland. I want you to stay here and . . . if there is any way you think you could learn to love me, too, I —"

"Michael." Violet's hand reached out and she gently touched his cheek once more. "I think I began to fall in love with you from the moment I walked into the parlor that first night. I've loved you for a good while now, and I've only dreamed that you might come to care for me, too."

Michael tipped her face up to his. "It seems we should have had this talk long before now. And I won't let another moment go by without asking you to marry me. Will you be my wife, Vi?"

Violet's heart flooded with happiness and love for this man. "Oh," she breathed, "yes, Michael, I will be honored to marry you."

"I love you with all my heart, Vi." Michael's head dipped and Violet stood on tiptoe as his lips grazed hers.

Suddenly, she realized that she finally had somewhere to call home. And it wasn't in Virginia. It wasn't New York City or even Heaton House. Home for Violet would always be right here in the circle of Michael's arms.

# EPILOGUE

*Heaton House*
*December 20, 1895*

Violet couldn't believe her wedding day was finally here. Michael had wanted to marry right away, but to please his mother, who wanted to give them the wedding she'd never been able to plan for her daughter, they agreed to a December 20 date. After all she'd done for her, Violet was more than glad to grant her request.

And it'd worked out fine; it gave them time to find a home of their own only a few blocks away. Michael had given her permission to work until they started a family and Butterick had reciprocated by providing Violet's wedding dress.

It was from their winter line, made of ivory satin and lace, and Mrs. Waters had made it for her. Violet felt beautiful in it, and as she stood at the landing at Heaton House, she thanked the Lord for the blessings He'd bestowed on her.

Now, Violet took a deep breath and held her bouquet with trembling fingers to her heart as Elizabeth straightened her skirts from behind.

"Just wait until Michael sees you," Elizabeth whispered. "He's going to fall in love all over again."

Violet smiled just thinking of her husband-to-be. Michael would be all she'd ever hoped for in a husband. He was loving and kind, affectionate, honest and strong. Best of all, he loved the Lord as much as she did.

"I hope so. Because I think I fall in love with him more each day," she whispered back.

She and Michael were going to spend a few days in her home in Ashland and try to decide whether to keep the house or sell it, then they'd return on Christmas Eve just in time to celebrate with Mrs. Heaton — Mother Heaton — and the boarders who'd been so happy for the two of them. The plan was to have everyone over to their house for New Year's.

As the "Wedding March" began playing in the parlor below, Elizabeth gave her a quick hug and started down the stairs before her. Violet's heart hammered against her ribs with each step she took as she followed her maid of honor down the stairs, into the foyer and on into the parlor.

She almost forgot to breathe as she saw Michael waiting for her, standing with Luke, his best man. They were in front of the Christmas tree his mother had made sure was up and decorated for this day. Garlands graced the mantel and the windows, and Violet couldn't think of a better setting for a wedding.

Michael looked regal and so very handsome standing there in his tuxedo, the expression in his eyes touching her heart, drawing her to him, past their friends from Ashland, Mrs. Waters and several of her coworkers and Michael's agents, too. Then there were Julia, John and Ben — the boarders she'd come to think of as family — and even Gretchen and Maida dressed in their finest and ready to serve the guests after the ceremony. How blessed they were to have so many friends.

She stopped beside Michael's mother and placed a kiss on her cheek as she handed her a flower from her bouquet. Then she took her place beside Michael and they turned to the minister.

Her fingers trembled holding the bouquet and only Michael's gaze kept her steady as they said their vows in front of the people they loved. They both promised to love and cherish each other for the rest of their lives and she handed her bouquet to Elizabeth before Michael slid the ring that'd been her mother's on her finger.

"I pronounce you husband and wife," the minister said. "You may kiss your bride, Michael."

Michael pushed back the veil and tipped Violet's face up. "I love you, Vi. Today, tomorrow and forever."

Violet barely got out, "I love you, too," before her new husband claimed her lips in the sweetest kiss she'd ever known — the very first one as Mrs. Michael Heaton.

Dear Reader,
After 9/11, watching how New Yorkers handled it and reached out to one another, New York City became a real place to me, with people and families who cared deeply for each other.

I became increasingly interested in the history of the city and found that at the end of the nineteenth century women flocked to New York City, finding work as seamstresses, telephone operators, department store clerks and lamp makers. Trying to support themselves or help their families, many of these young women lived away from their loved ones for the first time. But where did they live? In my research, I found that many lived in boardinghouses, where some even found their mates.

Michael Heaton and Violet Burton are two lonely hearts who need someone to love. I hope you enjoy their love story as much as I enjoyed writing it.

Blessings,
*Janet Lee Barton*

# QUESTIONS FOR DISCUSSION

1. When Harlan Black offered to forgive the loan if Violet agreed to marry him, she turned him down, deciding she'd lose her home before marrying the likes of him. What do you think most women in that time period would have done? Do you think Violet did the right thing?

2. Finding it hard to trust a man, Violet isn't really interested in finding a husband. Have you ever felt that way? How did you get past it?

3. Michael chose to search for his sister instead of staying in Virginia, and it prevented him from marrying the woman he loved. Did he do the right thing? Was his fiancée wrong or right in breaking off the engagement?

4. Even feeling that Lila doesn't like her,

Violet would like them to get along. Would you go out of your way to befriend someone who obviously didn't like you? What do you think the Lord would want you to do?

5. Michael didn't feel anyone would understand his need to look for his sister and help his mother after his fiancée broke the engagement. Did he have good reason to feel that way? Would you have felt the same way?

6. Sometimes things that happen in our past hinder our decisions in the future. How did past events hinder Violet and Michael's relationship? How did they get past that problem and move ahead?

7. Violet and Lila feel totally opposite in how they view Mrs. Heaton taking in temporary boarders. What do you think about it? Would it be something you'd do?

8. When Michael finds out about Harlan and that he's obsessed with finding Violet, he feels more responsible for her. Does that hinder his falling in love with her or

make him realize that he really cares about her?

9. Michael's fear is that Violet will return home once things are cleared up about her home. It keeps him from letting her know how he feels. Do you think he should have told her earlier? Or would you have done the same thing?

10. When Violet sees the tenements and the two little boys, her heart breaks for them and she has a hard time getting them out of her mind. Have you ever felt that way when you've seen poverty up close? Did it change you?

# ABOUT THE AUTHOR

**Janet Lee Barton** was born in New Mexico and has lived all over the South, in Arkansas, Florida, Louisiana, Mississippi, Oklahoma and Texas. She loves researching and writing heartwarming stories about faith, family, friends and love. Janet loves being able to share her faith and love of the Lord through her writing. She's very happy that the kind of romances the Lord has called her to write can be read and shared with women of all ages.

Janet and her husband now live in Oklahoma, and are part of what they laughingly call their "Generational Living Experiment" with their daughter and her husband, two wonderful granddaughters and a Shih Tzu called Bella. The experiment has turned into quite an adventure and so far, they think it's working out just fine. When Janet isn't writing or reading, she loves to travel, cook, work in the garden and sew.

You can visit Janet at www.janetleebarton.com.